Rag

MW00938682

A Mitchell Family Series

Book 3

By: Jennifer Foor

Check out the other books by Jennifer Foor

**Letting Go - A Mitchell Family Series Book One
(Contemporary Romance)**

Folding Hearts – A Mitchell Family Series Book Two

Hope's Chance (Contemporary Romance)

The Somnian Series (YA Paranormal)

Book One Ascension

Book Two Absum

Book Three Attero

Book Four Aduro

Book Five Abeo

Coming Soon

Tommy Ford Zombie Chronicles

I would like to thank everyone that continues to support
me.

Without you, I would never stay so determined.

Thanks to all of my new friends on my FB, Twitter and
Goodreads pages.

Thanks to all of my Independent Author Friends. (you know
who you are)

Thank you to all the book bloggers out there spreading the
word for me and others who write.

Special Thanks to:

Book Broads, Book Studs, Books Books Books, Reality Bites Books

What to read after fifty shades

ARC Readers

Amy Haigler, Glennis Ussery, Shannon Murphy, Jennifer Lafon, Jennifer Harried,

Erica Willis, Karrie Stewart, Kim Eckley, Lesley Ark,

Robin Harper, Heather Gunter, Angie Cowgill and Heather Collins

And everyone who has made this series the success that it is. I am forever grateful.

Thanks to my family and my faith

With them, all things are possible

Special Mentions in this book: Extreme Couponing, Twilight Zone, Lifetime Network

John Michael Montgomery – I can love you like that

Heartlands – I loved her first

Lowes

Chapter 1

Colt

I think it all started with Ty and Miranda getting married. I mean, it makes everything easier to be able to blame someone else other than myself for everything that was happening. For two years, I had given Savanna my heart and looked forward to our wedding. Everything was in order for the big day. We had restored the old red barn. Conner and I had spent hours installing overhead lights and running that damn speaker wire throughout the rafters in the ceiling. The decorations were delivered and beginning to be set up.

We were ready for this.

After the family had finally calmed down and realized that Ty and Miranda were in fact married and planned on raising her daughter Bella together, they wanted to do something for them. To be able to better accept things, we all agreed to let them renew their vows in the barn. It was decorated and setup for a wedding anyway. The family was already together, and although they didn't have a guest list anything like Savanna and I, they didn't care.

The service really helped everyone accept their unexpected relationship, myself included. I say unexpected lightly, because most of us could tell there was always some kind of attraction between them. Believing that either one of them would ever settle down was hard to do, especially with each other. It was extra hard for me because I was related to both of them. Miranda's mother and my mother were sisters and Ty's father and my father were brothers.

Ty and Miranda were not monogamous people. The fact that they were now so consumed in their relationship had left us all speechless. I think it was hardest on Van. I never doubted her love for me, but there were several recent circumstances that felt like a knife was being shoved directly into my chest. The first happened a couple months ago when Savanna went to North Carolina to get her car and go dress shopping. She walked in on Ty and Miranda, and from what she described, it was not something she would ever want to picture.

I knew that neither of them were modest, so I could only assume what she had exactly walked in on. Savanna was a more conservative kind of person. Every now and again, she would get a little freaky, but normally she was quiet and modest. There was no way in Hell she would ever be caught dead in anything Miranda considered going out attire. The girl left little to the imagination. I think that is what always got her into so much trouble. She dated the wrong guys because she liked the attention they gave her. Ty was the male version of Miranda. He cheated on Savanna for the attention they gave him. I'm not sorry he did either. If it weren't for his indiscretions, I wouldn't have found the love of my life.

Savanna was everything to me. That's why when she started acting funny, as a result of Ty; I started to get worried about our relationship. After her weekend in North Carolina, it took a good week for her to come clean and confess what she had caught them doing. Part of me wanted to drive out there and kick the shit out of Ty, but it takes two to tango, even Savanna and I knew that. After realizing that she was more hurt about the secret, instead of the fact that Ty was claiming to love another woman, especially one that was my family, it made it all easier to take.

We talked things out and prepared for when they came to Kentucky for our wedding. It was funny. I think at first they thought they could hide their relationship. On their first night here, Savanna and I had to pull them apart at a bar. I found out they had got married when I cornered Ty in the men's room. He got all defensive and insisted that he loved her. When I told him the family wouldn't stand for it, he blurted out how we couldn't do anything about it since they were married.

To keep my fiancée from going all crazy, I decided to keep it a secret for them. As much as I didn't want to believe this, I'm pretty sure that later that night they got it on in my bathroom at the house. They claimed that Miranda was throwing up, but it was a little too convenient for me to believe. I saw how fast Ty went up to bed and heard him leaving when everyone left that night.

The secret only lasted a few more hours. The moment that Bella saw Ty, she started running toward him calling him 'daddy'. The sudden gasps in the room were filled with an hour's worth of explaining.

Savanna really had a hard time dealing with their news. She saw that ring on Miranda's finger and bolted out of the room. I felt sick, almost like she was jealous of Miranda and wanted Ty back. She later explained that it wasn't anything like that. It was a good thing. I don't know if I could ever be able to take losing Savanna. That girl meant the world to me. When it was all said and done, Savanna agreed that they should renew their vows in the barn.

The service was short and sweet and the family really seemed to be accepting Ty and Miranda's marriage. Bella was a daddy's girl and Ty took his new title with determination. They were inseparable and if I ever doubted that he was serious, after seeing them for only a few days, I realized they really were crazy about each other.

In fact, for the next three days they were almost sickening. I showed affection with Savanna no matter where we were, but Ty and Miranda couldn't keep their hands off of each other. The only ones to appreciate their love more than them, was Miranda's mother and of course Bella. My aunt Karen had struggled as a single mother and I think all she ever wanted was for her daughter to calm down and settle into a more structured lifestyle. I never thought it would be with Ty, but he was very devoted to those girls.

Three days before our wedding is when everything really went to shit. The newspaper had a featured spot about me marrying Savanna at the ranch. I'm pretty sure that is how word got out about it being in the barn.

Ty and Miranda were staying in the main house, in Miranda's old room. Bella still had her own room there, so it was easier. We had all had a nice family dinner and sat around playing cards until around midnight. Savanna and I drove one of the golf carts back to our place and Conner and Aunt Karen did the same and headed to their place.

At three in the morning, we got the call from my mother. The phone ringing at that time of morning scares the bejesus out of anyone, because it is always an emergency. My mother's voice was so panicked. "COLT GET UP HERE FAST," she screamed into the phone.

I jumped out of bed and started throwing on a pair of jeans. Savanna sat up watching me. "What are you doing babe?"

"Somethin's wrong. I gotta get to the main house." I didn't even stop to kiss Savanna as I flew out the door.

Nothing could have prepared me for what I saw when I walked out onto my front porch.

I could see the flames even from my house. Something was on fire and it was big. I no sooner jumped on the golf cart and immediately heard the fire horns. We lived about ten miles from town, but late at night you could hear those sirens if they sounded.

I had forgotten my cell phone to call Conner, but hoped my mother had already done so. As I got closer, I saw exactly what was on fire.

It was the barn.

Giant flames were coming out of the main barn doors. The old hayloft was fully engulfed. Ty was running around without a shirt, trying to get a hose close enough to slow it down at least. "We have to do something," he yelled.

"There's nothing we can do," I said under my breath.

Being that the structure of the barn was made from wood, I knew there was little that we could do. I crouched down on the ground and threw my hands over my head. We had worked on that barn for months. For two years, it was all Savanna had talked about. At Ty and Miranda's party, she had been so excited. I didn't care about the money or even the barn; it was Savanna who my heart ached for.

She'd been through enough. This was going to send her over the edge.

Ty came and stood over me. He was breathing heavily from running around trying to do everything he could to save the barn. I saw headlights coming toward us from the back of the ranch and knew it was Conner. He left his lights on and jumped out of the truck. I could tell from the look on his face that he knew there was nothing that would be salvageable. He took off his hat and threw it on the ground, before kicking the tire to his truck.

All of our countless hours of working into the wee hours of the morning had nothing to show for now. Everything was gone. Ty put his hand on my shoulder and left it there while we both just watched the fire destroying my fiancée's happiness.

Of course, it didn't take long for Savanna to hop in my truck and come driving down that lane. I could see the flames against the windshield, but through the glass Savanna was breaking down, holding her hands over of her face. I got up and ran toward the truck, not knowing what I could say to make any of this better

for her.

Chapter 2

Savanna

All of my life I had pictured my wedding as the happiest day of my life. Of course, I had changed the person I thought I would marry, but the dream remained the same. I was marrying Colt Mitchell and the anticipation alone was killing me.

After Ty and Miranda had finally settled down, the family went back to being normal, with the exception of them being married now. I have to admit, they both hurt me. Don't get me wrong, I never wanted Ty back, but seeing him, so happy with someone else, someone that I was so close to, well it was like a punch in the gut. For years, I had been the best girlfriend possible, while he went behind my back cheating on me.

I loved Miranda, but as far as guys were concerned, she wasn't much better. She lost her father when she was little and I think once she hit puberty she sought out attention from the opposite sex to fill the void. She ended up getting pregnant by a total loser, who threatened the life of her and their daughter. His threats sent her to live with Ty and the rest is history.

I wanted to be happy for them, but I don't know if I could ever trust Ty. Maybe I just didn't want to, because then it would make our failed relationship somehow my fault. I wanted to be the best wife to Colt, so knowing that I never satisfied my last boyfriend really made me worry.

I couldn't help it that I was nothing like Miranda. She could walk around naked all day and be totally okay with it. When we went out places, she craved the attention. There was no way in Hell I could wear the things she put on her body. I could only imagine the things she did in bed. When I think about their relationship in that aspect I know why she tamed Ty.

He followed her around like she was his obsession. She didn't even realize how much he had changed for her. The most shocking thing to the whole family was his devotion to Bella. My God, he loved that kid like she was his own flesh and blood. She loved him too.

I will never forget hearing her call him 'Daddy' for the first time. The look in his eyes told me everything I needed to know. As shocked as we all were, I couldn't help but melt when I saw the two of them interacting.

I was jealous of their life. Colt was getting older and in the

fall would be turning twenty seven. He desperately wanted to start

having kids and was accepting when I told him we had to wait until

I was out of school. I went off the pill five months ago and we still

weren't pregnant. I guess that added to my sudden case of

emotional breakdowns regarding Ty and Miranda.

Anyone could tell they were happier than ever. I swear

they lived in their own little bubble and never worried about

anyone else. I wanted that so much, not with Ty of course, but with

Colt.

I loved him so much and marrying him was going to be the

happiest day of my life. I was hoping that once the stress of the

wedding was finally over, my body would just relax and I would

become instantly pregnant. Colt was optimistic, even as I began to

worry. He said when the time was right, we would get pregnant. I

appreciated his kind words, but I also knew some people couldn't

have children. That would break Colt's heart.

Since I had been so over-emotional lately, Colt was

especially sweet at night when it was just us. Sometimes he would

just hold me tight, stroking my arms, until I went to sleep. Other times he would hold me while I cried for reasons I wasn't even sure of. This night had been no different. We had a great dinner with the whole family and hung out afterwards.

Colt pried Bella away from her Daddy and was able to get some kisses from her finally. She had been stingy about only giving kisses to Ty. I teased him about brainwashing her, but ever since the child was born, she had claimed Ty as her favorite person in the world. It didn't even matter that they once lived in separate states; she never lost that love for him.

As much as I would like to hate Ty for hurting me, when I saw him being a husband and father, it made my heart just turn to pudding. I wanted Colt to feel that love from a child. I wanted him to talk to my belly and hold my hand when I went into labor. Obviously it was really bothering me.

My best friend Brina was in town and she and Conner seemed to be really hitting it off. We were all finally glad he hadn't brought Courtney around in a few days. I honestly could care less if Brina and he hooked up. Neither were looking for something serious so they may as well enjoy each other's company while she was visiting.

Colt and I went home from dinner and watched television in bed before finally going to sleep. Like every night lately, he made sure I fell asleep with either his arm around me, or my hand in his. When the phone started to ring, we both jumped up out of bed.

I watched as Colt's eyes got huge and he shot up out of bed. Once he got on some pants, he went flying out of the door without an explanation. For fear that, something had happened to a family member, I got myself dressed. Of course, I had been lying in only a pair of panties, so it took me a couple minutes to find my bra and then some clothes to put on.

Nothing could have prepared me for what I saw when I walked out of our house. Beyond the trees, I could see the flames of something on fire. Panic came over me when I started thinking it was the main house. I jumped in Colt's truck and grabbed the keys from the visor. I think I almost skidded off the dirt road that led to the main part of the ranch at least three times. Conner's truck sat in front of where I finally came to a stop, but nothing could block the site of the barn going up in flames.

Colt was ahead of me kneeling on the ground with his head down, while Ty and Conner stood behind him. They turned as I pulled up, but I couldn't get out of the truck. I couldn't move at all.

Colt got up and started running toward the truck, while fire trucks started to pour into the ranch. It was too late. There was nothing anyone could do to salvage anything in that barn.

"Savanna, Darlin' this changes nothin'," Colt said as he flung the door open. "Savanna, can you hear me?"

I looked at Colt, but words wouldn't come out of my mouth. Ty started walking toward us, I guess to check on me as well, but I didn't hear what he was saying. I felt Colt grabbing me by the arm and shaking me and still, I never moved. I guess I was just in shock.

We were supposed to be married in just three days.

How could it really be happening?

Was it just a bad dream?

Colt grabbed my hand and held it when he realized I was incoherent. He was brushing my hair out of my face and saying things to me, although I couldn't tell you what it was. He turned to look at me and past my watery eyes, I could see his mouth moving, but couldn't make out his words.

I turned to face the flaming building. The roof began to collapse. A loud cracking and falling sound erupted the ranch as the large structure fell to the ground in the midst of heated fire. The firefighters began hosing down the vicinity around the barn, to prevent it from spreading to any of the other buildings. All I could do was just sit there staring. I watched the fire consuming all of my happiness and turning it to ash.

Chapter 3

Colt

Savanna hadn't said a word after the fire had consumed the whole barn, leaving it as a pile of charred rubble. She managed to scoot over in the truck to enable me to drive us back to the house. I carried her in the house and put her in bed. She had anxiety medication she took when things got too hard for her to handle, it seemed like she was having to take at least two a week lately.

After getting her settled enough, I headed back to deal with the aftermath of the fire. At one point, there had been three ladder trucks and two engines here at the ranch. As I drove back, I noticed there were only two trucks left. Firefighters were walking through the still smoking debris. My mother was standing pretty far back talking to the fire chief. I recognized him from charity events we had both attended. I approached him and held out my hand. "Sorry you had to come out tonight."

"It's my job. I was just tellin' your mama that the inspector is goin' to need to come out for insurance purposes."

"Yeah I figured as much." I kicked a couple pieces of charred wood back toward the pile of ash.

"I'm guessin' this is where the big event was goin' to take place?" The fire chief wrote something else down in his clipboard and looked back up at us.

"It was. Now I have no clue what we are goin' to do," I said honestly.

My mother put her arm around my back and started rubbing it. "We will get it all figured out. Don't worry about that right now."

I nodded. There wasn't much to say. Everything for the wedding was in that barn. The only thing that we still had was Savanna's dress. This was a total fucking disaster. Conner was standing around talking to a firefighter, while Ty and Miranda were on my mother's front porch just watching from afar. I kept looking around at my family. I knew they were all concerned, but there wasn't shit anyone could do now.

The sheriff's department showed up about an hour later. I guess that was how long it took them to talk to some of the people who had worked hard to try to contain the fire. The fire department had just pulled away and my mother had taken everyone else inside. It had been daylight for about an hour so I estimated that it was around seven in the morning.

"Looks like you guys had a rough night," he said as he climbed out of his vehicle.

"You could say that." I shook his hand. "So what's goin' on?"

"I figured since this is goin' to be major news around town, I would get on top of this. I need to know if you think anyone could have started this fire. Is there anyone with a vendetta against your family? Anyone that you could think of that would hurt your family?"

As I was thinking about who could have done something like this, I saw Ty pulling a shirt over his head and walking toward us. "Hey man what's going on?" He asked.

"He was just askin' if we know anyone that could have done this on purpose."

Ty shook his head and let out a sigh. He got ready to say something, but we noticed Aunt Karen flying up the driveway. She jumped out of the car and came running toward us. "John, thanks for coming so fast. This is why I called you." She handed him a cell phone. I recognized it right away from all the bullshit we had gone through before. It was Miranda's.

Ty and I just looked at each other and watched the officer looking through the messages.

"They are all from a blocked number, but I'm sure it's him. We hadn't heard anything, but with the wedding being in the papers, I guess it gave him reason to believe she was back. Are they in any danger John? Do they need to leave the ranch? They have a small child to think about, you know."

"Karen, you need to calm down. I'm going to have to take this phone to the station. For now, I will post someone outside of the ranch keepin' an eye on anything suspicious. I know you will be havin' a lot of guests this weekend. Now, as far as these threats, since we don't have a number and nobody has seen Tucker Chase around, I can't really do much."

She shook her head. "This is why I had to send her away in the first place John. It has to be him. Did you read the message?"

I was curious. "Can I see the phone?"

Ty stood over my shoulder as I pulled up the messages.

I know u r back bitch. This is just the beginning.

It took everything I had not to throw the phone across the driveway. This fire was intentional. Miranda's ex was responsible. I knew it wasn't her fault, but because of her involvement with him, my girlfriend had to suffer. I wasn't okay with that.

"This guy is threatening my wife and child. There has to be something else you can do." Ty was beyond angry. He was literally shaking while talking.

"Son, I understand your concerns. I can bring Mr. Chase in for questioning," he offered.

"No!" I held my hand up for Ty to shut up and listen. "If they do that it will piss him off more. I think we have all lost enough here. You and Miranda need to stay inside. Don't go anywhere alone and don't let Bella out of your site."

"Like that would ever happen," Ty said sarcastically.

He never let her out of his sight; in fact he was attached to her hip for the most part.

"I think Colt is right. We need to just be careful. The inspector will be here later and maybe we will know more. We have to have proof before we can pick this guy up and keep him. If you want to put this kid away, we need to do it by the book." The sheriff kept looking at my aunt. It was obvious they had something going on. *Good for them and good for us. That meant he was going to bust his ass to get this shit handled.*

Miranda walked toward us. She had on one of Ty's college sweatshirts and it hung down to her knees. "What's goin' on?"

"They think it was Tucker. That son of a bitch sent more messages this morning. Do you believe this shit? We need to think about taking Izzy home baby. I can't have your lives being in danger."

I understood how Ty felt and if it was my family being threatened, I would want to leave town too, but them leaving would hurt Savanna even more. I didn't know how to selfishly ask them to stay just so that Savanna would be able to cope with what had already happened. This was too serious to take lightly. They were in danger; it was more obvious now than ever.

"If you need to leave, we will understand." I was disappointed, but I needed them to be safe.

Ty wrapped his arms around Miranda and kissed her head. "We can talk about it later."

My aunt Karen started walking to the police car with the sheriff. I turned to look at Ty and Miranda. It was clear that she'd been crying. Her eyes were blood red.

"I'm so sorry Colt. You have no idea how sorry I am. I don't even know what to say. This is all my fault." Ty comforted his wife and offered me an apologetic smile. For once he really didn't have anything to do with this.

"Don't blame yourself Miranda. None of us expected this."

Maybe we all did, but she couldn't have known this would happen.

"He would have never done this if I hadn't dated him," she cried.

I approached both of my cousins and grabbed Miranda's hand while Ty stood behind her. "If you didn't date him you wouldn't have Bella or Ty. Don't be so hard on yourself. He made the choices, not you."

"Savanna is going to hate me. Everything is ruined," she cried.

"She won't. She knows this isn't your fault." *Actually, she will probably blame you forever. I hated that she would, but I knew her and she will need someone to blame.*

I couldn't say that to her. Miranda and Ty had worked so hard to change their lives. Everyone has skeletons in their closet, how could she have known something like this could result in their relationship. He didn't even want to be with her in the first place.

"I hope you're right Colt. I know how much she wanted your wedding to be perfect. She didn't deserve this." Miranda pulled out of Ty's arms and started walking back to the house. She held her head down and continued to cry.

Ty turned to me and patted my shoulder. "Let me know if you need anything. I have to go try and calm her down. She's a mess right now."

I gestured toward the house. "Yeah, go ahead. I need to get back to my house too and check on Savanna. She ain't taking this good at all."

The truth was, I had no idea how she was taking things. She refused to speak to me when I took her home and got her into bed.

Ty turned around and started walking backwards. "You may want to give her some space. I know Van and she can't take stressful situations. She will hold it all in and then eventually explode and you definitely don't want to be around for that. It is the scariest shit I have ever seen."

I pulled my hat off and took a deep breath. I had seen her mad, but not like he was describing, although I knew they had some pretty heavy fights in the past. "Thanks for the warnin'."

"Seriously dude, be careful. It's scary!" I watched Ty walk into the house and started to head back to my truck.

Savanna was probably still asleep. I would make her some tea and convince her that we could get one of the other barns ready in three days. We would make it work. Things were going to be okay.

Chapter 4

Savanna

After Colt carried me upstairs and left to go deal with the aftermath of our newest catastrophe, I got up and went downstairs. I started looking for my medication and couldn't remember where I had put it. Knowing him it was on some shelf somewhere. He sat everything up high on account of him being so darn tall.

When I couldn't find the medicine, I headed straight to the liquor cabinet. If anything could calm my nerves it was Colt's private whiskey stash. I say private because he kept it hidden from everyone else. I happened to be excluded from the everyone else part since I was his lady.

I was so upset about the barn. All of my dream wedding plans were ruined. How could this have happened to me? I don't remember doing anything to piss off God or anyone else. I attended church regularly; I was a good girlfriend and fiancée to Colt. I always tried to live responsibly. It just made no sense.

I knew Colt was mad, especially when he had to rush back out of here. Sometimes I think he knew to avoid me when I got mad. I guess from being an only child my whole life, I had this complex that everything had to go my way, all of the time. When it didn't, well let's just say that I wasn't the nicest person. I had tried to be better, even to ask for forgiveness and guidance from up above, but my temper was something fierce.

With the whiskey finally in my grasp, I opened the cap and took a giant gulp. It burned from the first moment it hit my throat and I cringed at the kick it had as it went down. My stomach instantly began to warm and I giggled knowing that soon I wouldn't care about anything. I wasn't normally one to drown my sorrows, but nobody at this ranch could relate to what I was going through.

A knock at the door startled me. I took the bottle and hid it behind the couch cushion as I walked over to answer the door. Sam, our dog, went flying for the door. "Get down girl."

She sat next to me wagging her tail in anticipation of who could be on the other side. The deliveryman stood there with a package in his hands. "Hello there. You don't have to sign. Just wanted to say hello," he said as he handed me the package.

"Thanks. Have a good day."

He always seemed to give me googly eyes when I answered the door. I wondered if he had secret relationships with some of his regular delivery addresses. Since Ty had cheated on me, I assumed that every man, except Colt, had shady secrets. I don't know why I always kept Colt on some pedestal, but it worked for my happiness that I liked to keep us in.

I plopped myself back down on the couch and pulled out my hidden whiskey bottle. I was able to have already knocked off a quarter of it. The small box sat in my hand and I began opening it. Low and behold were photo books of Ty and Miranda's service that I had ordered with one day shipping. As I grabbed the first photo book, I feared what I would see as I looked down at it. Since I had designed them I knew that the pain would rip through me as I saw that decorated barn on the cover. Ty and Miranda were standing in front of it, with Bella in both of their arms. Their picture perfect moment captured just hours before it turned to rubble.

The page creaked as I opened the book for the first time. Page after page I studied the background and not the people in the images. In each one I could see Colt and Conner's hard work. Every little detail had been perfect for our big day. I grabbed the second book and took another three swigs of soothing liquor. There were pictures of the whole service; close ups of the alter Colt had built for us, the wooden dance floor that they stayed up late making level. It was all there in colorful photos.

I closed the book and stared at the cover again. They were so in love, so happy with their day. I took the book and chucked it across the room. A picture of a deer went crashing down to the floor, shattering upon impact. I pulled my knees up to my chest and buried my face into my hands. The tears poured out and I wasn't fighting them. It wasn't fair that they got to have my day. I knew it wasn't their fault, but it still wasn't fair. In some prissy pathetic way, I just wanted that perfect wedding to happen.

Without hesitation, I sat up and began gulping down the burning liquor. As the bottle went from almost full to almost empty, I started to relax. I could feel that my fingers were numb and I liked that the room was spinning around so fast that I couldn't remember what I was sad about.

I started belting out 'it's my party and I'll cry if I want to' over and over again, while sipping the heated liquor. Nobody could hear me, so I assume I was doing it for my own personal pity party.

I crawled up my stairs and headed into my bedroom where I found my wedding dress, in the zipper safe bag. I pulled it out and stripped out of my clothes. Once it was on, well halfway, since I couldn't fasten the back, I climbed up on my bed and finished off the whiskey. The ceiling started spinning around and I pretended I was moving around dancing with Colt on our big day.

"Savanna can you hear me? Wake up, Darlin'."

I opened my eyes and looked around the room. It was still spinning up a storm, but I was able to make out a very concerned Colt over top of me. I giggled when I saw him and reached for his beautiful face. "You forgot to shave tomorrow….I mean this morning," I giggled.

"Darlin' did you drink all of this?" He held up the bottle and shook his head.

"Yuppers!"

He shook his head. "Are you able to stand up?"

I shrugged and started to sit up. Immediately I felt nauseous. "The room is spinnnnnning."

"You need to get out of your dress. I'm tryin' real hard not to look at you in it."

Oh shit! No, he can't see me in this dress.

"I can't take it off myself." I stood up off the bed and began wobbling like I was going to flop to the ground. The dress was big and I couldn't find where it ended to grab it. I started throwing the underneath of it over my head in layers. After I got three layers of dress over my head, I realized I was completely stuck inside of it. Colt had originally turned around to prevent getting a good look at it, but I knew I was never going to be able to functionally remove it myself.

"I need your help."

I felt a few tugs and the dress lifting off of my head. When my face was free from fabric, I noticed he was helping me with his eyes closed.

What guy does that?

My guy does, that's who!

I climbed back on the bed and reached for the dress bag, but noticed that the bed felt so completely comfortable. I kicked the dress to the floor and backed up on the bed, staring at my hot ass fiancée standing over me with his eyes closed. It was probably wrong to be seducing him with my drunken eyes, but that was exactly what I was doing. Colt was the finest man I had ever laid eyes on. Every inch of him was a sculpted masterpiece. I dreamed about his arms holding me and the things he did to me with his body. I had studied every inch of him so many times.

"Is it put away?" He asked.

"Nope," I said as I licked my lips, knowing damn well that he wasn't going to be patient forever.

I maneuvered myself to the edge of the bed and put two fingers inside of his pants, in order to pull him toward the bed. Once he was standing at the edge, he opened his eyes, but I was already starting to undress him. I was drunk and extremely horny. I needed him in the worst way. I wanted him to make all of the pain go away.

"I want you." I grabbed his shirt and pulled it over his head.

Colt's chest was like licking heaven. I ran both of my hands up and down each side and over his little nipples. "You are drunk."

"I want you Colt. Please…" I backed myself onto the bed and tried to seduce him with my eyes. The problem with that was that Colt had the most beautiful light green eyes that I had ever seen, well besides Conner who had the same. Colt could look at me and melt me within seconds. His eyelashes were so dark and his full eyebrows matched his dark head of hair. Since he hadn't had time to shave, his facial hair had come in and covered most of his face making him look older and more distinguished. Colt licked his lips as he watched me watching him.

He leaned down over the bed and came within inches of my body. "You know I don't like being with you when you are incoherent. I want every time to be just as enjoyable for you as it always is for me."

His words melt me.

"Baby, I will enjoy every second of this." I grabbed him by wrapping my legs around his waist and pulled him over top of me. I had no balance, but Colt managed to catch himself before his body toppled on top of mine. I didn't let him pull away. Instead, I grabbed him by the ear and pulled him toward my mouth. Our first kiss was rough, as our mouths crashed together. The stressful day mixed with the liquor caused me to want him like it had been months. I yearned for his touch and wanted his hands all over me, especially while I was laying there naked.

"Touch me Colt, lick my nipples," I slurred.

He buried his head into my neck and began laughing. "It's better if you don't talk."

I grabbed his face and stopped him from kissing my chest. "Why can't I talk?"

Colt drug his lips over mine slowly, causing me to close my eyes and gasp. "Because you are sayin' things you would never say. As much as I like it, I know it's the liquor talkin'."

I sat up and pushed him onto the bed. When he began to roll over I forced myself on top of him. With my legs straddling him, he laid there looking defeated. "I want you to fuck me right now."

Colt burst into a laughing fit. He was making me so mad, but still wouldn't let go of my waist when I tried to hop off of him. As I did try to move, I could feel his hard erection pressing against my butt. I grinded myself against him. "Savanna, stop!"

Colt was getting mad too. It made me want him even more. I ran my hands through my hair and shook it around. I had to admit that it made me feel like I was going to pass out, but I closed my eyes for a second and let the dizziness subside. Colt loved how my hair was long enough to just reach my nipples. I pulled a strand from each side and let it fall over them. Letting my fingers slide over each side, I continued running them over my stomach and then finally, I reached one hand between my legs.

I saw Colt's adam's apple move as he swallowed and tried to stay focused on *not* having sex with me. I ran two fingers down and penetrated beneath the folds. I wasn't doing it for my own pleasure, but after a few slow-paced movements it started to feel real good. Colt licked his lips and tried to sit still. I could feel him trying to reposition underneath of me.

"You like it don't you?" I teased.

"Shit, Savanna. You're killin' me."

I started rubbing myself harder; not knowing which one of us was more turned on. "Oh God, it feels so good, Colt. Touch me please."

With his strong arms, Colt flipped us around and was sprawled over top of me. Ultimately, it freed my hands from where they were and left me panting. "You aren't playin' fair Darlin'."

I bit down on my lip and watched him tracing his hand down between my breasts. He kept moving it until I felt him drive a finger into my sex. I spread my legs further, letting him know I wanted whatever he would give. He pulled his finger out abruptly and before I could even react he slid down and buried his face between my legs.

Oh yes oh yes oh yes…oh right there.

Colt had taught me so much about myself and my body, but the things the man could do with his tongue were AMAZING. I felt him flicking my most sensitive spot over and over. My toes began to clench up and I let the magical feeling overcome me as I screamed out in pleasure. "Yessssss."

Even after he knew I had climaxed, Colt placed small kisses on my inner thighs, even knowing how much it tickled me. He kissed my belly button and let his wet saliva leave a trail up to one of my nipples. I loved to watch him touch me with his tongue. The moment it made contact with any part of my skin made me want to yell his name. He sent chills all over my body by just looking at me.

I ran my hands over my face just as he was coming up to kiss me. I felt his wet lips on my chin and then finally my lips. I could taste myself as he stroked his tongue over mine. It made me excited in a dirty way. Before I could comment, I was being turned around. Colt grabbed my hips and pulled me back against his erection. I could feel him positioning himself behind me, right before he forced himself inside of me. With each individual thrust He pushed my body forward. I grabbed the headboard and held on to it as his naked body slapped against mine. Colt held my hip with one hand and ran his other one up and down the small of my back. I could feel his body tensing up behind me right before he eventually collapsed over my back.

I flipped myself over and accepted my lover to rest his head across my breasts. I was looking straight up at the ceiling. He played with my fingers and twisted the large ring on my finger.

"Feel better now, Tiger?"

"Mmmm, a little bit," I teased.

He brought my hand to his lips. "I love you Darlin', even when you drink yourself silly."

I squeezed his hand tight. "I love you too, Colt Mitchell. I can't wait to be your wife."

He turned to face me and leaned himself on his own hands. "We will make it perfect. I promise you that."

I kissed him quickly. "I know."

Chapter 5

Colt

I had no idea I would find Savanna in the condition she was

in. Her drunk ass was sprawled out on the bed while wearing her

wedding dress, incoherent. When I finally did get her to wake up,

she decided that she wanted to get all freaky on me. I mean, how

was I supposed to tell her no, when she was flaunting it in front of

me. I did well for a couple of minutes, but the alcohol had caused

her to be way more adventurous then I was used to. Here lately,

since we had been trying to get pregnant, we had sex all of the

time. Sometimes it felt forced and I hated that, so when she

started touching all over herself, it made me crazy.

I wanted to stay in bed with her all day and pretend that

the fire never happened, but with a guest list of over two hundred

people due to arrive in just three days, there was a lot of work that

needed to be done. I had to figure out where we could move the

site of the wedding to and how we could make it look remotely like

the barn had. We still had two old barns from the original farm, but

they were filled with old equipment and one was all the way out by

my aunt's house. I was going to have to hire someone to come in to help move all of the shit out of it to see if it was even stable enough to house all of those people.

My mother and Aunt Karen could take charge of the decorations and everything else we had to replace; while Conner, Ty and I did all that we could to make everything else work.

While Savanna slept off her liquor binge, Sam and I headed out to look around the ranch. There had to be a way to make all of this happen and give Savanna the wedding she deserved. I needed her to look back and think that our wedding was one of the most beautiful moments of her life.

I found Ty leaning over the kitchen counter talking to Miranda. Bella was running around the island as usual, swinging something in her hands.

"Hey guys."

"Hey Cuz. So what's the plan? What can we do to help?" Ty asked.

Bella came up and hugged my leg. I picked her up and realized she was holding a pickle. It had been chewed to hell and apparently dropped on the floor a few times. "Do you have a pickle?" I teased.

She shook her head 'yes'. "Daddy gib me."

"He did? Well it looks like a good tastin' pickle."

Of course she pushed it up toward my mouth. "Bite."

I sat her down before I could have a dirty pickle shoved in my mouth. She started running around like I disappeared into thin air.

I leaned over the opposite side of the kitchen island. "I was thinkin' that we should look around the two old barns and figure out which one we could get cleaned out faster. I can hire some people to come haul out all the stuff while we run into town and get the new speaker wire and lighting. If we start on this today, we might be able to surprise Savanna and make it happen."

"Count me in. I can do whatever you need." Ty handed Bella a new pickle and took the old one. "Eat this one instead baby."

"Mommy yook." She held up the pickle to show Miranda.

"I see it. I bet it tastes good." Miranda pretended to take a bite. I knew for a fact that she hated pickles. We used to hold her down and make her drink pickle juice

As Miranda bent down to give Bella attention, I watched Ty watching them intently. He wasn't looking at his wife because she was bent over; it was more like he was admiring her being a mother. He focused on them interacting, and seemed so content with himself. I still couldn't get over the way he loved them, but the longer I spent with them, it was obvious it was real.

He turned and noticed that I was watching him and smiled, letting out an air filled laugh. "Baby, I'm going to walk out with Colt. Be back in a sec."

"K!"

Ty followed me outside and we hopped on the golf cart. "I still can't get over it man." I confessed.

"Well, it's real. You all can think whatever you want. Nothing will change the way I feel about them. I have never in my life been more happy as when I'm with the two of them. When I go to work, I think about them all day. I can't wait to get home at night and see them and tuck Izzy into bed."

"She really seems to love you, but I guess she always did, even when she was a baby."

We pulled up at the barn near my Aunt Karen's house. The door had broken hinges and hung crooked. I sighed as we jumped off and started walking toward it.

"I can't remember a time where I didn't love Izzy. I don't give a damn what the blood tests say, she is mine Colt. Being a dad is the most satisfying feeling. In fact, when she called me Daddy for the first time, I actually cried. There ain't much to make me cry, but damn she gets to me like no other ever has."

"Savanna and I are tryin' to get pregnant. We've only been tryin' for a couple of months. I can't wait for it to happen." We both pulled a side of the barn door and walked it open. Aside from the hayloft being full of old hay, and probably a few critters, the first floor wasn't that bad. There was a bunch of metal pieces from the tractors, a few tires and even some old barrels. It wouldn't take much time at all to get it cleaned out. Of course, it was very filthy. Twenty years of cobwebs and dirt filled every inch of the inside of the barn.

"So what do you think? You think we can make this work in three days?" Ty asked.

We started walking back out and closed the doors behind us. "Let's go check out the other one."

We hopped back on the golf cart and headed to the oldest barn on the property. In my honest opinion, it should have been torn down years ago. It was made from wooden planks and you could see through every single one. It used to be red, but now had cracked away to a peeled hue of brown. Ty and I approached the barn and I realized right away that it didn't look promising. After opening the door, I realized there was no way in Hell we could use this barn. "This one's a no-go!"

"Yeah, I can see that," Ty laughed.

We shut the doors and climbed back on the golf cart. "Looks like we are cleaning out the other one. I'm goin' to go back to the office and make some calls. I know a crew that can come in and gut the place. Do you mind findin' Conner?"

"Nah, I will round him up and meet you back at the office. You mind if I let Miranda know what we're doing? I just want to grab my phone so that if she needs me she can call."

I started shaking my head. He knew I had my phone. He just wanted to see Miranda. "You're obsessed!"

"Whatever dude! I prefer devoted. They are my girls. One day you will understand. Just wait until Van gets pregnant and you hold that baby for the first time. Then I will be calling you the pussy."

We both laughed. "Is that how you felt with Bella? Did you always feel like you were her father, cause that's kind of weird."

"Nah, it wasn't like that. I mean, I felt like she was special and I needed to be near her. I can't explain it. I guess the bond was there, even if I hadn't realized it. That day changed my life. *She* changed my life."

I watched Ty again as he talked about Bella. It was like he was under some kind of spell. There was no doubt that everything he was saying was true. Anyone could see he was smitten. It was just so strange to see him like that. For so long he was only worried about one thing. I don't have a clue what Miranda did to him, but the old Ty was gone. "You can add whipped," I joked.

"Don't hit me dude, but if you experienced the things that I have with Miranda, you wouldn't look at or even think of another woman. That woman does things to me that I have never experienced."

I guess Ty sensed me clenching my jaw. He held up his hand. "I don't mean sexual, well not completely. She just, well she just gets me. We are a team. Marrying her was the best decision I ever made."

I shook my head. "Enough about it. Your making me sick. I adore Savanna and I already know what you mean when you say you don't want to be with anyone else. I get it. It's just strange seein' this come of out your mouth. I never thought this would happen to either of you. I'm happy for you. No matter how much I joke, we are family and nothin' will change that. Just keep lovin' em Ty. You need each other and it's important. I hope you never forget how you feel right now."

He patted me on the shoulder. "Awww, your being such a good cousin. Does Van know how sappy you can be?" Ty asked sarcastically.

"You're a dick. I was bein' serious. Go check in with the wife and make sure you ask for her permission to do manly things."

"I'm only helping you if I can wear pink panties," Ty mocked.

I gave him the finger as I pulled away from the house and headed toward my office. The old sarcastic Ty was still in there, but he had also become a romantic, which was convoluted and just plain strange. If he acted that way around Conner, we would never hear the end of it.

Savanna was lying on the couch when I got there. She was curled up under a blanket and smiled as I walked in the door. "Hey babe."

"Hey yourself. You feelin' any better?"

She shrugged. "My head is pounding, but aside from that I'm okay. I cleaned up the picture mess. Sorry about that."

I leaned down and kissed her forehead. "No worries, I knew you would figure out a way to redecorate."

We both laughed. "Shut up! I never said that I wanted to."

"Savanna, our bedroom went from being brown to purple. I hardly think I had anything to do with that," I teased.

She pulled me down onto the couch. Our mouths banged into each other and I could feel her laughing against my body. She wrapped her arms around my neck. "You know you love it."

She kissed my upper lip and held her mouth there. I pulled away and kissed her nose. "I love you, I know that."

"Should we cancel the wedding?"

I buried my head into her neck and kissed up to her ear. "Nope." I whispered.

"Where are we going to put all of those people?" She asked.

I sat up and slid off the couch, positioning myself in front of her. "I will take care of everything. Just go about the plans like nothin' ever happened."

She gave me a funny look and raised one eyebrow. "You're not going to tell me what you're up to?"

"Nope!"

"I hate that word. It so, ...so short."

"No is shorter."

She laughed and shook her head. "Never mind. Are you home for good?"

I stood up and held my hand out for her. "I need to do some work in the office. You want to eat somethin' for lunch before I get started? I can make us somethin'," I offered.

She grabbed my hand and stood up. "I will make it for you babe. You know I love spending time with you."

We held hands and walked into the kitchen. Savanna led the way and I appreciated the view of her backside. She knew how much I loved her ass. I think I talked about it more than the normal person would.

My woman made me grilled cheese. She wasn't the best cook in the world, but she could make a damn good grilled cheese, of course she burned the first one, because I sat her on the countertop and started getting frisky with her. It wasn't until we smelled it burning that we realized how long we were preoccupied with each other.

After lunch I headed into the office to start making calls about getting some help. I managed to find a crew that could start as early as the next day. According to the crew chief, it would only take them half the day to get it all cleaned out. Feeling satisfied that we would have two full days to get everything decorated the best we could; I sat back and made a list of everything we would need in town.

After about a half hour, I heard the door opening and voices filling the house. I walked out and found Miranda, Ty and Conner standing in the living room with Savanna. "What's up man?" Conner asked.

I gave him a quick nod. "Everything's a go. You guys ready to head out?"

Miranda and Savanna looked at me for an explanation. "Where you going Babe?"

"We need to run into town to get some top secret wedding supplies. You need anything while we're gone?" I asked.

"Since I have no idea what you are doing or even where you are going, I will say 'no'," she laughed.

I walked over and kissed her goodbye, while Ty grabbed Miranda and pulled her in for something that lasted entirely too long for anyone else in the room to feel comfortable. As Conner and I stood there clearing our voices, they continued to have their tongues down each other's throats. "Get a fuckin' room," Conner said while shaking his head.

Ty pulled away from Miranda, but went back in for one more peck. "We just came from our room if you must know. Miranda was showing me some new moves, " he said.

"Do ya'll seriously have to talk about sex all of the time. Damn, it gets old," Conner said as he walked out the door.

"He must not be getting any. Van you need to get Brina to get right on that. As long as he stays satisfied, he doesn't want to beat my ass so much," Ty joked. He slapped Miranda on her ass and kissed her cheek. "Be back later, Baby. We can start where we left off, I promise."

She giggled and watched him leave. I let out a laugh. "Unbelievable!"

I caught up to the guys, who were standing by one of the ranch trucks.

"Rock, paper, scissors, shoot!" They said together.

"Damn, I never get it!" Ty announced as Conner jumped in the front seat.

"What are you two five?" I asked.

Ty climbed in the back and leaned over the seat. "I never get to sit in the front," he said in a baby voice.

"You are such a douche," Conner laughed.

"I know you are but what am I?" He pushed Conner's buttons on purpose. It was like the two of them had to be at each other all of the time. It had to drive Miranda crazy. The worst part was that they were both so damn similar. Neither one of them had any room to talk.

"You need to stop groping my sister around me. Have some respect." Conner threatened.

Ty laughed and started looking at his phone. He never looked up from it while he spoke. "I'm respectful of your sister. You do know she is an adult and we are married. If I want to touch her, I can. Just so you know, she wants to touch me too. She tells me all of the time. Do you want to see the messages?" He handed Conner his phone.

Conner took one look and the phone went flying in the backseat. "What the fuck dude! You're sick!"

"Seriously you two. We have a lot of shit to do today. Can you please act like adults for a few hours?" I begged.

"I just saw my sister's naked breasts man. I can't help it." Conner said defensively.

Ty sat in the back seat laughing his ass off. "Did you see the message?"

"Yeah, I saw it. Fuck you. Don't show me that shit again." Conner added.

Without me asking what exactly he showed him Ty started to explain. "They weren't her naked tits. She had her nipples covered. I was just trying to show you that it isn't always me. Miranda loves it. She is the one always initiating it. She can't get enough of my meat."

Conner went flying toward the back, swinging at Ty. I pulled the truck over and let my head fall to the steering wheel. As Ty continued to laugh and Conner had smoke blowing out of his ears, I jumped out and stood on the side of the road until the truck stopped moving from them trying to bust each other up while still inside.

The power window rolled down. "You can get in now Colt. We're done."

When I got in the vehicle, neither of them said a word. I looked in the backseat to double check Ty was alive. He was still playing on his phone and I could hear messages coming in. Every message made him laugh more. I looked over to Conner who rolled his eyes. "First he was my cousin, and now he is my brother. I can't kill him. I can't even hate him. I know they are perfect together, but I hate that he rubs it in my face. All those damn times I warned him to not touch her. I think I have a right to be at least a little upset still."

Ty leaned over the seat. "I swear to God that I never touched your sister in all the times I came to visit, not even when we were teenagers. I may have thought about it in the past two years, but that's it. Nothing happened until she showed up at my farm."

Conner turned to face the backseat and I considered pulling over again.

"I believe you, but only because I can see how crazy she is about you, and if you were involved before she never would have been able to keep it a secret. I know her and Bella are happy. It's all that matters. Just don't show me her tits again. She's my sister for shits sake."

Ty continued to laugh. "It was her idea. Besides, she was wearing a bra. You act like I was really showing you skin. Nobody is allowed to see what I see. Just so you know."

"Keep it that way. Don't make me regret forgiving you for all of this."

I figured they would finally give up, but no, Ty had to get the last word in. "You should have never been mad. It ain't like I ever hurt her, or ever will. Just admit it that you were wrong and we can be even."

Conner turned around again and looked at Ty. "Are you serious right now? I was mad because you didn't keep a promise. It was never about how well you can take care of Randa. We already talked about this the night ya'll renewed your vows. Just drop the shit!"

"You need to get laid!" Ty added.

"Fuck off. I got some last night."

"Well trust me when I say that I know it was no good. After five minutes with Miranda, I'm good for a week, not that we ever go that long. I mean some days we.."

"Okay Ty, cut the shit out. I'm half-tempted to let him beat your ass when you get out of this truck. And Conner, you know he is saying this shit to get a rouse out of you. Why do you let it get to you in the first place?"

I looked in the rear view mirror at my cousin, who was laughing his ass off. As serious as Conner was being, I don't think Ty was serious about one single thing.

They stayed quiet for the rest of the ride. Once we made it into town they started to get serious about everything we needed to do in the next couple of days. As long as they didn't kill each other, we could get it done.

We had to, because I wanted Van to have her perfect day. It meant everything to me.

Chapter 6

Savanna

I tried to pry what Colt's big secret was out of Miranda, but she must have either promised Ty she wouldn't say anything, or he hadn't told her. I really wanted to know. It wasn't like I would interfere with Colt's plans, I was just so eager to know what was going on.

Since Miranda and Ty were staying here until the wedding, Aunt Karen had been spending all of her time with Bella. It must have been hard to know that her daughter would never be moving back home, well unless Ty really messed up, but I couldn't for the life of me think he would ever do that to her.

She seemed so happy, and it was weird to me considering how sad she had been the months before she left to stay at Ty's farm. Once I had seen the two of them together, it was obvious that they were involved and in love. I knew why Miranda fell in love with Ty. Aside from the way he cheated on me, he was an awesome person. No matter how serious anything was, he could make people laugh. His sense of humor was often annoying, but he meant well. He was a good listener and would do anything for one of his friends. I knew he and Miranda had been talking for months about what each of them was going through, because Miranda would tell me.

We used to talk about Ty and his cheating ways. I have no idea what made her take that step into giving him a chance with her. Maybe it was just the building attraction they had for one another. Conner claimed that it was just him who noticed, but I knew Ty and I could tell he was interested in her. It didn't help that she was drop dead gorgeous and showed off every perfect inch of her body.

Nowadays she didn't dress like that unless we were going out. Today she was wearing a little sweat suit. It covered her whole body, but still showed off her cute little curves. Knowing that they are a couple I had to laugh. If I could have described Ty's perfect girl in the past, I would have been describing Miranda. She was beautiful and seductive, not to mention a complete nymphomaniac. The girl loved sex and that is what got her into so much trouble in the past. The thing was, she and Ty needed that kind of relationship and they were perfect for each other.

Colt always knew how to touch me to make my body quiver. His strong hands always made me feel safe and I can't remember a time when I didn't get his complete attention. He was a faithful man, which set my mind at ease considering I had been cheated on before. Looking back now, I wouldn't change a thing. Everyone was so happy. We were a family and in some convoluted way, we were always going to be together.

Miranda was flipping through the television looking for something to watch. She'd been quiet around me lately and I couldn't help wonder if she didn't feel uneasy being near me, due to her relationship with Ty. Neither one of us had really had a private kind of conversation about them, on account of it being just too darn awkward. The silence in the room was really getting to me, in fact, I wanted to jump up and down and scream for no apparent reason.

"So, are you having a good visit now that the cat is out of the bag?" I just blurted it out. I couldn't take it anymore. She and Ty were my closest friends, besides Brina, who really wasn't that close to me anymore. I wanted to just get the weirdness out of the room.

Miranda giggled and turned to face me. "With the exception of the fire, yes. You have no idea how scared I was for everyone to find out. Ty and I never planned this. I had no idea he had feelin's for me. We were such good friends and he just loved Bella so much. Maybe I should have stopped myself. I just wanted him so much. I guess I should have talked to you about it first."

I took a deep breath. I couldn't believe she thought I was mad. "Miranda, you and Ty were a shocker, but you're good together. You're honestly perfect for each other. I know you both must think that this is especially hard for me, but you're wrong. I'm about to marry the single most beautiful man on the planet. If anything, I'm glad I get to keep you both in our lives. It means a lot to Colt and to me too. Now I wouldn't go telling Ty that, cause he will get a big head about it, but it is the truth. I never thought he would settle down with anyone, especially not so soon, but he loves you Miranda. Ty and I were many things, but he never loved me like he loves you and I'm okay with that."

Miranda jumped off the couch and came running over to where I was sitting. She gave me a big hug. "You don't understand how much that means to me. I never wanted to lose your friendship, but I couldn't give up Ty. Every bone in my body pushed me right to him."

She sat down beside me and had tears in her eyes. "Don't cry."

"I'm so sorry……. I'm just so happy. I never thought my life could be like this. After my dad died, I just went crazy. As soon as I got boobs, I used my body to get attention from anyone that would give it. I know it was wrong, but it was like I had to get attention. I was horrible, Van. All of the names everyone called me were true. "

She started to cry more and I wrapped my arms around her. She was the type of girl that Ty would cheat on me with, but for some reason, I didn't think of Miranda that way. I saw her as a broken girl who lost one of the most important people in her life, way too soon. She just needed to feel loved, even if it wasn't real. I'm definitely not making excuses for any other girls, but Miranda was a damn good friend and mother. Even if she wasn't related to Colt, I know she wouldn't have ever tried to seduce him or hurt me. "I love you dearly and if any of those people really knew you, they wouldn't have said those things. Everyone makes mistakes

Miranda. What I know is that you are a fantastic mother and you would do anything for your daughter. Ty would have been a fool not to fall in love with you. I'm surprised it took him as long as it did to admit it."

I continued to hold Miranda. She was no longer crying but still sniffling. "I love him with all of my heart, Van. I can't even explain to you how wonderful he makes me feel." She wiped her eyes.

"Not to mention his undeniable devotion to Bella. My God, I have never seen anything like the two of them. What he said at your service to her, was incredibly perfect. I could see tears in Colt's eyes the whole time. I don't know what it is like to be a parent, but he seems to naturally know how to do it."

She looked up at me and seemed sad again. "Would you be mad if we had children together?"

"Of course not. In fact, Colt and I are already trying to get pregnant right now. It's only been a couple of months, but we are hopeful it will happen anytime now. Colt wants at least two children. I can't wait. I mean, I know it will hurt, but I want to have his babies and be a mother so much. I can picture them walking around with Colt's eyes."

"Oh they will be so cute," Miranda agreed.

"Our children can be close in age and grow up having cousins like the boys do. It's kind of exciting isn't it?" For the first time since their big news, I was actually looking past their relationship and seeing a future for all of us. Our children were going to be blood, my children and Ty's children would be related. How crazy was that?

"It's going to be at least a year before Ty and I can start tryin'. I got the shot right after Bella was born and it lasts for three years. Ty did say that he wants children as soon as we can start tryin'. We don't want Bella to be too much older than her brother or sister."

I started thinking about how Miranda got pregnant by Tucker so easily, while Colt and I were tryin' so hard with no result. I suddenly didn't want to talk about pregnancy anymore. "So I know this is random, but do you and Ty go out a lot at home? I know there isn't much to do."

She smiled. "Since we have Bella we spend most of our time at home. Ty likes it to be just us during the week. On the weekends we eat at his parents, especially Sunday's after church. We always end up stayin' late playin' cards."

I had to laugh. "I can't believe you actually get along with that woman. She never liked me at all. When I was younger she tolerated me, I mean I spent all of my time there, but she wasn't exactly loving."

Miranda's phone vibrated and she looked at it and typed something, while smiling the whole time. "Sorry, it was Ty. He likes to text me random messages when we are apart." She sat the phone back down. "Ty said at first she warned him about me using him. He said he told her it wasn't her business and that he cared about me and Bella. From the moment she saw us with Ty for the first time, she has treated me great. She even told me to call her Mom."

I was amazed. I had to admit, it hurt a little. I had never done anything but love that woman's son with my whole heart, but she never really accepted me. She had welcomed Miranda into the family instantly. How could I not be a little hurt by that? "You are so lucky. She must really like you." It was easier than telling her the truth.

"She said that Ty was in a really bad place before Bella and I showed up. He wasn't hangin' out with friends and didn't seem interested in doin' anything outside of work. To be honest, I hadn't exactly been very nice to him months before I showed up at his house. The last time he visited Kentucky, when Tucker attacked me, something started happenin' between us, but neither of us would admit it. I felt so embarrassed, thinkin' he didn't feel the same way, that I stopped talkin' to him. I still let him video chat with Bella, but I was really short with him. So when we finally showed up at his door, there was a lot of pent up feelin's. I guess his mother sensed how excited he was to see us there."

"Can I ask you something personal, between us?" There were a lot of questions that I had for Miranda. Obviously the girl knew what she was doin'.

"Sure, you know you can ask me anything. We are family." Miranda pulled her knees up to her chest and waited for me to respond.

"I feel embarrassed asking this. I guess I want to know how you know you are good in bed." There I just came out with it.

"What do you mean? It is different with every person, especially if you have real feelin's."

"I've only been with two people and one of them is your husband now. I guess I just want to know what you did to make Ty feel so satisfied. Our sex was always so rushed it seemed. Then I get with Colt and he takes things slow and is so gentle. I could never ask for a better lover. Never mind, it's really not a question to be asking." I felt so stupid. She must think I'm such a prissy little virgin*ette*.

She reached over and grabbed my hand. "It's different with Colt because you two love each other. When it's just sex for one or both of the people, the emotional connection isn't there. You may be new at a lot of things, but one thing I never experienced was what it felt like to make love to someone. I never had that until I met Ty. In all of my endeavors, I have never trembled and been so terrified. Once I felt that, it changed everything I ever knew about sex. Now as far as tamin' Ty, let's just say that he and I share the same extracurricular interests."

"When you got drunk the other day, you told me how good he was at ," I had to take a breath, like I couldn't say the words. "going down."

She cocked an eyebrow and looked like she did something wrong. "He never did that to you?"

"Barely ever and it was not because he wanted to. He would only do it so I would return the favor, which I hated doing."

Miranda started laughing. "I don't know what to say to that. I'm not tryin' to make you mad, but Ty seems to really enjoy doin' it to me, of course, he and I have had a lot of firsts since we have been together. Sometimes our feelin's are so intense." She paused as if she were trying to wait for my reaction. "Do you really hate it, or are you just not sure how to do it good?"

She didn't say it in a snotty way, she was genuinely trying to help me. "I do it now. I think my technique is getting good. Colt goes crazy over it, so it must not be too bad."

"Men love it. As far as techniques go, well everyone is different. Listen, I have this silly book about sex in my room. Remind me before I go to give it to you. It has all kinds of details and peoples own stories in it. I learned a bunch from reading it."

A book, like with pictures? I need visual help here!

"I need to see and read that book. I want to." I had almost forgotten all about her pictures, ever since I threw them up against the wall earlier. "Speaking of books, I have something for you. Hang on and let me go get it."

I got up and walked into the office. The box of photo books were sitting on the desk still. I grabbed the whole box and carried it into the living room. "Look what came in the mail today."

"Oh my gosh, they are amazin' Van." She started opening them up and looking through them. I was pretty sure they didn't have family photos. I made sure to take a bunch of the three of them.

"I had some bigger prints made too. Look at these two." I reached in the box and handed her two larger wall pictures, done on a canvas.

She held them both and just smiled. "Ty is going to love these."

I grabbed the last photo in the box. The picture was just of Ty and Bella. They were dancing and she was kissing him. It was such a random shot when I took it, but when I saw it later on, I knew I had to blow it up. I held it up so Miranda could see. "I got this one for Ty."

She put her hand over her mouth. "It's beautiful. She loves him so much. Van he will go nuts over this picture."

"I know, that's why I got a big one. I figured you guys could use some pictures for the house."

"They are all perfect. Thank you so much!"

Miranda spent a good twenty minutes looking at every picture over and over. I could tell she was touched by each one. I thought about mine and Colt's first real pictures together, and how after the first few, I started taking them all the time. Our house was filled with pictures of the two of us. It was like we had been together for ten years instead of two.

As mad as I was about the pictures coming in and seeing the barn in a bunch of them, it made my day to be able to see Miranda's face when she looked at them for the first time.

Chapter 7

Colt

The drive back from town was a lot less eventful, as far as

the bickering between Ty and Conner. Once we got the truck

loaded, they seemed to both be motivated. Sitting back and

looking at the two of them was entertaining. I think they only

fought because they were so similar. The only difference was that

Ty had grown up and become a husband and parent, while Conner

was determined to hit every piece of ass in the state of Kentucky.

I think sometimes Conner hated Ty, because he knew how

he was himself. I could honestly say that Ty was head over heels in

love with Miranda and Bella. He was happy and maybe his

happiness was what made Conner so upset. Sure, I knew deep

down he wanted Miranda to be happy and Bella to have a father

and a family, but it was hard to be able to accept Ty as that person.

When we got back to the ranch, the first thing Ty wanted

to do was see Miranda. Apparently they had been texting and he

said he had to make a pit stop. If he thought the two of them were

going to get busy in the bathroom again, he had another thing

coming. It wasn't happening.

Both Miranda and Savanna were sitting on the couch, looking at all of the pictures. When we walked in, I watched Ty walk over to his wife and kiss her. It wasn't a normal peck like I gave Savanna; it was a more full-blown kind of passion, like they hadn't seen each other in months. I shook my head and tried not to watch them swooning.

Conner walked right past them and headed into the kitchen. I could hear the fridge opening and a beer cracking open. Being that we had so much shit to do, I followed suit. We both stood in the kitchen, leaning up against the counter.

I could hear Savanna in the other room talking to Ty about the photos. She had showed me the one of him and Bella, and I knew he would love it. Savanna made a point to order the pictures as a way to let them know she was completely okay with them being together. I had no reason to worry about either of them having feelings for one another. Savanna found Ty to be annoying and immature, while Ty constantly got on Savanna for being uptight. They loved each other, but there wasn't an inch of romance involved. I often found myself wondering what they were like as a couple. They had no chemistry and although I know, it hurt

Savanna deeply when they broke up, I don't really think Ty was ever that serious about her.

My wife to be always seemed to end up a victim. She had the worst luck, and the newest of such luck resulted in us having to bust our asses to create a new wedding location. After Conner and I both had a beer, we walked back out into the living room and found Miranda in Ty's lap. They were still looking at the photo books with Savanna.

"You ready to get to work, or do ya want to hang out and watch Lifetime Network all afternoon?" Conner teased.

Ty got a big smile on his face. "You're just jealous cause you weren't invited."

Here we go again!

"There ain't nothin' about you to make me jealous," Conner said defensively.

"Till I take off my pants. Then you will be." Conner started approaching Ty and Miranda held her hands up blocking her brother from her husband. She was laughing so hard she couldn't speak.

Conner turned around and walked out of the door. "Forget this shit! Let's roll Colt."

Once Conner was out of the house, I turned to look at Ty. He and Miranda were already back to their cuddle fest. "Seriously, can you just keep your mouth shut until we get finished workin'?"

"He was taunting me."

"Act your age, instead of five, please," I begged.

Ty scooted himself off of the couch. He leaned down and kissed Miranda again. I watched their eyes intently focused on each other. It was like they were having mind sex or something. I shook my head and turned to Savanna. "We have to get to work on your surprise. Love you, Darlin'." To prove a point to myself, and everyone in the room, I let my kiss linger over Savanna's lips. As I walked out the door I laughed at myself for being jealous of Ty and Miranda's kissing.

Damn, he is rubbing off on me!

I was blown away when we got to the barn and the cleanout crew had shown up early. I hadn't expected it, but when someone in our town needed help, people showed up. It was even better that they brought a roll off dumpster. A group of four guys were pulling out large metal tractor parts as we approached the barn. Ty started to unload the generator, while Conner grabbed the pressure washer. My intent was to pressure wash the entire outside and take the tractor around to cut the high grass that had grown all around the outside of the barn.

With every prayer I had focused on my two cousins working together proficiently, I started walking back to get the tractor. It took me a good fifteen minutes, but I was more than pleased when I arrived back to find Ty and Conner working together. Instead of cutting the grass and having it uneven, I had bought a whole truckload of sod that was to be delivered the next day. I took the tractor and tore up the existing weed filled grass to give the dirt a nice even bed. When the landscapers arrived all they would have to do was roll them out evenly.

It took the guys a few hours to pressure wash the whole outside of the barn. For the most part, all of the old paint came right off. The sun was shining down, drying the wood quickly. To give the barn the exact look of the original, we picked out the same red paint and had to rebuild the barn doors from scratch. Conner worked on the doors, while Ty painted all of the white trim.

As the sun began to set, we started spraying the outside the deep color. I had rented the sprayer for two days and it worked so much faster than rolling it. Since the roof was metal, we climbed on top and sprayed it the dark gray color that it once had.

When the moon replaced the sun, we had already painted the whole roof, the front and one side. The cleanout crew finished in less time than they had expected and we were able to get into the empty barn right away. Since there was nothing in it, and the paint on the outside had dried for the most part, we started gently spraying the inside. I knew the outside would need another coat, especially since we had sprayed some of it with water, but we had a good head start.

We called it a night around ten in the evening. After dropping off the guys at the other two houses, I headed back to find Savanna asleep on the couch. Without waking her, I carried her up to our bed and tucked her in. I was working so hard to give her the perfect day she always dreamed of. I climbed in bed beside her and pushed the hair out of her face. She was so beautiful to me. I loved her full lips and the tiny freckles on the bridge of her nose. Her dark hair was longer now and it fell past her breasts.

Savanna was everything I had wanted in a woman. She was so innocent and it was something that I cherished about her. I'd been in bad relationships, some in which I never even gave a damn about. I had treated my fair share of women terribly, especially after I got cheated on in college. I found it so hard to trust anyone that I just couldn't let myself care enough in any relationship. Savanna changed me.

Being there for her and feeling the pain of what she went through, it opened my heart. At first I fought it, but the more time I spent with her, the more I knew how real my feelings were. I wanted every part of her for myself. I had to touch her and have her heart. She was my everything. I never wanted to let her go.

To be able to open up my heart again didn't exactly come with instructions, especially on how to deal with things, when she still loved my cousin. Looking at them now, I would never think they even liked each other, but I guess neither of them really considered what else was out there. Ty was never mean to Savanna, in fact she was more like a treasure to him. He kept her locked away, even from the real person he was.

Savanna started to stir and nestled her body into mine. Since neither of us liked sweating in bed, we kept the window cracked so we could touch while we slept. With her arm on my chest, I fell fast asleep knowing everything was going to work out.

The next morning I got up early. Ty and Conner were already at the barn waiting for me. As I got closer it looked as if they were fighting, but instead they were playing some stupid slap game from when we were kids. I started to yell at them, but the truck full of sod came rolling in. I shook my head as I walked by them and started directing the truck in.

Ty and Conner must have sensed my frustration with their love hate relationship, because they got right to working. The entire inside of the barn needed to be sprayed white. I left Conner and Ty to the task. They each took a spray machine and did opposite sides. Of course, I should have never trusted that they could go for a long period of time without acting like total morons. I came in to check on their progress and they were both covered in white paint from head to toe. They were back to work, but after they spotted me coming toward them, they both pointed to each other.

Instead of playing into their drama, I walked back out of the barn, knowing they would work harder to try and not piss me off again. The sod was looking seamless and I decided to have the landscapers come back and lay flowers all around the edges of the barn.

Savanna had planned on riding Daisy, her horse, up to the barn. I decided to make Daisy her own little corral with a little white picket fenced in area. Since our wedding flowers were lilies, we could have some draped around the small fencing.

When the jokesters were done painting the inside, they came outside and we got right on to finishing the outside, with a second coat of paint all over. When it finally started to get dark, we went inside and got to installing the floor. The floor was dirt, so we needed to frame out an almost deck formation, in order to lay the plywood down flat.

Conner was amazing at construction while Ty and I were great at the mathematical aspect of it. Ty made the measurements while I cut the wood, then finally Conner installed it. We had a great system going and at about midnight, we were all starving to death and exhausted.

The wedding wasn't until four in the afternoon, so we had plenty of time to run all of the electric and get ready without Savanna having to worry.

Since she and I were being married and we didn't want to jinx anything, she chose to sleep at the main house with all of the girls. Plus her parents and my aunt and uncle had arrived and they were also staying in the guest rooms. Us guys came back to my place to a tray of lasagna and a fridge full of beer. We were too tired to stay up and party, and after about an hour, Ty finally snuck away from us to sleep with Miranda. He claimed that she couldn't sleep, but Conner and I thought he was the one who couldn't handle being away.

The following morning came too soon and my nerves were getting the best of me. I don't know why I was nervous. I had wanted to marry Savanna for so long. There wasn't a doubtful bone in my body. I think I was more worried about her not showing up. I let myself love her with everything I had, so the thought of losing her was just too hard to ever imagine.

Ty was already at the barn when Conner and I arrived. A truck full of flowers and another full of tables and chairs had arrived. We hadn't had time to paint the wooden floor, but with everything being decorated and set up, the brown floor just wasn't an issue. The white inside walls of the barn gave it a clean look. People from different companies started decorating and setting up with chairs, tables, balloons and other things to make it perfect.

I felt a hand on my shoulder and turned to see Ty standing there. His hair was all sweaty like it was hot out, but it really wasn't at all. "What the Hell? Did you run here or somethin'?"

"Nope, got up early and made you something. Come out back and look." Ty suggested.

We walked out back and I stood there shocked. It wasn't anything fancy, but Ty had made a trellis out of lattice to use on the altar. "I didn't have time to do this. Thanks Cuz. This is fantastic." I patted Ty on the shoulder and went over to thoroughly look at it.

"The paint is still wet. I just finished spraying it. I figured after it dries we could put flowers all over it. So you think she'll like it?"

I turned to face Ty. "I think she will love it. She is goin' to be so surprised about all of this, but I will make sure she knows you did this for her."

"For you both Colt. I did it for both of you. I'm glad she's marrying you. You were always the right choice you know."

I didn't answer him. We both knew it was true, so I didn't have to agree. Ty was so overly happy about his own life, that I would never in a million years think he wasn't being genuine. His priorities were on his own family now. I used to picture him trying to have one last plea with Savanna to not marry me, but seeing him now, I knew it was never going to happen. He might tease Savanna, but there was nothing between them.

"So what do we have left to do?" Ty asked.

"Yeah, what do we have left? Brina said she'd meet me before the service if I hurried up." Conner interrupted.

"T.M.I. brother." Ty joked.

"Brother, my ass. Stop callin' me that you cock sucker."

"Speaking of cock sucking, you should have seen your sist......."

I had to interrupt them before they went wrestling through one of the barn walls. "Can you two just shut the Hell up for one Goddamn day? Jesus, you may as well be in kindergarten. Neither one of you fought like this when we were little. Conner, just get over it. They're happy together and there ain't nothin' you can do to change it, and honestly I know you don't really want to. In my opinion, you're just jealous of them. You want to settle down, but don't want to admit it. How long are you two goin' to do this shit? Make amends, were family for Christ sakes."

I'd had enough of the bickering. Two grown ass men arguing for no reason. Yeah, Ty went behind everyone's back, but so did I. I snuck around to be with Savanna on Ty's own farm. I knew the consequences to my actions and did it anyway, with no regrets. Conner needed to let it go. He was going to lose his sister if he continued, because I knew for a fact that she would be with Ty without a single regretful thought.

"I don't have a beef with Conner. He just can't accept that both of the girls chose me." Ty stood there waiting for Conner to reply.

He just stood there staring at Ty. We had been through this for almost a week. Every time we thought things were good between them, they would go all hog wild again. If they didn't quit it would cause problems with the family. As much as Ty tried to make things a joke, I knew it was his way of dealing with feeling uncomfortable. He did feel bad about lying to Conner, but he wouldn't regret it.

"I don't want to be like you. Let's just get that out in the open right now."

Ty took a big gulp from his water bottle and poured some over his head. He was listening to Conner, but making a point to not give him direct attention. "Conner, it doesn't bother me if you dislike me, but don't ever doubt my intentions. I love her like no other man could ever love her. Izzy is my daughter in every way and I would never hurt either of them. I would die before I let anything happen to my family. You can say whatever you want about me, but don't you ever say my feelings for them aren't real. If you need me to repeat this every day for the rest of our lives, then so be it, but just know, it will always sound exactly the same."

Ty didn't wait for Conner to react, he just walked away from both of us.

I thought Conner would say something smart about Ty since he walked away, but instead, he walked up to me. "I ain't jealous Colt. You both can have that monogamous shit."

I threw my hands in the air and watched him walk in the opposite direction. For the next two hours, we worked without talking about anything other than the task at hand. Conner and Ty never even made eye contact with each other.

With the wiring run through the rafters and the lighting working properly, we gassed up all of the generators and set them out back, to hide them from the guests. The caterers were starting to arrive and we needed to start getting ourselves ready. The three of us jumped on the golf carts and headed to get cleaned up. In just two hours I would be marrying Savanna. It was really happening.

My house was so quiet and if it wasn't for my dog Sam following me around, I think I would have gone a bit crazy with anticipation. After showering, shaving and getting my tux on, I heard the guys coming into the house. Sam went flying down the steps to greet them. I could hear them telling her to stop jumping. It was a good thing it hadn't been muddy outside, or she would have made a mess out of their tuxes.

I came downstairs to Ty and Conner fixing each other's jackets and flowers. "Good to see you're getting along."

"It's just a show. We can hate each other tomorrow," Ty joked.

Conner didn't say anything and I didn't give a damn. They needed to shut up until Savanna's day was over with. I had about two hundred people coming to the ranch. My grandparents were deceased, but Savanna still had two sets and she hadn't seen either of them in two years, on account of them living in California and Florida. She was more than excited to see them and impress them with the life and future that we had here. Of course my mother was a nervous wreck, running around making sure that everything was in order.

"You ready to get this over with Cuz?" Conner asked.

I took a deep breath and looked at the clock. Conner was right, we needed to head over there. "I've been ready for this for two years."

Ty put his arm around me while we were heading out. "Hey man, I never said thanks to you."

"For what?"

"For taking her from me." I pulled away and gave him a dirty look. "If you wouldn't have taken her from me, I never would have my girls. Maybe it sounds terrible saying it that way, but you gave me my future, at least that is how I see it."

Conner was already on the golf cart. "You guys comin'?"

I held up my finger for him to hold on. "I never thought you'd be here with me today. I wanted to regret lovin' her but I just couldn't, not for one second. I never meant to hurt you, even if it was temporary. I know you were in a bad way last year, while Savanna and I were planning our future. I should have been there more, but I didn't know what to say. I felt like I was the reason for ruinin' your happiness. When I found out about you and Miranda and then saw you two for myself, it was like a weight lifted off of me. I could tell immediately that you were crazy about each other. I'm real glad that everything has worked out Ty. Your my cousin, my blood, and nothin' will ever change that."

"Love you too man. Let's get you hitched dude." Ty pushed me off the porch as if he were more eager to get there than me.

"Bout time!" Conner said as we hopped on and headed to the barn.

Crowds of people were already outside. Soft music was coming from inside and we were greeted with lots of familiar faces. Ty pushed me toward a group of elderly people standing with Savanna's parents and I leaned over and greeted them first. Even Ty reached in and shook Savanna's dad's hand and gave her mother a quick hug.

"I heard you got married. I never thought I would hear that, but congrats Ty," her mother said.

"Thanks. Have you met my girls yet?" He asked.

"As a matter of fact, your mother introduced us earlier. Bella was running around looking for you. She is adorable."

Ty got a huge smile on his face and spotted his parents. "Colt would like to meet both of your parents." He waved to his mother and father. "Excuse me, I need to say hi to them."

I met the two couples and talked to them for a short while before my mother blessed us with her loud voice over the microphone.

"Attention everyone. The girls are on their way here. Guys, you need to take your places and everyone else needs to find a seat. My son is getting married!" She was more excited than me.

We took our places and stood there waiting in anticipation. Beads of sweat were running down my head. My heart was racing and I stared at that barn door just waiting to see my beautiful bride for the first time.

Chapter 8

Savanna

It was my big day and I'd already thrown up twice. Aside from Colt leaving me messages on my phone, I hadn't talked to him at all. Brina and Miranda were trying to keep me from freaking out, but I was so nervous.

As if that were the only thing I had to worry about, I still had no idea where the wedding service was taking place. Everyone had been so secretive including Miranda, who I knew for a fact had been told by Ty.

My parents and grandparents had kept me company all night and it was awesome to see them all after so long. I wish I could have told all of them that I was pregnant, sadly I wasn't, but today was about me marrying Colt, not about our failed attempts at conceiving. We had all our lives to be able to announce things like that.

Miranda had spent the last two hours doing my hair and makeup. If I wasn't in my own body, I wouldn't have recognized myself. I'd never looked so beautiful and it was hard not to cry.

Miranda came into the room with Bella by her side. "It's time."

I took some deep breaths and grabbed as much of my dress as my hands could handle. Miranda looked so beautiful in her dress. I had changed my mind at the last minute and picked light blue dresses. Brina kept bitching at me that it was the only color that looked good with her pale skin, not that it was her decision, but I wanted them to both be happy. Of course Miranda looked good in anything she put on, she could wear a sheet and make it look beautiful. Ty was a very lucky guy.

I didn't say much on the way over to where they had Daisy waiting for me. Our wedding planner was all smiles as I made my way across the yard to the horse pastures on the golf cart. He held out a hand to help me off of the golf cart. "We need to get you up on that horse without messing up your dress. We put a white fabric over the saddle so that you wouldn't get your dress dirty."

"Thank you. Where am I supposed to be riding to?" Before he could answer I saw a horse and buggy pulling up in front of Daisy and I. Miranda smiled and winked as she and Bella climbed in behind Brina.

"Just follow them. I will meet you there." He assured me.

It took a good five minutes to get me on that horse. Between the high heels and the dress, it was hard as hell. Once on it, I had to sit sideways, and I feared falling off and landing in a pile of dirt. As Daisy and I followed the buggy, I could hear Bella calling out for me. I was afraid to let go to wave to her, on account of losing my balance.

Nothing could have prepared me for what I saw once we got closer to Miranda's mother's house. An old barn that had once looked like it was falling down, was painted red and looked even more perfect than the one that had burned down. Green grass surrounded the building and flowers had been planted everywhere. The photographer was steady taking our pictures as we got closer. I held my hand over my mouth and tried so hard to hold back the tears. For three days Colt had been working on my secret. I had no idea that he was giving me my barn wedding that I had always dreamed of. Miranda and Bella climbed out of the buggy and came to stand near Daisy. My father started walking toward me and held his arms out for me to fall into them. I could hear the camera clicking as I released my hold on the horse. Of course, my father caught me and sat me down with ease. "You look beautiful."

"Thank you Daddy."

"Shall we?" He held out his arm for me to take.

Colt and I had sat Brina down and asked if she and Conner could walk first so that Miranda and Ty could be together and Miranda could walk with Bella down the aisle. Brina didn't seem to care as long as she walked with Conner. Apparently they had hooked up a few times, after she had made friends with Courtney, his newest ex. It was weird, but it was Brina and she wasn't exactly hard to get.

When Brina disappeared in the barn, I started shaking. My father tried to steady me, but I was trembling. Miranda and Bella waved before heading into the barn. I could see her trying to get Bella to throw the flowers as they were going.

Right before walking in I heard Bella yelling 'Daddy', followed by the crowd of people inside going 'awww'. Of course Ty got attention at my wedding. He must have been laughing his head off.

"You ready for this?" My father asked.

"Definitely."

The photographer opened both of the barn doors before my dad and I came into view. I wanted to close my eyes to avoid seeing Colt. Feeling like I was going to pass out, I kept my head down and my veil over my eyes. With each step I counted and took deep breaths, trying to focus on not falling. I avoided making eye contact with anyone and squeezed my hold on my father tighter. The decorations were beautiful and everything looked more perfect than I could have ever pictured.

We were getting toward the end of the aisle and I could feel everyone's eyes on me, but only one set of eyes were making me weak in the knees. Reluctantly, I looked up at Colt. His half smile and beautiful eyes were fixed on me. I couldn't take my eyes off of how beautifully perfect the man was. It wasn't the tux, or the way he had styled his hair. He was just breathtaking.

I was in awe over the man.

I don't remember taking that step up to that altar, but I was suddenly reaching my hands out to Colt, while my father lifted my veil and kissed my cheek. After agreeing to give me away, he went and took his seat, while my eyes never left Colt's.

His hands found mine and he held them tight. I thought I was shaking until he was holding me. He was shaking so bad that his lip was quivering. I found his gaze and his eyes were full of wetness.

No...no....no..you can't cry!

I tried to look away but I just couldn't. I was mesmerized by Colt's love for me. He blinked his dark eyelashes and tears fell down each of his cheeks. I could feel the burning in my eyes and fought so hard to not lose it, knowing once I started I wouldn't be able to stop.

The pastor started talking but I never took my eyes off of Colts.

"Dearly beloved. We are gathered here today to unite Colton and Savanna in holy matrimony. Do you Colton take Savanna to be your wife, to have and to hold from this day forward, for better or for worse, for richer, for poorer, in sickness and in health, to love and to cherish; from this day forward until death do you part?"

Colt squeezed my hands and let out a very hoarse 'I do'.

"And do you Savanna take Colton to be your husband, to have and to hold from this day forward, for better or for worse, for richer, for poorer, in sickness and in health, to love and to cherish; from this day forward until death do you part?"

I clenched my jaw and focused on saying the two words without crying. "I do."

"At this time Colton and Savanna have chose to say their own vows to each other." He handed Colt the microphone first.

Oh no! I can't do this. Just pronounce us husband and wife. I can tell him mine later.

Colt cleared his throat and put one arm around my waist. "Savanna," He took a deep breath and shook his head, trying to calm his nerves. "I pretty much knew I loved you from the beginnin'. Your beauty caught my eye, but your heart took my breath away. When I look to my future, all I know is that you're in it. I want to hold you every single night, laugh with you every single day and love you for the rest of our lives." Colt started to break down and I could tell he was having trouble speaking without losing himself completely with his emotions. When he spoke, I could feel the tears filling my own eyes then finally falling down my face. As he continued, I began to sob. "Darlin' you are my whole world and I promise to do whatever it takes to make sure every day of our lives leaves you with a smile on your pretty face and a heart that is always full of love."

Colt handed me the microphone and wiped his face, waiting for me to start. I tried to wipe the tears away, but the mic kept screeching and causing the audience to gasp. I closed my eyes and focused on being in a room alone with Colt. I thought about the millions of things that I had thought about saying to him. "Colt, you know you've always owned my heart. That day you came walking into my life two years ago changed everything. From our first kiss, I felt as if I couldn't breathe without you beside me. The way you love me amazes me every single day and I can't help falling in love with you more and more each day." My lips started shaking and I had to take a second to calm down. I knew I shouldn't but I looked right up into Colt's burning eyes. I could feel his thumb moving over my waist as his hand held me. I looked around the beautiful barn and thought about the sacrifices he had made to make this all happen. I literally began to sob, but through the tears I managed to say one more sentence. "You are my best friend, I love you so much Colt Mitchell."

Thank Goodness we didn't ask for a traditional service.

"Can we have the rings please?" The pastor asked.

Ty scooted up and handed Colt our rings. He gave me a quick wink before ducking back behind Colt. Even he had tears in his eyes.

I can do this. A few more words.

Colt slipped the ring on my finger and then my engagement ring over top of it. It was a lot of ring and under the lights it sparkled like crazy. "With this ring I thee wed." He brought my rings to his lips and kissed them.

I let out a small giggle, in between tears. I grabbed his ring and slid it onto his finger. I had wanted to do that for so long. He was mine in every way. "With this ring I thee wed."

Colt took both of my hands in his and waited patiently for the go-ahead we were both waiting for.

"I now pronounce you husband and wife. Ladies and Gentleman, let's give a round of applause to Mr. and Mrs. Colton Mitchell. You can kiss your bride now."

The room filled with clapping but once Colt's lips reached mine, everything went quiet. We entered into our own little world and nobody else existed. I had imagined this kiss since I was about eight years old, of course as I got older the kiss got deeper, but nothing could have prepared me for the kiss Colt was giving. His soft lips covered mine, while his tongue stroked my bottom lip. Soon our tongues began to mingle and we were completely caught up in each other to pay any attention to the loud whistling in the crowd.

I used to be so worried about my grandparents seeing me kiss like this, but I was married now. I was allowed to kiss and have as much sex as I wanted. I had the paper to prove it.

Colt finally pulled away and rested his head on my shoulder. "I love ya Darlin'."

"I love you too baby, so much..... Colt, this is amazing. I can't believe you managed to do this. It's perfect."

Clanking of glasses got everyone to quiet down. My biggest fear was upon us as I stared at Ty and Conner, fighting over the microphone. Finally Conner grabbed it and switched it on. "Can ya'll hear me?"

"My family and I would like to thank you all for comin' out to celebrate with us tonight. I just have a couple things I'd like to say about Colt and Van." Ty stood back and patiently waited his turn. It worried me that he was going to get the last word in.

"As everyone knows, Colt is my cousin, so I have obviously known him my whole life. He is a great all around guy, and has been hunted by every chick that's ever come in contact with him." The crowd started laughing. "The funny thing was that Colt never really noticed it. That is why we were all so surprised when he came back from an out of town visit, head over heels in love with someone. Van captured his heart and he never gave up until he had her for himself. What you all might not know, is that Van used to be ……….."

Holy shit! No No No!

"Give me that thing before I shove it so far up your ass you can't find it." Ty yanked the microphone out of Conner's hand.

The crowd of people were dead silent. Colt grabbed my arm and held me still. "Excuse my brother in-law, he has had a bit too much to drink." Ty started to laugh a little and the crowd seemed to relax. "I have known Van, Savanna, since we were little kids. Colt knew her back then as well. He used to come and visit during the summer. All of the girls would go nuts over him there too. Van was different. She was a late bloomer and Colt made it a point to tease her for it. When he went off to college and stopped visiting, Van changed from a little girl, into a beautiful woman. Two years ago when he came to help out my family, he saw her again. I'm pretty sure she took his breath away and you all know the rest of the story. Besides my own wife, Colt and Van are my best friends. I love them and wish them a long and happy life together. Everyone hold up your glasses," He pointed to Conner. "except you

Conner, you're officially cut off." Everyone started laughing and raised their glasses.

"To Colt and Savanna."

Colt rubbed my back and kissed the top of my head. Ty walked by Conner and came over to us. "You want me to fuck him up?"

I gave Ty a big hug. "No, but thank you for fixing things. That was uncomfortable."

"He didn't do it to piss you off Savanna. He did it to get to Ty. He wanted him to look like a sap."

"He's the sap." We saw Miranda standing by her brother, arguing with him. He had issues.

The next twenty minutes flew by. Between everyone congratulating us and the photographer trying to take pictures of everyone, I was glad to finally get to the first dance. We had picked a song called "I can love you like that." It was older, but the words were so beautiful. The music started and I paid no attention to Colt reaching for something behind my back. To my utter shock, I felt the vibrations of Colt's voice as he began singing the words to the song.

"They read you Cinderella

You hoped it would come true

That one day your Prince Charming

Would come rescue you

You like romantic movies

You never will forget

The way you felt when Romeo kissed Juliet

All this time that you've been waiting

You don't have to wait no more"

Colt held me tight against his body while he sang every single word to me. Our family and friends had all stood up and some were even crying, as they listened to every word coming out of Colt's beautifully talented body.

"I can love you like that

I would make you my world

Move Heaven and Earth if you were my girl

I will give you my heart

Be all that you need

Show you you're everything that's precious to me

If you give me a chance

I can love you like that"

I looked over toward Brina and Conner who had now come out to the dance floor. They had their hands all over each other, almost like they were having some kind of sex, right here in front of everyone. I shook my head and looked toward Ty and Miranda. With Bella in their arms, they swayed to Colt's beautiful voice. Ty placed small kisses on Miranda and Bella's foreheads, before resting his head into both of theirs. It was beautiful to watch them.

I never make a promise I don't intend to keep

So when I say forever, forever's what I mean

I'm no Casanova but I swear this much is true

I'll be holdin' nothing back when it comes to you

You dream of love that`s everlasting

Well baby open up your eyes

I can love you like that

I would make you my world

Move Heaven and Earth if you were my girl

I will give you my heart

Be all that you need

Show you you're everything that's precious to me

If you give me a chance

I can love you like that

You want tenderness-I got tenderness

And I see through to the heart of you

If you want a man who understands

You don't have to look very far

I love you Darlin' "

Someone came and grabbed the microphone from Colt as the music finally faded into another song. He pulled me into his embrace and kissed me deeply. I was still speechless. I couldn't believe he had sang to me in front of everyone. I had never heard him do anything like that before. Sure, he had sang to me as we danced, but never for everyone else to hear. I was overwhelmed with happiness.

"That was amazing."

"Could you tell how nervous I was?" Colt got this embarrassed look across his face.

I looked into those green eyes that made me melt every time I saw them. "Are you kidding me, you totally owned it baby."

"I used to sing in church when I was a kid. I hated people watchin' me. I just wanted to give you everything today. Were you surprised with the barn?"

"You have no idea. My God, it is more beautiful than the other one. I can't believe you did this for us."

"For you Savanna. I did it for you. I would have married you anywhere, but I knew how important this was to you. I needed to make it happen Darlin'."

"I love you so much Colt. I have never been happier in my whole life."

We swayed to the music and he held me so tight in his arms. "Just wait until we fill that house with little feet. We are just beginning Savanna."

Colt and I broke away after the second dance and started on our wedding to-do list. I had originally planned it all out, but after his vows and his song to me, I just couldn't think straight.

Ty grabbed me and pulled me in for a hug. "Congrats Van." He took both of his hands and grabbed my face to plant a kiss over my mouth. Miranda stood behind him laughing the whole time.

"Thanks." I started wiping my lips. Bella came up and grabbed my dress while she jumped up and down. I picked her up and got a giant slobber kiss. "Aunt Van loves you."

She poked me in the nose. "Van."

Colt came up and grabbed her, spinning her on to the dance floor in his arms. She wrapped her arms around his neck as he danced around wildly, while she clung to him laughing.

I needed to be pregnant.

The food was even better than when we had sampled it and the cake was to die for. Colt and I agreed to not make a mess with our first taste, but Ty and Conner taunted him so badly that at the very last second, I got it smashed all over my face and up my nose. As Colt began trying to lick it off my face, I grabbed his neck and pulled his face into the mess over mine. Instead of pulling away, he pushed his face all over mine, gathering the icing with his own skin. He pulled away licking his lips, smiling at me.

How could anyone be mad at someone that looked like Colt?

After we had done everything traditional on my list, we met everyone out on the dance floor. Even my grandparents were dancing, as best as four very old people could. Colt's mother was dancing with Ty's dad, while Ty's mother danced all around with Bella.

Miranda and Ty finally had a second to themselves, since Bella was occupied. Instead of dancing to the melody of the song, they were in a deep embrace with their faces buried into each other's bodies. The old Ty would have been groping all over someone while he danced, but he held his wife so passionately, it made me so happy for them. I regretted all of the terrible things I had said to him when I caught them together. They were truly, madly and deeply in love with each other. It was picturesque. While Ty and Miranda fell in love with each other, Bella had made them a family from the beginning.

Just as I was thinking about the little beauty, I watched her spot her parents and go flying toward them. Ty startled when her little body smacked right into his leg. With one arm still around Miranda, he picked her up and held her between them. She giggled as he placed kisses all over her face.

"They're beautiful aren't they?" Colt asked as he watched them with me.

"I want that." I confessed.

Colt pulled my gaze to his face. "We *will* have it Darlin'. Be patient. It *will* happen. Besides, not only do we have our whole lives together, but I'm really liking the tryin' part of it all. Anything that gives me a reason to make love to my wife is a good reason to me."

We both started laughing as my father approached me. "I think they want to do the father daughter dance now Honey."

I had purposely requested this dance to be one of the last of the night. Marrying Colt while he cried was hard, but dancing with my father, at this particular moment was like sealing my childhood away. I know it was juvenile to think like that, but I couldn't help be a little irrational about it.

I could hear the music to Heartland's "I loved her first" coming on. My father reached out his hands and took me in his arms. I buried my head into his broad chest and tried so hard not to cry. He started rubbing my back and I could feel him crying against my body. Saying goodbye to my parents when I moved to Kentucky was a rushed decision. They wanted me to finally be happy after so many years of uncertainty with Ty. Colt changed my life, at a time when all I had on my side was my parents. Sure, they had respected my decision, but I knew they missed me terribly.

"I love you Daddy." I cried on his shoulder, forgetting all about my perfect wedding face of makeup. The cameras flashed like crazy around us, but my father never let go of me. He squeezed my hand and held me tight.

"I love you too Honey. I'm so proud of the woman you have become. Please promise you will come to visit as much as you can. I miss you so much already."

I saw Colt watching us, he was dancing with his mother. She was much shorter than he was so just watching them was really cute. I knew what they were talking about and it made me even more emotional. As the song ended, my father kissed me on the cheek and slowly let go. He gave Colt a quick hug before finding my mother.

"You okay Darlin'?"

"I am now." I smiled and accepted his gentle kisses to my lips.

"I know we live together, but for some reason, I can't wait to get you home and strip off your clothes tonight."

I ran my hands around his perfect butt and pulled his body toward mine. "I can't wait either."

"So did I do good?"

He spun me around and pulled me back into his arms. "You have no idea how happy you've made me. This day was more perfect than I had ever imagined."

"You know I aim to please." He teased.

"Well, I can't wait to show you how grateful I am to be your wife." I ran my lips over his, causing an instant heat between my legs.

People around us were starting to get rowdy, including Conner and Ty. I wasn't exactly sure where Bella had gone, but the music got a lot more clubby and Ty and Miranda were lighting up the dance floor with their provocative dancing. It wasn't classy, but it wasn't as dirty as I had seen them dance in the past. They were both good dancers to begin with and together, they were fun to watch. Of course, Brina and Conner took it as a challenge and began trying to out dance them.

Miranda and Ty had them from the beginning, in fact they never changed their pace, while Conner was reaching under Brina's dress and grinding her into his body. Since they'd already hooked up, I knew where it was leading, in fact everyone there did. Ty and Miranda knew they were together, so the chase wasn't an issue for them. As much as Conner tried, everyone watched Ty and Miranda who were so in sync you would think they rehearsed.

Colt and I stood back and started clapping and egging them on. Even the older guests were getting a kick out of the two guys competing for bragging rights.

"I think Ty's got it." Colt laughed.

I shook my body to the beat of the song. "Yeah, Brina has nothing on Miranda. Ty told me one time that Miranda danced better than any stripper or Porn star he had ever watched. Since I have no idea what they dance like, what do you think?"

He started laughing hysterically. "Yeah, she's pretty good, but she's my younger cousin and I hate comparin' her like that, besides, I think it's okay for Ty to say that but he wouldn't want anyone else doin' it."

Colt was right. Ty was a protective person. He could brag all he wanted, but if someone said anything about either of those girls, it was on like Donkey Kong.

After three more long songs, Conner and Ty finally high fived and went back to their seats. Even with everyone seemingly entertained by their immaturity, it was good to have a break from laughing. People were starting to head out, so Colt and I made it a point to walk around and make sure we thanked everyone for joining us.

When it was just our immediate family, Colt's mother came up and told us to just head home. She said that she had arranged for the cleanup and we needed to enjoy our night.

I didn't want to leave my parents since I barely ever got to see them, but they also insisted it was our night to enjoy.

Daisy had already been taken back to her own personal corral, so Colt and I rode away in a very fancy decorated golf cart. Between the beer cans, the bells, the shaving cream, and the opened condoms, it was hard not to laugh, while we made our way down the gravel and dirt lane. The cans were so loud, and the condoms were unsticking and hitting us in the face. Unfortunately they bought lubricated, which in turn stuck to us, as they flung off the dash. When we stopped at the house, I found myself pulling them out of my hair and off my dress.

Colt laughed as he grabbed me and lifted me up to carry me into the house.

He had remembered every detail to my perfect day, and I would never forget the most unbelievable day of our lives.

Chapter 9

Colt

I couldn't believe that I had pulled off everything without

a hitch. When Savanna came walking into that barn she took my

breath away. I couldn't believe how perfectly beautiful she

looked. She radiated with beauty and I knew everyone in that

barn felt the same way. I tried to hold it together, but I couldn't

hold in my emotions.

I was finally married to my best friend, the one girl that I

had finally given my whole heart to. Carrying her over that

threshold felt so different than all of the other nights. She was

mine in every way and this was the first day of the rest of our

lives.

I had planned for us to go away for a week to Hawaii and

as a treat; we had invited Ty and Miranda to tag along for the

first three days. It was part of their wedding present from

Savanna and I. They were shocked that I could get them a last

minute reservation, and begged both of their bosses for the

extra days of vacation. While they went away, Ty's parents were going to drive Bella back home with them. As much as my Aunt Karen wanted her to stay, it was just too much of a worry with Tucker still out there somewhere.

Ty and Miranda weren't too worried about losing money and taking a couple extra days. It wasn't like they had a lot of bills. My uncle's farm was finally making them money and his life insurance had paid everything off. They never had to worry about money, and Ty knew the farm would one day be his and Miranda's.

Knowing that Savanna and I wouldn't be alone for the first couple of days, I had made the decision to give her the most fulfilling wedding night possible. I had got the best wine and had it chilling next to our Jacuzzi tub. Savanna and I had gotten many baths together, but tonight was going to be the best one yet.

I was careful to grab Savanna's dress as I lifted her over my head. She screamed out when I did it, but I never sat her down. I continued to carry her over my shoulders until I sat her down in the bathroom. She sat down on the step to the tub, while I started the water. Once I got the temperature perfect, I knelt down in front of her.

I removed one shoe at a time, chucking them behind me. My hands slid up her sexy legs until I reached the tops of her stockings. I let my fingers brush across her panties before sliding the thigh highs down, the left one first and then the right. I ran both hands up her hips and onto her inner thighs. Her dress was so full and it was hard to maneuver. Savanna stood up slowly and turned around. Her face was so serious and I could tell how much she wanted me from her increased breathing. I started unfastening each little button to the back of the dress as slow as my eager fingers would let me go. With each button, I could see more of her bare skin. The pale blue strapless bra was sitting beneath the dress just waiting to be unfastened. I ran my fingers over the skin to her shoulder and then reached down to kiss it. My tongue just needed a taste before I pulled away to get the dress removed.

Savanna's chest was lifting higher and higher, the closer I came to undressing her. After enough of the buttons were removed, I reached my hands into either side and let it fall down to her feet. Before she turned around to face me, I got to see the matching pale blue bra and thong she was wearing. A soft moan came from deep inside of me, as I took in the site of her perfect ass.

I let my fingers trace the skin of her shoulders, as she finally turned around to face me. Her long hair hung down in random curls and the rest was pinned up in several intricate twists. I decided to save her hair for last and focus on the rest of what was still on my wife. With a one handed snap, I was able to remove her hook in the front bra. Her soft breasts bounced free as the bra fell to her feet.

I let my hands slide from her shoulders and down over each of her nipples. She gasped when I reached them and circled them with my fingers. "So beautiful," I said as I brushed my fingers over them again.

She bit down on her lip and watched my fingers touching such a sensitive part of her body. As I squatted down I slid my hands with me, tracing her perfect hips and tucking my fingers underneath her panties. I kissed her hips as I slid them down inch by inch, kissing her at every exposed area of skin.

She began to tremble as she watched me. I thought about the first time I had removed her clothes, before we had even had sex. I wanted her even then and now two years later, my mouth was just inches away from her hot sex. She shimmied her way out of the panties while I pushed her back to sit on the edge of the tub. I leaned over and turned the water off, before I stepped back and began to slowly remove my own clothes.

I hadn't wanted her to help, so when she stood up I shook my head and made her sit back down. I tossed the jacket to the floor and started to removed the dress shirt, while Savanna ran one of her hands over her own nipple. She never took her eyes off me while she did it, which in turn made me even harder than I already was. I tried to go slow with my pants, but Dammit if she wasn't setting me crazy by touching herself like that.

My pants and boxers came off within seconds and I rushed toward Savanna, meeting her lips with my own. Her tongue entered my mouth and pressed against mine, slinging away to only meet again for more. Her lips were wet and slippery and I found myself sucking on her lips as we pulled away and then came back in for more. She grabbed my hand and guided it between her legs, showing me how badly she needed me to touch her.

The ache between my legs needed to be attended to. I grabbed Savanna's hand and helped her step into the hot bubble bath. Her beautifully naked body disappeared into the deep water and I climbed in front of her to touch what I could no longer see. I slid right into her body and felt her slippery legs wrapping around me. Savanna leaned her body back so I could take the soap and wash each of her breasts. She reached over for the bottle of wine and handed me the corkscrew to open it. Once the cork went flying, Savanna took the bottle into her hand and drank it without taking her eyes off of me. She slid her body toward me and kissed me hard, before backing away and leaning up on the edge of the tub. I slid toward her, and watched as she slowly poured wine down over her breasts. I watched the red liquid naturally slide down every smooth inch of her skin until it came to rest between her legs.

I shoved my face in between her legs, lapping up every drop that had fallen there. It added a sweet fruity taste to her natural essence and I couldn't get enough. I grabbed the bottle and took a few drinks before pouring more right over her pussy. I caught some of it with my tongue while I poured and Savanna threw her head back after attempting to watch my tongue stroking her sensitive spot at the top.

She grabbed both of her breasts and squeezed each nipple as her face scrunched up and she came right into my thrashing tongue. While her body trembled against my mouth, she started to slip back down in the tub, positioning her body over top of mine. I pulled the main clip out of her hair and let it fall down into the water. Savanna ran her wet hands up and down my chest. She leaned into my chest and licked her way to one of my nipples. I cringed at her first bite of it, but got off when she did it a second time. She licked it again before moving to the opposite side. I lifted her chin up so that I could kiss the side of her lips and drag my tongue over them. She tried to touch me with hers, but I pulled away before she could. Her eyes were fixed on my mouth and I licked my lips just knowing how turned on she was for me.

"Please kiss me," she whispered.

I could feel her breath on my face, while I continued to tease her with my tongue.

The combination of the slipperiness of the water and the way her body glistened from being wet, sent me over the edge. I grabbed her body and let it float over my hard shaft. Savanna gasped as I slid right inside of her. The friction was so much tighter in the water, not allowing the natural lubrication of her body to help. She moved up and down slowly, using the water to allow her to go up and down while still floating. I wrapped my arms around her waist and held her lower back as she rocked her body over mine.

She leaned back enough to allow me to suck on each of her nipples. As they got hard in my mouth, I pulled away and blew on them. She was trying to keep her eyes on mine, but as the feelings became too much to take, I saw her closing her eyes and biting down on her lip. Savanna wrapped her legs tightly around me and began thrashing harder against me. The water was splashing all over the place, because with every thrust a loud pouring sound could be heard on the floor.

Savanna's ass muscles began to tighten and I could feel her internal walls closing as she came. Just feeling how tight she was, caused my own explosion to mimic hers. I stilled her in my arms and held her tightly by the back of her hair, kissing from her shoulder, to her neck, and then finally her full lips.

"I'm so glad you're my wife Savanna. Thank you for choosing me Darlin'."

"I will always choose you Colt. I love you so much."

Savanna only stayed in the tub for another couple of minutes. I got out first and grabbed her a towel. Neither of us bothered getting dressed. I knew that wasn't the only sex we would be having, besides, there wasn't anyone sleeping at our place. Everyone had gone somewhere else to give us privacy.

As we got in our bed, I watched Savanna drop her towel and watch me as I dropped mine. A low groan came from deep inside of me as I caught the site of her naked body. I knew we had just finished, but I still wanted more of her. We climbed on the bed to meet each other in the middle and my lips found hers right away. Our passion filled kisses increased the urgency to take her again. I could feel myself getting hard and it didn't take Savanna long to feel it for herself.

She let out little whimpers as I let it brush against her stomach. Her hand reached down and grabbed onto my girth. She purred as she pushed me down on the bed and began stroking me with one hand. Her free hand found mine and we intertwined our fingers together. Savanna licked my hard shaft before taking it into her mouth completely. When she pulled away she let her saliva build up on the tip, before sliding her soft lips over my hardness again. Because of the lubrication, she was able to slide up and down faster.

I tried to close my eyes, but watching her was even hotter. Her eyes continued to stare into mine, while her head bobbed. I squeezed her hand that I was holding and without even thinking I grabbed the back of her head, just to feel her actions even more. She continued moving faster with each motion of her head. My fingers became tangled in her hair, but she never tried to remove it. The sensations running through my hard cock were rapid and in no time, I could feel myself growing on the verge to come again.

Savanna kept thrusting her head down, taking my cock into her mouth further, but I didn't want to finish there. I took my tangled hand and lifted her head away from my throbbing shaft. "Not yet baby."

Savanna licked her lips and looked down at my dick, like she had enjoyed every second of it. To say that was a turn on was an understatement, because my god that was hot. She turned and did something else unexpected. Without speaking she got on all fours and stuck her ass right up toward me. I ran my hands up and down each cheek, while positioning myself behind her.

Apparently, she really got off having it in her mouth, because she was so slippery between her legs, that it slid in with ease. I reached around and grabbed her tits, using her own body to pound into her harder. She cried out, begging me to keep going. I reached down and started circling my fingers over her swollen sex. Savanna screamed my name in pure bliss as I collapsed over her back, giving her soft kisses all over the back of her shoulders.

We were both out of breath and exhausted. Once we fell onto the bed, it took only minutes for us to both fall asleep, our bodies still entangled together.

We woke up to the sound of Ty's big fat mouth yelling from downstairs. "Get your naked asses up, we need to roll."

I sat up and looked at the clock and realized we never set our alarm. We had two hours to get to the airport and we didn't live close at all.

Savanna and I jumped up and got dressed as fast as we could. She had already packed for our trip, and our luggage was downstairs. Savanna followed behind me as we walked down the steps. Ty and Miranda didn't seem to be in a hurry, they were having a full make out session on my couch. "Can't ya''ll wait till we get our own rooms?"

"She's never gone anywhere without Izzy. I was keeping her mind off of things." Ty winked at me and I shook my head.

"Bella will be fine. She's with her grandparents. My dad is going to drive my Jeep home so we can just fly back there instead. It's no sense of us having to come back here and then have to drive all that way home. Mom and Dad are going to stop

a few times and make sure they are driving at night so Izzy

sleeps most of the way," Ty explained.

Savanna came around and started grabbing our bags.

Sam must have sensed we were leaving, because she was

jumping all around. "Hey girl, Uncle Conner is goin' to keep you

company this week. Be a good girl and don't chew anything up."

I gave her a kiss and we headed out the door.

Conner was waiting outside, standing next to one of the

ranch trucks. "He's driving us to the airport." Miranda explained.

Ty and Miranda started climbing in the truck, while I

started loading our bags up in the back. Savanna hopped in the

back too, leaving me to sit in the front with Conner. I didn't

understand the whole grudge issue with Ty. Last night could

have been a disaster, of course I think Ty liked being the hero a

little too much. They obviously needed to spend time apart.

Conner needed to distance himself from the two of them until he

could get a grip.

We got about two miles down the road before Conner said a single word. " So, about last night..."

I held my hand up. "Just let it go."

But he didn't.....

"Nah, man I'm sorry. You were right the other day Colt. I see ya'll happy, while I'm alone. I never thought my sister and Ty would settle down before me, especially with each other. To make things worse, they are the happiest couple I have ever laid eyes on. I feel like ya'll are leaving me out. I've been a real ass, especially to you Ty." Conner looked in the rearview mirror at Ty. I looked back and saw him lean his head on Miranda. "I was thinkin' maybe I could come visit ya'll at your place sometime soon. I hate that Miranda just upped and moved clear out of the state. We've never been apart for this long. So, I apologize."

Ty reached over and put his hand on Conner's shoulder. "As long as you can be cool, you're welcome to visit whenever you want. This shit needs to be resolved. No matter what, we are all family, and at the end of the day, all we have is each other."

Miranda had done something to Ty. We couldn't explain what it was or how it happened, but his focus was on his family, like nothing else existed in the world. I could see how Savanna had loved him. He was a great man, who just needed to find that one person to give his heart to, just like me.

"Don't go searchin' for love Conner. It happens when you least expect it," Miranda added.

"For the record, it still makes me sick watchin' the two of you. If you could refrain from touchin' around me, it would help." Conner continued driving, but I caught him looking in the rear view mirror a few times. Miranda was his sister and all of his life he had been protecting her. For the first time she had found someone that he didn't need to protect her from and it scared the shit out of him.

The girls started singing a familiar song to the radio, so to break the animosity in the truck, I turned up the volume.

Conner pulled us right up to the airport doors. He climbed out and pulled his sister in for a big hug. Ty was already grabbing their bags out of the back. As he turned around,

Conner held his hand out to Ty. Of course, Ty grabbed his hand and pulled him in for a hug. Conner was reluctant at first, but Ty kept holding him there. "She's safe brother. I promise you she will always be taken care of."

Finally, Conner hugged Ty back. It was a real Kodak moment, if you ask me. Only time would tell if they could ever fully get along, but we had our whole lives to figure it out.

Since Miranda had never been on a plane before, she was a nervous wreck. She went from being excited, to full blown panic attack. At one point it got so bad, that she begged Ty to take her back and said they couldn't go. Savanna reached into her purse and handed her a tiny pill. "Just take half. It will help you relax. It's just a Xanax, so you won't go to sleep or anything."

I wasn't one to promote sharing medicine, but flights were difficult for some people. My poor cousin was terrified. I knew she wanted to get there and have some alone time with Ty. Miranda took the pill and rested her tear-filled eyes on Ty's chest. He rubbed her back until she finally started to relax.

Normally I would have expected Ty to joke about the plane going down, but he was so respectful around Miranda. He never let go of her hand. He kept her occupied and made sure she knew she wasn't alone. We played cards and guessing games to pass the time. After three hours in the air, Miranda was fine. She even managed to sleep the rest of the flight.

Savanna and I had all of our brochures of what we were planning to do while we were there, so we just sat there going over everything. At one point the stewardess came over and was flirting with Ty. For the first time in my life, I watched him blow a pretty woman off, the whole time kissing Miranda's sleeping head and messing around with her wedding ring on her finger.

The woman even made a second attempt, which in turn pissed Ty off. He woke Miranda up and told her all about it. The next time the woman came around he grabbed Miranda and started a full-blown make out session with her. He even added extra visuals by grabbing her breasts for everyone to see. To get the final point across, he pulled away from Miranda and looked up at the woman. "Have you met my beautiful wife? She is fucking amazing."

That was the last time any of us saw the woman and the last of Ty's entertainment for the flight, with the exception of him discussing getting lei'd when we got off the plane. He had everyone aboard in hysterics.

None of us had ever been to Hawaii and we had no idea how beautiful it would be when we stepped off that plane and looked outside. Savanna looked more excited than I had ever seen and I think she was excited about being able to share some of our time with Miranda and Ty. Since both of us already lived with our spouses, we weren't so worried about all day sex fests, well at least Savanna and I weren't. Ty and Miranda on the other hand, probably could have spent every second of their lives having sex. It would catch up to them one day and Ty would be the new spokesperson for Viagra.

I wasn't surprised when the taxi came to pick us up and Ty grabbed my hand and kissed me on the cheek like we were a couple. I tried to pull away, but he kept a death grip on my hand while he laughed his ass off.

"Can I take your bags?" The driver asked.

"Oh yes, my husband and I are so excited to be here, aren't we my Dark Stallion?" Ty kept a straight face, while the girls were cracking up behind us.

When I finally got free of his hand, he proceeded to slap me hard on the ass. "Oh, I can't wait to see how big our bed is. I know how much you like big things." Ty added.

We climbed in the taxi and I found my wife, so that my cousin couldn't touch me again. The taxi driver knew he was joking, but it was still funny.

Chapter 10

Savanna

I had this idea in my mind that asking Ty and Miranda to join us was going to be a disaster, but once we got into our rooms and agreed to meet later for dinner, Colt and I couldn't stop talking about how much fun we were having with them. Ty was a natural comedian and Miranda was his own personal cheering squad. Together, they were the most fun people to be around.

The room Colt reserved for us was amazing. I had never been anywhere like Hawaii, so the scenery was fascinating to me. I couldn't wait to get out and do things, as well as spend as much alone time with my new hubby as possible. I still couldn't believe he was all mine. How I managed to marry the most handsome man on the face of the planet still boggled my mind, not that I was complaining. Colt got me, he understood me more than anyone ever had.

There was not one single day since we had been together, that he didn't remind me of how much I meant to him. It wasn't like I ever expected him to say it all the time, he showed me in so many other ways. The way he worked me into every aspect of his life was amazing. In the past two years we had created something wonderful. The only thing missing was a baby, and we were working really hard for that to happen too.

I think both of us wanted to try as much as we could while we were here. I had already been paying attention to my cycle and knew exactly when I was going to be ovulating. It ended up working out to where I wouldn't start until the night that Ty and Miranda left. I wanted to be able to spend time with them, but also give them some alone time. They didn't get to go home at night like Colt and I. Ty and Miranda had Bella, and even though neither of them complained about it, I knew they appreciated the time to themselves when they got it.

I still couldn't believe Ty had chose being a husband and father over his old lifestyle, but it was clear that Miranda and Bella were the missing piece in his life. I wanted to be focused on Colt and I, but my not being pregnant was causing me to focus more on how happy they were and how desperate I was. Colt was a very forgiving man. I knew he would never leave me if I couldn't conceive, nevertheless, it would kill me if I couldn't give him the one thing he yearned for.

I needed to stay positive and not get so stressed out about it. Colt had already started unpacking his things. To follow suit, I grabbed my bag and started removing the items. Of course, Miranda had given me that sex book and for hours before my wedding, I found myself staring at every page. She had also given me a bunch of pointers and advice, that somehow made me feel optimistic I could take my sexual experiences to a whole new level. Our sex last night had benefited significantly already.

Miranda had also gone out and bought some raunchy little numbers to bring with us, of course she gladly handed me the pile and told me to pick two. I still couldn't believe it was Ty's wife teaching me about my body and what I could do with it, but hey, she was family and I needed the help.

She was so confident about her body, where I was only confident sometimes. Colt loved my body, that was never a secret, but it was me who wasn't really sure of myself, especially next to Miranda. I feared the moment we stepped onto that beach, because the girl could easily be a swimsuit model. I had

hated being at the ranch pool some days.

"You finished unpackin' Darlin?" Colt's arms wrapped

around me.

"Yeah, you ready to go to the beach?" I asked.

He pulled away and turned me around. Colt was wearing

Aviator sunglasses and swimming trunks. My mouth dropped

open.

Holy crap! That is sexy!

"What do ya think?" He asked.

I wrapped my arms around him. "Do I have to share you

with the whole beach? I'm kind of thinking that I shouldn't have

married the hottest man on the planet."

He rolled his eyes. "You are the only person that thinks

that Darlin'. It doesn't matter anyway, because they will be

lookin' at you, not me."

I shook my head and grabbed my swimsuit. While

walking to the bathroom, Colt stopped me. He shook his head

and started lifting off my shirt. He licked his lips and unhooked my bra, then immediately started removing my shorts and panties. I stood there in front of him completely naked. He backed away while he grabbed the bikini. Slowly, he bent down and let me step into the bottoms. When he got them up he kissed the fabric between my legs. Colt then took my bikini top and turned me around to tie it. He pulled my hair out of the clip and let it fall down my back, before stepping back and giving my body a once over. "Beautiful."

"You're just saying that." I worried that it wasn't the truth. I knew I wasn't ugly, but my boobs weren't gigantic and I always felt like my ass wasn't made for my slender body.

Colt started laughing. "Darlin', you can go ahead and think whatever you want, but you are the sexiest little thing I have ever laid eyes on. There ain't one girl out there that can do what you do to me Savanna." He pulled me toward a full size mirror near the bathroom. Colt stood behind me and ran his hands down one of my arms. "Your skin is perfect." He kissed my ear. "I love the way your hair smells." He kissed my neck. "Your breasts fill my hands and are sexy as all hell." He kissed my chin and ran his hands down over my hips. "These here, are my most favorite part of your body. I love these hips and this ass." His hands cupped my ass cheeks.

Colt turned me around and looked into my eyes. "I love every single thing about you, Savanna. You're a beautiful woman and if I have to remind you of it every single day, I will."

Aside from leaving me completely breathless, Colt stood there waiting for me to respond. I stood on my tippy toes and brushed my lips over his. With my eyes still closed, I kissed him once more. "Best.Husband.Ever."

He smacked my butt. "I better be, cause I'm the only one you will ever have."

I turned to see Colt wink at me and then put his sunglasses back over his eyes. "We need to get going or I'm going to suggest we stay here and take off everything we just put on."

Colt laughed and grabbed the beach bag from me. I found my sunglasses and cover-up and we headed out to find Ty and Miranda.

I pictured them hiding in some cabana, already half naked, but instead they were in the water, wrestling around and laughing. They waved as they saw us coming and pointed to which chairs were theirs. Colt and I took the ones next to them. I saw him clenching his jaw, waiting for me to take off the cover-up. "Do I have to?"

He pushed his glasses down so I could see those sexy eyes. "Now!"

He didn't say it in an angry way. He wanted it off because *he* wanted to see me. Just thinking about it gave me goose bumps. I considered taking it off slowly and attempting to be super sexy, but as I hesitated, I felt cold arms wrapping around me. Ty's wet body pressed against me, sending a cold chill all over me. It also instantly made my nipples rock hard. At that very moment, Colt grabbed the string and opened up the cover-up, revealing how cold I had become. Colt and Ty just stood there staring at my chest.

I pulled off the cover-up and threw it at both of them. "Assholes!"

I went running for the water.

Miranda was already there waiting for me. When I got in to about my waist I went under the water and swam the rest of the way out to her. She wrapped her arms around me and giggled. "Isn't this amazing?"

It took me a second to get over the guys embarrassing me, but once I looked around at the blue water and the tropical surroundings, I started to smile. "It's stunning."

I saw her eyes get big and I turned around just in time to get dunked. Colt came in and attacked Ty, shoving him down further into the water. They were playing around like they were teenagers again. After another five minutes they decided they were going to ride waves until they either died or collapsed from exhaustion. Miranda and I got out of the water and got comfortable on our chaise lounges. A cute teenage boy came up and brought us frozen drinks whenever our glasses were starting to get empty. By the time the guys came back in from their amateur body surfing competition, she and I were pretty drunk. We couldn't stop laughing at everything we saw or talked about.

I had been so worried about Miranda being so beautiful, but we were both getting whistled at, well, at least we were, until the guys came up and sent our audience away crying. Colt was the hottest thing ever, but Ty came in a close second, so to other guys, they knew they didn't stand a chance. Miranda and I had already applied lotion to our bodies, but Ty came up and straddled his wife with the lotion in his hands. "Baby, I think you are burning. I need to reapply this shit everywhere, especially where the sun can't see." He buried his head in between her big breasts and shook it around, giving her a motorboat. She laughed hysterically, but never pushed him away.

"I hope you know that you just put sunscreen all over your face. I hope it's uneven," I teased.

"Shiiit, that is the best way to apply it to the face, right baby?" Miranda nodded and laughed again.

Colt held up our glasses and looked from Miranda then back to me. "How many of these have you had?"

"Three or four," I giggled after hearing Miranda confess.

"Fuck, I can't get all freaky with you if you pass out on me." Ty teased Miranda.

She wrapped her arms around him as he pulled her on top of him. "We can do it right now."

I stood up, frantic to get her to recall that we were on a public beach. "Whoa! Not here guys."

Ty stopped kissing her and looked over at us. "She's joking Van, calm down. Besides, I would never let anyone else see my goods." He grabbed her butt. "There are certain things that are only for my eyes."

In his own perverted way, Ty was being protective of Miranda. I noticed Colt laughing at the two of them. He held his hand out for me and we walked away from the two sex maniacs.

"I'm surprised they aren't expecting," Colt said as we walked toward the water.

"Miranda had that three year shot. She said they aren't going to get it again. They want to have another baby before Bella gets too big."

"It makes sense, plus Ty loves being a father. I can see them having lots of kids, and lots of fun making them." Colt started laughing and spun me around in his arms. "I sure am having a good time making them with you."

He picked me up and I wrapped my legs around his waist. "Having a reason to make love to you is always a good thing."

The cool wind was blowing and Colt's wet body gave me chills as his lips found mine. He backed us slowly into the water and once we got far enough, he let us fall back into the water together. I screamed at first, until he grabbed me and put my legs around his waist again. The water at this particular beach wasn't totally clear, but you could definitely see our bodies. I felt Colt reaching up and untying my bathing suit top. "What are you doing?"

"Shhh, nobody can see this far. I will leave it around your neck. Just let me play for a minute. Colt pushed me back and ran his hands on both of my breasts while my legs held on to his body.

"What if they have binoculars?" I worried.

We were in the water to our necks and the probability of someone actually seeing what Colt was doing was low, but it still made me uneasy. "Darlin', we are on our honeymoon. I don't think anyone else at this resort cares about what you and I are doing out here in the water. Besides, I'm sure anyone would enjoy the view."

I couldn't possibly consider this, could I?

I dunked Colt into the water. After he came back up he carefully placed my legs around his body again. "Live a little." Colt's hand pulled over the bottoms of my bikini as he slipped his finger inside of me. "Put your arms around me."

I did as he said, just when he began moving his finger in and out of me. I didn't know if it was the fact that we were out in the open, but I was instantly turned on. I pressed my mouth over Colt's chin and used my tongue to taste his salty skin. He nudged my face over enough to kiss me full on the mouth. Our tongues met and I was captured in his essence. Just like always, I was too engulfed in Colt's burning hotness to care about anything else.

Pretend we are invisible.....

I reached down and felt his growing erection and couldn't help but reach inside of his shorts and feel the girth for myself. Fire blazed between my legs as Colt's fingers worked their magic. With his lips still against mine and both of our breathing becoming rapid, I tugged down on his shorts. Colt used one hand and grabbed my ass, while he removed his fingers and positioned his hard shaft where his fingers had just been. The friction of the water and his pure size sent a jolt of pain and pleasure all at once. The more he entered me, the more I burned for him to continue.

We moved slowly in order to not be too obvious, but at that moment, I couldn't have cared who was watching us. Our bodies were under the water, and aside from sudden movements, from far away it would be impossible to decipher what was going on. I wasn't a fool, I knew people could figure it out, but this gorgeous man was all mine and I wanted him inside of me, filling me with his beautiful sperm.

Our tongues mingled, while our bodies thrashed under the water. The slow movements became rapid and I couldn't keep from reaching around and digging my nails into Colt's back as I started to feel him seizing within me. He buried his head into my shoulder and held me there tightly. "That was..."

"Hot," he whispered into my skin.

I laughed. "I was going to say unexpected, but I have a feeling you knew what you were planning all along."

"I couldn't take watching you in that swimsuit any longer. It was hard as hell not to pounce on that chaise with you."

"Is it possible to be sweating while in the water, because I'm burning up right now," I confessed.

We both started laughing. I felt Colt reaching back and tying my top. My bottoms had naturally went back to covering me, once Colt pulled out. He was so large that whenever our sexcapades ended, I would feel empty the first couple of minutes following. I lowered my legs but never let go of my hold around Colt's body, and neither did he. We continued kissing and holding each other until our hands were too pruned up to feel each other's touches.

Colt took my hand as we walked out of the water. When we approached Ty and Miranda, we noticed they had pushed their chaises together and were laying side by side, hand in hand asleep. It was such a cute sight that I had to grab my camera and take some pictures. The coolest part was that they had no idea I had captured such a perfect moment between them.

Colt grabbed my camera and started taking pictures of me chasing after him. Once I had gotten a hold of him, he pulled me close and started snapping more pictures of us together. His final picture came with him kissing me, which turned into something hot again, resulting in our falling into the sand on top of each other. Our fast giggles and playful touches had gotten the attention of other people around us. As soon as I noticed, I jumped up and started brushing off the sand, feeling a bit embarrassed.

To my surprise a little older woman approached us. "Would you like me to take some photos of the two of you together?"

I handed her our camera and wrapped my arms around my husband. The nice lady took a few pictures before handing us back the camera. "You two are a good looking couple. I wish you a happy life together," she said as she walked away from us.

Colt and I walked with our arms around each other, making our way back to Ty and Miranda. Since they were still sound asleep, holding hands, I thought it would be a great idea to prank Ty. I grabbed two empty glasses and went running toward the cold water. I was careful carrying them back, making sure I spilled little on the way. It was hard to contain my laughing, especially when I looked over to Colt who was beside himself just watching me.

All at once I poured the freezing water over Ty's back. He jumped up with super speed and turned with startled eyes to face me. I started backing up, even before he made it off the lounge, but knowing he was still faster than me, made me run my hardest. I could feel him closing in on me as I reached the edge of the water. Arms grabbed me by the waist and threw me right into the water. I clung to his arms, causing him to tumble in with me as I screamed loudly. We both stood up and gained our balance, before splashing the hell out of each other.

I held my hands up while still being splashed. "Okay, okay, truce?"

"That fucking sucked," he let out a chuckle as he shook his head to dry his hair.

I couldn't help but laugh as I started trudging out of the water. Ty came running behind me and smacked me hard on the ass as he ran by. "Paybacks are a bitch Van. I will get you when you least expect it." His smile didn't make me feel any better. When Ty wanted paybacks, he ended up totally embarrassing the person. I was really in for it, but even with the knowledge of something resulting in my prank, just seeing his face was priceless.

"Bring it on bitch," I taunted.

Colt was rolling and Miranda just sat there shaking her head. Ty turned to Colt and pointed his finger at me. "Did you know what she was doing?"

Colt started laughing harder. All he could do was shake his head to agree.

"You both suck. That shit was freezing." Ty started laughing as he climbed onto the chair behind Miranda. He wrapped his wet body over hers, making her jump. He held her tighter. "I need something hot to warm me up baby."

She put her arms over his and accepted his kisses on her neck.

"You guys going to stay down here much longer? I'm gettin' kind of hungry." Colt rubbed his stomach like he was a child explaining how he was starving to death.

"You're always hungry," I teased.

He held his arms out for me and I gladly walked over and sat in between his legs. "I know one thing I'm always hungry for." His lips brushed my shoulder, sending tingles to my nipples.

"Yeah, we saw how hungry you were earlier. Why do you think we turned our heads and fell asleep. It was too much to watch." I could tell Ty was joking, especially with the look he got from his wife.

"Whatever, you saw nothing."

"I have to give it to my dear cousin. He got you to have sex in public, in the DAYTIME," he added.

My face turned blood red. Colt didn't have to look at me to know I was totally embarrassed. "He's just jealous we did it first."

"In the water. We already hit the balcony and gave everyone a good show, right baby?" Ty's sexual confession did not make me feel any better about being caught.

Instead of letting him get the best of me, I stood and reached for my man's hand. "The balcony sounds sexy. Come on babe; let's go show em how it's done."

Oh, shit! Was I really considering it?

Colt said nothing and I could see him clenching his jaw. He wanted to laugh, or say something smart, but he knew better. Ty and Miranda just sat there with their jaws dropped. I held up my hand while Colt grabbed our bag. "It could take us a while. Colt can last for hours."

Once we got far enough away, I thought Colt was going to pee himself. He hunched over and tears were coming out of his eyes. "Did you see his face?"

I couldn't help but laugh. My heart was beating so fast from my big fat lie, but it was worth it. "Yeah, I'm pretty sure we just started a war over who can have the most sex in the most places."

Colt calmed down and got a little serious as we made it back to our room. He stroked the hair out of my face. "I wouldn't fight you if you wanted to actually go through with it."

"With what?" I asked.

"Desperately makin' love to your husband in random places."

"Oh," I started to giggle thinking he was teasing, but then I saw that he wasn't. "OH! Seriously? We could get arrested you know."

He tossed the beach bag on the floor and pressed me against the wall. His fingers gently ran over my lips and I eagerly opened them. He bit down on his lip and looked at me with a creased brow. "Darlin', bein' with you is worth the risk. I would never force you into doin' somethin' you didn't want to do, but Sugar you are so breathtaking that I would do just about anything to be inside of you."

Breathe Savanna.....just breathe. Stop panting!

Chapter 11

Colt

Savanna stood there breathing heavy in my arms. She had to know how much she drove me crazy. I was in awe of the woman. Her salty hair fell down over the breasts of her bathing suit and I pushed it aside. She still hadn't said a word, but I had a feeling she was considering my idea.

Savanna was modest and I loved that about her, but we weren't at home, in fact nobody knew us here, aside from my cousins. We could explore each other in ways that we had never done before. It was appealing to even think about.

Without a single word, Savanna came at me, while reaching up and ripping off her top. Her hands pushed me back toward the balcony and once I hit the glass door, she ran her tongue over my nipple and looked intently into my eyes. I felt her reach behind me and open the door, swinging it open and allowing us to back out. The balcony consisted of two regular chairs and one lounge. Savanna pushed me down on the lounge chair, never even looking to see if anyone was watching us.

She dropped her bikini bottoms and climbed over top of me, straddling me with her legs. I watched as she let her hair fall down over her breasts as she began rocking all over my groin. "Jesus Darlin' are you for real?"

"Don't talk." Her hands went for the fly of my swimming trunks and she rapidly pulled them open, grabbing my whole cock and pulling it out.

Fuck...that's my girl!

It made me groan when I felt her maneuvering herself to slide right over me. I entered her hot sex and grabbed her waist, running my hands up to her chest. She ran her hands in her hair, making her perfect breasts stick out for me. I couldn't help but reach up and touch them. Her sudden courage was sexy as hell and I had no idea how long it would last. Just knowing that forced me to take advantage of all that she was offering.

Savanna moved her body slowly over top of mine. She knew just how to rock her hips to send me begging for more.

She could tell I was going crazy and decided to pick up the pace, which would only make it worse. I grabbed her awesome ass and started grinding her into me harder. Her facial expression let me know she liked it. She put two fingers into her mouth and I watched her tongue them. I pulled her hands down and offered her my fingers instead. She took them right into her mouth and started sucking them, as if it were my cock. When I pulled them away from her lips, she licked them once more before directing them to one of her nipples. As my wet fingertips circled her hard little mounds, I felt her insides tightening around me. Just seeing her face was so hot and I felt myself trying to still her eager body. Savanna let out tiny cries and she fell onto my chest. We lay there panting, covered in sweat.

Whistles from below were coming in different directions and Savanna instantly became aware of what we had just done. She covered her chest with her hands and ran for the door. I fastened my shorts and followed behind her, never looking out to see how many people had got an eye full.

Thank you Ty!

Savanna must have ran right into the bathroom. I found her leaning against the shower, with water trickling down her stunning body. Without startling her, I let my shorts fall to the floor and joined her. She didn't even flinch as my arms reached around her waist and pulled her back up against my chest.

I grabbed the shampoo and started washing her hair, making it a point to massage her scalp as I did it. Once I got her head lathered up, it was easy to run the suds down her body, spreading them over each of her breasts. I washed Savanna's entire body while she stood there with her eyes shut. If only I had super powers to be able to perform over and over again without taking breaks. I would have loved to slide right back inside of her. Her slippery, wet body, combined with a great tan, was tantalizing to look at. I kissed the back of her shoulder. "Darlin' you are so sexy."

She turned around to face me, wrapping her arms around my neck. Her tongue slid from my chest and then up my neck. Savanna kissed my chin and pulled my face down to hers. She stroked my lips with her tongue and ended with her mouth pressed to mine.

As she pulled away and opened her eyes, she smiled and grabbed my ass. "So are you baby."

Now, I have absolutely no idea what had gotten into her, but it was hot and I was in no hurry for it to stop. I liked this new playful side of Savanna that she had kept hidden from me until now.

Our shower ended sooner than I would have liked and Savanna got dressed quickly. I knew we were meeting Ty and Miranda for dinner and that they were probably already waiting for us, well that is what I thought. It turned out that we sat down in the hotel lobby for a good twenty minutes before they came walking down, completely engulfed in each other.

"Took you long enough," I said sarcastically.

"We were busy," Ty laughed and buried his head into Miranda's neck. We could tell he was whispering, but I was pretty sure we didn't want to know what was being said.

Right off of our resort was an outdoor restaurant and bar. It was already getting dark outside and a band was playing as we approached. While Savanna wore a sundress, Miranda wore a small top that showed off her whole stomach and full chest with a long skirt. She immediately started dancing around, enticing Ty to grab onto her exposed hips. "Save it for after we eat guys." I couldn't help laugh after I said it. Had it been Savanna, I would have done the same thing.

Dinner was fantastic and we stayed for a while after to dance to the Caribbean music the band was playing. Savanna and I danced close together, focusing on each other and appreciating our private moments, while Ty and Miranda had everyone watching them. They needed their own Vegas show for erotic dancing. The crowd gathered around them and watched as they danced in sync, basically having mind sex with each other the whole time.

Even Savanna stopped dancing to watch the two of them doing their thing. Savanna got all into it and pulled me in the center of the dance floor. She started swaying her hips and matching Miranda's moves. As the crowd started cheering us on, Miranda and Savanna thought it would be more fun to erotically dance with each other instead. In a couple swift moves, Ty and I were pushed to the sidelines, while the two of them entertained everyone around us.

Ty stood there next to me smiling the whole time. "If you are picturing some sick threesome, you need to get it out of your head right now," I warned.

"Sorry," He teased and nudged me while he started laughing. "As hot as that would be, I couldn't ever share my wife, not even with another woman. In fact, that shit would devastate me more than her cheating. I can't compete with that, therefore I would lose."

"The fact that you have actually thought about it that much to come to that conclusion is very disturbing."

He chuckled but continued to watch his wife. "Shut up dude. Threesomes are hot and I have no problem if you want me to watch Van and another chick, just as long as my wife is sitting on my lap the whole time."

"You're sick man."

Ty started laughing. "Although, I am at an advantage since I have seen both of them naked."

I shook my head and couldn't even get mad. He was joking and I knew he had no interest in Savanna. Not only was he obsessed with Miranda, but Savanna thought he was an ass most of the time.

The song finally ended, considering it was the longest song in the history of songs, and the girls came over and grabbed both of us guys.

"Colt was hoping you guys were going to start making out," Ty announced.

Savanna looked shocked, while my open-minded cousin Miranda smiled and smacked Ty on the chest. She turned around toward us. "No worries Van, Ty wouldn't let me even if I wanted to."

"Jesus, you talked about it?" She asked.

They both were laughing this time. "Not really, he just tells me all the time when I say a woman looks pretty or hot. He is a little protective of me." She reached up and kissed his sad face. "Not that I mind at all babe. It makes me love you more."

"I'd never share you." Ty was dead serious too. He had joked with me about it, but Miranda talking had put the most depressed look on his face. He needed to go to Miranda Anonymous meetings.

"Ty knows I would never do that either. You're actually lucky, he used to beg me to have threesomes." Savanna just shook her head at him.

"Sleeping with Miranda is like being with four women at once. It's fucktastic!"

He turned her around so her back was against his chest, then wrapped his arms around her waist. She shook her head and continued to laugh. He was pushing Savanna, like he loved to do, but something was making her act different. She turned around and stuck her hand right down the front of my shorts, clearly making it obvious she was grabbing my cock. "I couldn't share you either. There is no way I would ever share that huge dick with anyone else." She winked at me, before hugging me, with her hand still holding my junk.

"Damn, maybe ya'll need to go back to your room," Miranda suggested.

"Actually, we have already had sex on the balcony. I was thinking we could take a hot walk on the beach instead." Savanna bit her bottom lip and finally let go of my dick, so that she could grab my hand and start pulling me toward the beach.

We didn't wait to say goodbye to our family, instead we just kept walking away from them. Once we hit the sandy beach, I pulled Savanna into my arms. "What has gotten into you Darlin'?"

"I just want to enjoy every single second of our honeymoon and hopefully go home with a souvenir. Nothing else matters except being here with you Colt. I love you so much and I want to satisfy you in every way possible."

"Please don't take this the wrong way, but Darlin' I am lovin' this side of you."

She reached around and grabbed my ass as we walked. "Really?" She seemed shocked.

"What am I missin'?"

She started to laugh and shake her head. "I kind of went to Miranda for advice. I wanted to be all hot for you while we were here. She gave me a book to read and told me some things you might like."

"Are you freakin' kiddin' me? Why would you go and do somethin' like that? You don't have to change for me Savanna. I love you exactly the way you are."

She turned to face me and put her hands on her hips. "I know for a fact that you have enjoyed your day immensely, don't go trying to deny it."

I reached my hands around her waist. "My wife is throwing herself at me, of course I like it. I'm human and in love with you. I would be a fool not to like it, but you don't have to change for me, not ever."

Savanna stared at me and I could tell she was thinking about what to say. She looked down instead of straight into my eyes. "I just want to satisfy you in every way possible Colt. I don't want you to ever wish you had something else."

"Darlin' you never have to worry about that with me. I realize what happened to you in your first relationship makes you leery, but I promise you that there will never come a time where I wished you were someone else."

She hugged me tight and then pulled away. Slowly, while I watched her, she started pushing down the straps to her dress, letting it fall to the sandy beach at her feet. "What if I like feeling this way?"

I took a step toward her and she stepped back. "Do you now?"

"Maybe I do," she flirted.

My wife continued to back up, wearing nothing but a small pair of panties. I bit down on my lip as I took small steps forward toward her. She started to turn around, I ran faster catching her into my arms. She let out a little scream as I pulled her down to the soft ground. Savanna turned to face me lingering over her body. She reached up and grabbed my cheek, running her sandy fingers over my face. "I want you."

It was a command and I planned on satisfying her every desire.

Savanna smelled like her body lotion and I appreciated that she had allowed me to apply it to her legs after our shower. The pomegranate fragrance filled my nostrils, making me salivate. I sat up on my legs and pushed her knees up, while spreading her legs open.

It was dark outside and the sound of the ocean was all we could hear. I wiped the sand off of my hands and ran my hands up her inner thighs. I could feel her leg muscles tensing to my touch. I leaned down and licked the fabric to her panties, causing her to cry out into the dark night. "Oh fuck yes...."

I licked her panties again, this time forcing my tongue to press harder against her pussy. Savanna's hands found her breasts and she began massaging them while trying to also watch what I was doing. I could smell the musk of her wetness and I had to taste her. With one hand, I slid my fingers into the side of her panties and moved them out of the way. "I need to taste you."

As my head moved toward her sweet sex, Savanna's body vibrated with the sounds of her being completely turned on. "Mmmmm, please don't stop."

I covered my mouth over her whole pussy, thrusting my tongue inside of her, then pulling out to circle it around her swollen clit. Savanna knew I got off by making her come. She moved her body against my mouth, as I pushed my tongue harder and harder against her little nub.

As I continued to lick, I thrusted two fingers inside of her, pounding them against her tight walls. She grinded herself into my hand, making sure my fingers were in as far as they could go. When I felt my fingers being forced out by her orgasm, my cock started to throb for her. I need to be inside of her, to feel her wetness coating my dick.

Savanna's hands were opening the fly to my shorts and her feet were kicking them down around my ankles. With one quick thrust I drove my eagerness inside of her, jolting my throbbing cock deeper as I penetrated her tight walls. Her body accepted mine, like it always did.

The cool air chilled our bodies while the friction of our hot sex made us burn with pleasure. It was a happy median, considering how brave we were both being to be fucking on a public beach, for anyone to discover us. My wife had turned into a voyeur and I wasn't sure I wanted her to ever stop. Being on the beach like this was something I had never experienced. It was hot and explosive and I felt myself coming far too soon.

Even after I was spent, we lay on the soft ground, still attached. Her legs were wrapped around me, while her fingertips circled the cheeks of my ass.

"Jesus Christ Savanna, that was.......awe....Hell, I don't even know what to say."

"Tell me you love me," she whispered against my ear.

"You know I do." I ran my fingers over her lips before kissing them. "I love you so much."

Our moment was cut short when we saw a group of flashlights coming up on the beach, in the distance.

"Oh shit! Sugar, we need to get dressed." I stood up and pulled up my shorts, while pulling Savanna to her feet. She rushed over and grabbed her dress, throwing it over her head. I reached my hand out for her and we started running in the opposite direction of the lights.

Once we made it back to the resort, and into our room, we broke out into extreme laughter. We were acting like teenagers, running free and doing crazy things. I was excited and I couldn't get enough of it.

Chapter 12

Savanna

After reading Miranda's book cover to cover a few times, I felt adventurous. Colt didn't seem to mind my new curiosity, and accepted every sexual innuendo I sent his way. My husband was so sexy that being wild and crazy for him was easy. It turned me on to turn him on.

We spent the next two days spending our days with Ty and Miranda, but our nights discovering each other's deepest fantasies. After Ty and Miranda left, Colt and I treated ourselves to a spa day, we went snorkeling and even traveled to a place that had private waterfalls and hiking trails. Since Colt and I were being so frivolous, we decided to visit them alone. It was a good thing because once we got into that water underneath those falls, Colt went all buck wild with me. He bent me over behind the waterfall and then we later made love at the bottom where the bubbly water secluded our naked bodies.

Our honeymoon was both beautiful and educational. Colt and I discovered so many things about each other, that we hadn't known in the past two years. When we left we felt fulfilled and more in love than we had ever been. I'd like to say that I learned it all from my nympho cousin's sex book, but most I learned from opening myself up to exploring both mine and Colt's bodies. Leaving Hawaii didn't end our new addiction either, I almost tempted Colt into entering the Mile High Club. It wasn't like I had changed as a person, it was just that I wanted to be desired. I wanted to get that look from Colt that Miranda got; that look like they knew they had hot secrets between each other and they couldn't wait to have an alone moment again soon. Maybe I was wrong to idolize parts of their relationship, but if I hadn't asked, I would have never known how good it could be.

The feeling of being with Colt was the same, but the excitement was what made it even better.

I knew we were going to go home and have sex in crazy places, but just knowing that we HAD done that got me all excited again.

Since Colt and I were desperately trying to make a baby, we started really paying attention to my ovulation cycle. After four months worth of cycles went by, I was losing all hope of being able to ever get pregnant. Colt never gave up hope and assured me that it would happen for us. He said we were meant to be parents.

Five months after our honeymoon I was on my way to the pharmacy to buy a test. It was the first time I had been late since we had been trying. I remember my hands profusely shaking as I paid the cashier for the little box with two sticks inside that could determine our future. I was half-tempted to run into the bathroom in the back and pee on them before even leaving the store.

My breasts had been tender and I felt so irritable a week before purchasing the tests. Colt was so sure of himself, never giving up hope that I had a baby growing inside of me. It was hard peeing on the stick while he stood there watching me, but I knew he was just as excited as I was. This was an unforgettable moment and I knew he wanted to be there for every second of it. It turned out he had to turn the water on so that my bladder would actually wet the stick. We stood there like two little kids waiting for Christmas, just watching for two blue lines. Finally, after about thirty seconds I pulled him out of the bathroom. We stood at the edge of the door like it had some magic barrier preventing us from entering until the three minutes were up.

We didn't have a stopwatch and hadn't noted the time when we exited, so we just stood there staring at each other. After what felt like twenty minutes, but was actually four or five, we ran into the bathroom and stood there staring at the little blue lines. Of course, I couldn't believe it was positive, so I ended up peeing on the second stick and waiting another three minutes to see the same results.

Colt hugged me so tight, kissing me all over my face. He picked me up and started spinning me around the bathroom. "We're goin' to have a baby. Woohoo! Oh Darlin', I'm just so excited."

He finally set me down, but not before he kissed me again. "I can't believe this is finally happenin'."

"When can we tell everyone?" He asked excited.

I stood there and just started crying against his chest. For so long I had been afraid that we couldn't conceive. I was overwhelmed with emotions just knowing that I had a real baby growing inside of me, a baby that was made out of pure love and passion for each other. It was the most amazing feeling I had ever experienced.

"Oh Colt, I can't believe this is finally happening. We're going to be a family, a real family baby." He held me tight, spinning me around in circles.

Happy tears were shared between both of us, leaving us in momentary bliss. I was happier than I had ever been in my entire life. I had the most handsome and loving man as my husband, a beautiful home, a family that loved me, wonderful friends and my first child growing inside of me. Our life was perfect and Colt was the reason. He gave me it all, and I would be forever in awe with his devotion to me.

For the next four weeks, we managed to keep my pregnancy a secret. Colt had a more difficult time than me, especially being around his mother all of the time. For a while I thought he caved and told her, but I knew he hadn't when I saw the look on her face when she did find out.

We had our normal family Sunday dinner. Conner had already left and Lucy was doing the dinner dishes. While Aunt Karen and my mother in law were gossiping during our card game, Colt cleared his throat and stood up from the table. They both looked and watched as he pulled me to stand next to him. He looked down into my eyes with the biggest smile I had ever seen before. He never looked away from me as he began to speak. "Savanna and I have somethin' important to share."

Colt's mother literally yelped and stood up holding her hand on her heart. "OH MY GOD, YOUR PREGNANT?"

We both turned to face her as we started laughing and shaking our heads to confirm. Both of the middle-aged women came running to our side of the table, throwing their arms around us and feeling on my belly.

His mother cried for nearly an hour, pulling us into the living room to talk about her excitement some more. She offered to basically buy me anything my heart desired in preparation for our special delivery. As much as I appreciated her thought, Colt and I could afford to do it all ourselves and we wanted to. This was our first child and we were ecstatic.

For the past six months, I had done nothing but think about baby matters. I had a nursery designed in my head. I knew what bedding I wanted and what kind of diapers I preferred. I had already filled out information on cloth diapers and had them mailing me several coupons a month. I researched nipples and what type of bottles gave the least amount of gas. One day I had gone out to a department store and ended up trying out several strollers and car seats. I was so ready for this, so ready to give Colt the family that he wanted so badly.

My first doctor's appointment was at ten weeks. The doctor wasn't optimistic at first, but she was able to find the perfect little heartbeat. Colt held my hand as we listened to it for the first time. It was the most rapid, most beautiful thing to hear. While the doctor wrote me my prescription for prenatal vitamins, she kept the monitor over my belly so we could continue to listen.

We left the office hand in hand. Even though we already had known we were pregnant, hearing the heartbeat made it all real. There was a little baby growing inside of me; a little Colt perhaps.

Ty and Miranda were just as excited when we shared the news with them. Miranda had checked with her doctor and they still had a little under a year to go before they could start trying themselves. They were completely happy with Bella, but I think Ty was hoping for a little boy to complete his perfect little family. They really were perfect too. Their friendship and love for each other was amazing to experience. If I had ever doubted them before, it was proven beyond a doubt that I had been wrong.

Miranda was really happy with the salon she was working at. She had made great friends there and she and Ty had even joined a local billiards league for a night out together. Ty's mother was madly in love with Bella, apparently spoiling her like crazy. After four months, Ty and his father managed to do a complete renovation to the Carriage house. They had taken the back storage part, which had been a barn, and converted it to more living space. They had restored the original roof and gave the living room higher ceilings with exposed beams. It was such a big change, and looked like their own little cottage.

Of course, Bella got her own bedroom and playroom, as well as her own little bathroom. In fact, the full addition added three bedrooms and a bathroom to the house. To make up for the loss of storage space, Ty got his father a pole-building and had it installed. They seemed happy living on the farm. It wasn't like they didn't have privacy. The houses weren't right up against one another and Ty and Miranda's front door faced the opposite direction.

Colt and I had gone to visit them twice and for now, they had made one room for guests. Bella made it a point to drag us down the new hallway and show us her new rooms. The best part was when she made Colt sit on the floor while she handed him each toy in her room, one at a time.

We had a really great visit and didn't want it to end. I no longer even considered Ty an ex-lover. Instead, he was a great friend and cousin. Miranda had helped me learn to discover myself and my body resulting in a deeper connection with Colt. We'd have secret conversations labeled 'girl talk' and she never shared my private information with Ty. I had no idea if they ever talked about me, but Ty never mentioned it, so I assumed she hadn't.

Ty's mother also had changed her opinion of me. For so long I had wanted her to accept me and love me. On one of our visits, she pulled me aside and profusely apologized for being such a hardcore bitch. Ty was happier than he had ever been, which meant she was happy. Maybe she had known all along that we weren't meant for each other. Either way, to hear her saying those words to me made me so happy. From then on, she was never bitter.

We must have gotten pregnant right after our last visit to North Carolina. Colt came back to some issues with the ventilation in two of our chicken houses, so he had spent a whole week working late getting them up to par. He was so tired when he finally came in at night that we didn't have sex for over a week. I only remember because it was the longest we had ever gone without it. The night he finally had everything working, he came home and pretty much attacked me, pulling me in the shower with him first, then taking me back to our bed.

It had been so intense from the sexual tension building up between us, that we just had an entire night of making love to each other. We slept the whole next day, only getting up to eat, drink and use the bathroom. I never wanted to go that long without being with Colt, but I will never forget how awesome it was when we finally did it.

The first trimester of my pregnancy was perfect. I was tired at first, but it subsided and I felt fantastic and excited. I never really got morning sickness. It was cool to finally start getting a little baby bump to my belly. It was not noticeable unless I was naked, but Colt was the only one feeling around every night anyway. He would always lay next to me, kissing and rubbing my belly, sometimes even talking to it.

My mother was freaking out, knowing that she and my father were so far away, but I wasn't really scared about being alone, besides Colt told them that he would fly them down immediately when the baby was coming.

One morning Colt went out to work somewhere on the ranch. We were running low on groceries and I refused to let Lucy do our shopping for us, so I grabbed my purse and headed out toward town. For some reason I had become obsessed with couponing, after watching the extreme couponing show on television. We didn't need to necessarily save money, but I did it as more of something to do with my extra time. We may have been well off, but I liked to get good deals still.

I went into the store with my book of coupons and the list of what I was going to buy. Early in the mornings, the stores weren't ever busy, so I could take my time without dealing with long lines of people.

After checking out, I headed toward my car, hitting the trunk button on my key ring.

As I started unloading the groceries, I heard someone come up behind me and grab me. Something hard pointed into my side. "If you fucking scream, I will kill you right here."

I froze, trying not to make a sound as he pushed me toward the passenger side of my car. The man opened the door and shoved me inside. "Don't look up. Keep your god damn head down."

I looked to the floor, hoping and praying he would just take my purse and leave me. I didn't want to die. I couldn't even remember if I had told Colt how much I loved him this morning.

How could this be happening to me? We lived in such a small town.

"Please don't hurt me. Just take my whole purse. There is over a hundred dollars in there and several credit cards. I won't say anything. I swear." I pleaded with my eyes closed the entire time, just praying to myself that he would listen.

My body began to tremble and I could feel my teeth chattering, not from being cold, but from being completely petrified. I started crying out loud and I felt the car door slam next to me. For a brief moment, I thought he had left, but then the driver's side opened. At that very precise moment, I had looked up to see if the coast was clear. I got one brief look at the perpetrator before feeling a blow to my face.

When I came to, I tried to move, but my hands were restrained behind my back. Something was tied around my head and stuffed into my mouth. My tongue lay dry against it. I began to gag, but no one came to help me or relieve the bindings. I sat there on some sort of dirty basement floor and cried, with nobody to hear me.

Some time had passed before I was awoken suddenly to someone slapping me in the face. I realized that I must have fallen asleep from crying so badly. I looked up to see the shadow of a man standing behind me. He was tapping on something that looked big and long in the shadow. As he smacked it repeatedly against his hand, I could tell that it was not metal, but more of a plastic sound. His country accent filled my ears. "You just sit still and mind your business and I won't hurt you. I bet you thought you were lucky marryin' someone like Colt Mitchell. Miranda thinks she can just get me locked up while she is livin' all large somewhere, well that shit is about to change. I seen her and that cousin getting' all cozy. It's kinda funny how I wasn't good enough, but they accept her havin' some kind of incest relationship."

Oh God! I have been kidnapped by Tucker Chase.

'That is some kind of sick shit. It don't matter to me who that little whore is bangin'. I'm gonna gets me some of that money and get the fuck out of this town. Once I gets mines I will let you go."

This can't be happening to me. I just want to go home. I want to forget this day ever happened to me.

I was mumbling words from beneath the cloth shoved in my mouth, but Tucker never relieved me from it. I could hear him pacing behind me and when he began to talk again, the sound of his voice startled me. I hadn't noticed before, but my head was throbbing and when I moved my eyebrows, my forehead and cheek felt weird, like when I wore face masks for my skin. With the pain coming from my eye, I realized I must have had dried blood from where he had originally hit me to knock me unconscious.

Tears streamed down my eyes as I listened to Tucker talking on the phone to someone. "I did everything as planned. Yeah, I gots her tied up, what do you think I'm an idiot or somethin'? No Mamma, she is fine. YES, I WILL GET THE DAMN MONEY. Stop your whinin'. Do you think I would have been lyin' low all of these months if I wanted to get caught? I had Charlie make the call already. It's all takin' care of. Just calm down and wait for my call."

What the fuck? His mother was also in on this?

Tucker must have got off the phone. He stopped talking and even pacing. He was so quiet for a few seconds that I considered he was right behind me, preparing to kill me here on this dirty floor, with whatever object he was holding in his hand. I could see his shadow and he was just standing behind me.

I tried to silence my tears enough where my body wasn't trembling so much, but I was afraid for my life and it was just impossible to try and be calm. Eventually, I saw the dark shadow move and finally heard him climbing up the steps, and then shutting a door. As soon as I heard that door shutting, I tried to wiggle my way around to decipher just how my hands were bound and if there was any way, I could possibly free myself.

I had to give it to the little redneck creep; he must have used zip ties on my wrists. The more I fought to free myself, the more the plastic rubbed against my skin. I was apparently tied to some kind of pole in the basement and from the feel of it against my skin; I would say it was old and rusty.

If I wanted to get free, I would have to inflict major pain on my wrists, but I was desperate. I needed to get me and my baby out of this house. I knew Colt would come looking for me, but he didn't know where to look. I was alone for right now, but determined to get out in one piece.

I started lifting my arms up and down against the coarse metal pole; the plastic pressing and ripping the skin on my wrist as I did it. The pain was agonizing when inflicting it on yourself, but it was necessary if I wanted to get out of this place. I could see a window straight in front of me. It had a sheet over it, but the light shined through enough to know it was an escape. Against one wall, I spotted a broom and a shovel. If I could manage my hands free, I could untie my feet and grab the shovel for protection.

The metal pole wasn't making a dent in the plastic, so I decided on taking a different approach to the plastic restraints. I twisted and turned my wrists in opposite directions, hoping to break the clasping mechanism to the stupid ties. The basement was freezing, considering it was unfinished and I was sitting on a concrete floor, but beads of sweat were rolling down my aching head. Pain shot through my wrists and up my arms, as warm liquid oozed down from them. I had broken the skin and was bleeding from where the plastic was now digging into my skin.

My arms were exhausted and I wanted to give up, but knowing that Tucker could come down any second and see that I was fighting to get free, well it scared the bejesus out of me. I had to keep trying until I was free. I was glad that I hadn't given up, because just seconds later I felt the resistance give and my hands freeing themselves, at the exact moment the basement door creaked open.

Chapter 13

Colt

I had been helping Conner work on installing a new manufacturer's part to one of our combines all day. The day had gotten away from me and I found myself heading home as the sun was starting to set. It was weird not hearing from Savanna all day, considering she always called at least once. I remembered she said she was going into town to get some things we needed, so I figured maybe she and my mother, or even Lucy caught an afternoon movie or something.

Nothing could have prepared me for walking into the dark house, seeing that she had never returned home. Her purse wasn't on the counter, suggesting she had gone to the ranch house. The refrigerator was still pretty empty and nothing was picked up from this morning.

I reached in my pocket to grab my cell phone and realized I had left it back inside of the combine. Worry rushed over me as I ran out of my house, Sam following, to get to my cell phone. After driving as fast as the golf cart could take me, I grabbed my phone out of the combine and noticed missed calls. There had been just one call from Savanna at nine in the morning, but nothing since. The other calls were from a blocked number. I dialed into my voicemail and started listening to the messages.

Colt....Colt Mitchell. We have your wife and if you know what's good for you, you will get us fifty thousand dollars. If we don't hear from you, she will die. I reckon you best be gettin' to the bank. We will call you back later today with a place to make the exchange.

Somehow hearing the message was like being in the Twilight Zone. After the first moments of utter shock, I reached down and dialed my mother. I should have called the police first, but something made me call her. Maybe it was some inclination that she was always my mother and could protect me from anything painful. The thought left my mind when I snapped back into reality and realized she was on the other end of the phone waiting for me to respond. "Colt? Can you hear me dear?"

"Mom......I don't.....something.....someone took Savanna, Mom. I need your help." I was frantically pacing around the living room.

"What do you mean someone took her? Where is she?"

I sat down and ran my hand through my hair. "I don't know. She wasn't home when I got here. I had missed calls from some unknown number and a message demanding fifty thousand dollars or I would never see her again." Just the thought of never seeing my beautiful Savanna, my wife, the mother to my unborn child, made me cringe with sickness.

"You need to call the police Son. I'm coming over there right now. Sit tight. I will grab John. He is over at your aunt Karen's tonight for dinner."

How convenient. The sheriff was already at the ranch.

I contemplated calling the police, but with Savanna being kidnapped, I couldn't take the chance of having the authorities fucking up my chances of her getting home to me in one piece. I had seen too many things go bad in movies and television shows to know it didn't always have a happy ending.

My mother came rushing in the door, followed by the sound of a car slamming on their breaks in my gravel driveway. My little mother came rushing over to me, grabbing my hand, while Aunt Karen and Sheriff John followed in. "Colt, tell me everything you told your mother. Don't leave anything out. We need all the details that we get."

"I hadn't talked to Savanna all day and when I got home she wasn't here. After locatin' my phone, I had a missed call from an unknown number and one message statin' that they had Savanna and if I didn't give them fifty grand, I wouldn't see her again." I really started to panic. "She is pregnant John. We have to get that money and do whatever it takes to get her home safe. She can't handle stress John. Please tell me what to do."

He held his hands up, telling me to calm down; even though I knew it was an impossible gesture. "They never said where to meet?"

"It said they would call back." My mother rubbed my shoulders.

Aunt Karen walked over to John and grabbed his hand, getting her attention. "John, we can't just assume the best here. We need to figure out how to get her and that baby back in one piece.

"The money isn't a problem." My mother interrupted.

John put his hands up again. He was obviously accustomed to trying to calm seriously frustrated victims and criminals down. "Now let's not jump to conclusions. The next time they call, you will ask to speak to Savanna, for proof of life."

"Proof of life? Heavens to Betsy, this can't be happening right now." My mother buried her hands into her face.

I was trying so hard to remain calm and focused on just getting my wife home safely, but we had nothing to go on. To make matters worse, the banks were all closed and I had no idea how we were going to get fifty grand at six o'clock at night. "What happens if they need the money tonight? We can't get that kind of money tonight." I stood up and started pacing around the living room.

"Colt, listen here Son, if they are in it for the money, they will expect to have to provide proof of life. We have no reason to believe they have harmed her in any way," John explained.

"Can we trace the call? Is there a way to trace a blocked number?" I asked.

He shook his head and sat down on the couch, finally looking up at me after rubbing his hands together. My Aunt Karen sat down beside my mother and grabbed her hand. "It's not that simple. In most cases the phone used is called a burner phone. You can pick one up at any gas station or grocery store.

The phones are untraceable, especially without knowing the number. I'm afraid we are going to have to wait it out."

That was not what I wanted to hear coming from the sheriff himself. I guess I expected he would just be able to bring her home to me immediately. I realize that it was stupid to assume, but the thought of my Savanna out there somewhere scared, and God only knows what else, made me cringe. I needed to find her, to save her, and to bring her home. I couldn't live with myself if anything ever happened to her over my parent's wealth. It wasn't fair. She never asked for this life. In fact, she came here *because* of me.

Guilt washed over me and the pain of realization.

My wife had been kidnapped.

For the next hour, the four of us brainstormed different scenarios back and forth. I don't know how she did it, but my mother left and came back about thirty minutes later with a suit case full of cash. For some reason, I knew I wasn't meant to ask questions. My parents were loaded, but who the Hell keeps fifty grand at their house? It's like having a sign on your front door saying 'rob me'.

I never snooped around my house, but I assumed they probably had some hidden safe somewhere. My mother was a smart woman and my father even wiser. It wasn't hard to admit that they always had a rainy day stash lying around. My mother saw me giving her the curious eye. She came over toward me and reached for my hand. "It's our emergency fund. Your dad started it when you were in high school. He was afraid he might have to bail you out of some trouble," she whispered.

"That's crazy. I wasn't that bad."

She cocked an eyebrow and gave me a snarky look. "I beg to differ, Colton."

I pulled her into my arms. "Thank you for this, Mom."

My cell phone started ringing from across the room, grabbing our immediate attention. Before opening it, John gave me certain instructions. I wasn't to plea with them at all. I had to stick with one simple question.

"Hello?"

"Colt Mitchell?" The voice was distorted.

"Yeah."

"You got our money?"

"Yeah. Is Savanna okay?"

"The girl is fine."

"I need to hear her voice."

The phone went quiet for a second, like he held his hand over it. "We will call you back and let you talk to her. Stay by your phone."

They hung up before I could say any more. I looked around the room at the three of them waiting for an explanation. "He said they will call back and let me hear her voice."

"Oh thank God she is okay." My mother announced.

I put my head down and waited for the phone to ring. I hoped that she was right, but after forty minutes we still had no call and that just didn't sit right with me at all.

Chapter 14

With my hands freed, I reached down for my feet, but was startled by the door opening, followed by feet coming down the stairs. The shovel was too far away to grab and I would have been seen by the person coming down the steps, causing them to come at me faster.

I gathered my hands back together, as Tucker rounded the corner and headed in my direction. He stood over me, scratching his head and squinting his eyes like he was in deep thought. "I'm goin' to make a call and you are only going to say hello and tell them you are okay. Do you understand bitch?"

I nodded my head, but said nothing. He started reaching in his pockets and obviously couldn't find what he was looking for. "Shit. This phone doesn't have the number in it." He headed toward the stairs and ran up them, two at a time.

I reached for my feet and used my bleeding hands and wrists to free them. As I heard the door squeaking open, I ran for the shovel. I could hear him coming at me as I grabbed the handle and swung it around. It hit him across the jaw, sending him falling to the floor. I was breathing heavy and could feel my heart beating out of my chest, but I had no time to panic, as Tucker began to stand on his feet again.

I had never physically inflicted pain on anyone in my entire life, but my life and my unborn child's life was in danger. With all of my might I swung that shovel again. He turned as a natural reaction to it heading toward his face and it got a chunk of the back of his head. He went down fast. His head hitting the floor as blood started forming a pool around him.

At this point I had begun crying my eyes out. The shovel felt loose in my hands and I let it fall to floor, thinking I had really killed him. He was a bad man, but I was no killer. My natural instinct was to check for a pulse, but thank God my adrenaline kicked in and made me rationalize with such an idiotic decision I was about to make. I could hear voices coming from the first floor and looked back down at Tucker bleeding out on the ground.

I climbed onto the shelf in front of me and started to push open the hatch window. When I got it good enough to slide my body out of, I grabbed a hold of the sides and dove for it. My feet dangled against the wall as I used all of my might to pull myself up and outside of the house.

I'd got about half through when I heard someone screaming and then felt the hands grabbing both of my feet. With one rapid pull I went flying back into the house, falling about seven feet down onto the hard ground. The pain of hitting the floor was agonizing and for a few moments I couldn't even move. Aside from having the wind knocked out of me, I couldn't shake the tremendous amount of pain coming from my stomach.

"Get her hands," someone yelled.

I struggled to move away from them, but it hurt to even try to roll. A boot came crashing into my jaw, sending my face and head in the opposite direction it was facing. A ringing started in my ears and although I knew the two people were talking, I could only hear the muffled sounds of voices. I brought my hand up to my ear and it was wet with blood. I brought my knees to my chest and cringed in pain, both from my stomach and my back.

After at least five minutes of them not coming near me, and me lying there in utter pain, someone came over and kicked me in my back once more. I cried out, but there was nobody there to help me. I knew what was happening to my body, but I just couldn't admit it to myself yet. This was probably going to be my last day on this earth and the fact that my last moments of life were losing the baby that I had wanted my whole entire life, well it was indescribably terrible.

It was as if all of the visions of me being a mother were disappearing right in front of my eyes. Just knowing that made me want to give up. They were destroying my heart, my future, my life.

I managed to put my hand over my bad ear and could hear a bit of what they were saying. The female was arguing with the male about taking Tucker to the hospital. The male was saying that Tucker would go to jail for setting fire at the barn and he would be locked up and convicted of my kidnapping as well. The girl was crying and pleading with the guy, almost begging him to reconsider. I heard one of them walking up the steps and then slamming the door closed.

At first I thought maybe they both had gone up and I just didn't notice it, but low cries were coming from the opposite side of the room. While covering my face, I turned to see a redheaded girl hovered over Tucker. She was crying and rocking back and forth.

When she spotted me looking at her, I could sense the hate in her eyes. She stood up and walked toward me, but for some reason she just stood there over me, holding her hands over her mouth. She started backing away, shaking her head and repeating the word 'no,no,no'.

I tried to sit up and she turned around to start walking away. While still crying she turned one last time. "God, I'm so sorry. You weren't supposed to get hurt. This wasn't part of the plan. We just wanted the money. I swear." She went running up the stairs and I even heard the front door being slammed shut. Voices could be heard out of the open window and moments later a car started and pulled away.

I don't know how long I waited before trying to get up, but it was at least ten minutes. Instead of attempting to stand, I crawled over to Tucker's body to check for a phone first. After searching every pocket, I found the phone, under his body. I wasn't worried about him waking up. With the amount of blood loss and the way his eyes were open, I knew he was dead.

Calling Colt first would have been pointless. I had no idea where I was. The only way for me to be found would be to have my call traced. I open the phone and hit the emergency button.

"Nine one, one what is your emergency?"

"Please help me," I cried. "I've been kidnapped, bound and beaten. I'm in a basement and I have no idea where I am." My voice began to fade and the tears were streaming down my face. "I'm having a miscarriage. Please help me."

The phone fell out of my hands as I collapsed onto the floor. Saying the words made it a reality. I just wanted to die, to just close my eyes and not feel the physical and emotional pain that was tearing through my body. How could this have happened to me. What did I ever do to deserve this?

I have no idea how long it was, but I finally picked the phone back up to hear the operator still there.

She told me they could search the vicinity of where the call was coming from and there were only a couple of residencies to search through. I stayed on the line and listened for the Ambulance. As it got closer I relayed it to the operator. When it was its loudest, I heard the doors slamming and soon a bunch of voices were in the house. I never hung up the phone, but continued to cry as the emergency crews came down to help me and handle the crime scene.

The paramedics were as gentle as they could be with me, while getting me onto the stretcher and carrying me up the flight of stairs. Police had already started arriving and the yard was full of officers. Once I was in the ambulance and the paramedic was trying to get my vitals, I reached over and grabbed his arm. "Please call my husband. My name is Savanna Mitchell, my husband is Colt. Please find him."

"We know who you are Mrs. Mitchell. He's already on his way." I heard someone say before everything went black.

The next thing I remember was waking up in the hospital. I was hooked up to all kinds of monitors. The buzzing in my one ear was constant, and the pain in my stomach was worse. I tried to open my mouth to speak, but my jaw was stuck shut. A hand on my arm caused me to turn my head. Colt stood there over me. Tears filled his eyes and everything that had happened to me came all back to replay in my mind.

"No! No! No! Please tell me it isn't true. Please Colt. Tell me it isn't true." I pleaded through my tight jaw. It was hard to talk, but I couldn't help myself from expressing my pain. "Please, God, tell me this is a bad dream. Tell me this isn't real. My baby.....our baby. Our.Baby."

He knew I was referring to our baby. I didn't have to keep saying it. He couldn't look into my eyes, but as the tears fell from his own, he shook his head from side to side, right before covering his face into his hands.

He tried to shush me, to get me to calm down, but the tears flooded my vision. "Try not to talk Darlin'. They had to wire part of your jaw. Please don't cry, Sugar. I'm so sorry Savanna. I'm just so darn sorry."

Our baby was gone.

There would be no calming down. No being grateful I made it out of there alive. I caused this to happen. The red head told me they weren't going to hurt me. Me trying to escape is what killed my baby. It was all my fault.

My emotional breakdown became so uncontrolled that the doctors came and eventually sedated me. The last face I saw was Colt's. The pain I saw in his eyes was worse than anything physical I was feeling myself.

I was in the hospital for nine days. I had a broken jaw, a busted ear drum, two broken ribs and had lost our baby. To make matters worse, they had to surgically go in and remove the deceased baby from my body. They said I went into shock, but I couldn't remember anything after the ambulance.

A psychiatrist came in every day and sat with me, trying to console me and get me to be okay with everything that happened. Of course they insisted I was already having PTSD and that I needed to be on a medication regiment until they knew for sure I had recovered fully from what had happened to me.

Tucker had died from blunt force trauma to the head. I was never charged on account of it being ruled out self defense. They never caught the other two people and they didn't have enough evidence to convict his mother of being in on the crime. With Tucker Chase dead our family knew that we wouldn't be bothered anymore.

Our family was not sad to hear of his demise and I did know that someone like him didn't deserve to be alive, but it still didn't help with the repeated nightmares of me killing him. I couldn't shake what I had done, not even with my therapists help.

For three weeks I stayed in my bed at the house. Colt flew my mother in to Kentucky and she stayed with me for two weeks. I barely ate and I never came out of my room. Colt tried to comfort me, but in my eyes I had taken his heart and ripped it to shreds. I couldn't tell him the truth about what I had done. If he ever found out that everything was my fault, he would never be able to look at me, and especially be with me again.

Our sex life was non-existent, in fact, after several attempts, Colt had stopped trying to touch me. I read all kinds of books about self help and losing children, but nothing filled the void of feeling my baby growing inside of me.

After two months, I started to come out of the bedroom. I missed Colt and even though I had this huge secret, I knew he was all I had left. The doctors said that the miscarriage had left a bunch of scar tissue and being able to conceive naturally could be even more difficult than it was before. With all hopes of getting pregnant again almost gone, Colt did his best to coax me into our old life again.

It took about a week for me to get back into my normal routine. I never went anywhere besides the ranch, but my therapist insisted it was a good start. Lucy would get my groceries and run errands in town so I wouldn't have to. Colt spent more time working from his home office and when he didn't he still came home for lunch and was always home in time for dinner. We still ate in silence, but we were together, taking baby steps to get back to how things used to be.

One morning I woke up feeling like I was at peace for some reason. Colt was still asleep next me and I reached over to kiss him. His lips brushed over mine and he woke up and wrapped his arms around me. It was the first time that I had wanted him since my accident. He slipped the nightgown down off of my shoulders and kissed me gently on my neck. "I miss you so much, Darlin'."

"Make love to me Colt."

He gently pushed my head down on the pillow and slipped the nightgown down off of my waist and then my feet. He removed my panties and ran his hands down my naked body. "Are you sure?"

"Please."

It was more like I was begging him to touch me, like I needed to feel him as close as he could get. I didn't want to be alone anymore, in fact, I couldn't bear it anymore.

His gentle hands stroked my lips right before he leaned down and kissed them. Colt cupped my breast and sucked on it, before removing his boxers and sliding on top of me. It had been so long for both of us. I didn't want the foreplay, or to take our time. I needed him to be inside of me.

I reached down and felt the girth of his immediate erection. Just knowing he still wanted me made me hot between my legs. There was this burn for him that I needed to calm. I thrusted my hips up, touching his hardness with my naked skin. He groaned and positioned it so that he could slide right in. Colt moaned as he entered me. It was so tight and even hurt at first like our first time had. He went slow, his body trembling over top of me. I grabbed his naked ass with my hands and pulled him into me harder. His strong arms held his body up from crushing mine and I ran my hands over the muscles of them. Colt's gorgeous green eyes found mine and he stared into them as he thrusted faster, picking up the pace to signal he was about to come. His eyes closed tightly and his body tensed up over top of mine. I could feel him exploding inside of me, making me feel like I was full of his love. In hindsight, I knew it was just semen, but at the time, it was pure bliss.

He rolled us over and stroked my hair as he placed gentle kisses all over my face. "God I missed this."

I wrapped my arms around him and began to cry. "I did too, Baby."

I made Colt breakfast that morning and we drank coffee on the porch while swinging and looking out at the pasture. Sam was already running around chasing squirrels. I felt euphoric, like I had overcome the treacherous last bit of months. When my husband left for work, I got myself inside and started cleaning the house, and thinking about what we could have for dinner. I turned my favorite music up and danced around as I worked. I had a great life and I wanted to be happy again.

A knock at the door startled me. I turned down the music and headed toward it. All of our family would open the door and call out for me, and I knew it wasn't locked. I opened the door to two people in business suits. A black SUV was sitting in our driveway. "Mrs. Mitchell?"

"Yes?"

I thought they were just there to go over something to close Tucker's case.

"Can we come in Ma'am? Is your husband around?" A gentleman asked.

"He is out on the ranch somewhere. What is this about?" I asked.

They hadn't come into the house yet and my vision of the second person, a woman, was obscured by the first guy standing in my way. "We really need you to get him to come home Ma'am. We can explain everything once he is here."

Before I could turn to grab my phone, I saw Colt pulling up on the golf cart. He must have seen them coming in the Ranch's main entrance. As he made it up the steps the man moved to the side, leaving me to be able to see the woman, who was holding the hand of a child. Colt walked past them, until he reached where I was standing. "Can I help you with something?"

"Mr. Mitchell? Hi, I'm Roger Nesbitt. I'm with the Department of Social Services. I'm sorry to just come by unannounced. We don't get many of these kind of cases. Do you mind if we come in to explain?"

I was just staring at the little hand that was attached to the woman.

"Sure come on in." Colt opened the door and let the man in.

As the man came through the door, the woman smiled. "Hi, I'm Sarah Forrester and this is Noah. Noah, can you say hi to the lady." The little boy, who looked to be about three or four, came looking around the woman's legs and I bent down to greet him, but what I saw in his eyes made me collapse.

I came to and noticed I was on the couch. Three adults surrounded my vision, while the little boy sat in the chair across from me. Ignoring the people talking to me, I got up and crawled over to where he sat. His hands were folded together and he was swinging his feet looking down at his pants. I kneeled in front of him and placed my hands over his knees, causing him to look up at me.

Those eyes...

Those beautiful green eyes that I knew so well...

Chapter 15

Colt

"Colt?" Savanna was kneeled down in front of the child. Her voice was weak and I could tell she was struggling. I knew what she saw because I saw it too. I was in too much shock to actually understand what the hell was going on though.

I reached down and grabbed her by the arms, lifting her to sit beside me. She gave me a worried look and I tried to smile, even though I had no idea what to say. I saw his eyes and there was only one person in my life that had those eyes. They couldn't be looking for me if this had anything to do with Conner.

"Mr. Mitchell, we are very sorry to barge in like this, but last week there was a fatal accident on route ten. The driver and passenger of the vehicle died on impact, but the child survived. Since I can see the look on your face, excuse me for asking, but you do know Krista Nichols, don't you?"

Oh God, it's true.

I grabbed Savanna's shaking hand and squeezed it tight. "Yeah, she was my ex. We ended things almost four years ago." *I was trying to do the calculations in my head.*

"I'm sorry to tell you this but Ms. Nichols and her fiancée were killed in the crash. We notified the next of kin, but the only person we had listed was her father. He just underwent a triple bypass and wasn't able to care for the child."

Just because I needed more confirmation than a pair of eyes, I had to ask. "What does all of this have to do with me?"

The gentleman seemed uneasy with my question. "Were you not aware that Ms. Nichols was ever pregnant?"

I ran my free hand through my hair. "I wasn't. I never spoke to her after she moved out."

"I'm very sorry we just showed up like this. I'm sure you can understand that this isn't something we could discuss over the phone. Ms. Nichols listed you on the birth certificate as the father."

Savanna's hand went limp and I didn't know what to say or do to make her feel better. I glanced over at the little boy who was still staring down at his legs. My heartbeat picked up and something forced me up off of that couch. I stood over where the little boy sat and when he refused to look up, I crouched down and patted him on the head. He looked right at me, with the same eyes as mine. I was so choked up that I couldn't say anything. He kept staring at me and finally his little voice filled the room. "My mommy says that I look like you."

I sat down in front of the little boy and just took him in. His perfect little fingers were still folded together across his lap. I couldn't speak. There was no way this could be happening to me, no way I had a child and didn't know about it.

Say something to the kid, you idiot.....

Savanna's voice broke my train of thought. "What do we have to do next? Are there papers we need to sign? A paternity test?"

"Yes, all of the above Ma'am. We do require a paternity test if the father has no knowledge of the child, for legality purposes of course. The paperwork is standard. We have a list of his medical history as well as a psychological report from the hospital that treated him. It would be best if we took care of this as soon as possible. We would also need to know that you have room in your home for him, which obviously you do," the gentleman explained.

I stood up and held my hand out for the little boy. "It's very nice to meet you, Noah."

He shook my hand and looked at my wedding ring. "Are you married to that pretty lady?" He pointed to Savanna. "My mommy was getting married before she had her accident." His eyes got sad and he looked down at his lap again.

"Noah, would you like that pretty lady, whose name is Savanna, to give you a tour of the house?"

He smiled and looked at her as she approached. "Okay."

Oh God! I needed to talk to my wife. How could I expect her to be okay with something like this?

She reached out her hand and he promptly took it, trusting her already. When I saw them getting to the top of the stairs, I turned to face the two agents. "After seein' him with my own eyes, I would be a fool to deny that he is my child. I will take any test you need and sign all of the documents. I don't know why she kept somethin' like this from me. She knew I always wanted kids."

The woman caught me off guard when she spoke. "When we visited with her father, he told us she didn't think you wanted children with her. When she finally had decided to tell you, you were already engaged to be married to someone else. She thought telling you would ruin your happiness. By that time, she had met someone herself and they were raising him together."

"But my name is on the birth certificate?"

"Yes Sir, it was the first documentation we pulled."

"How old is he?"

"His birthday is January 4, he is three and a half years old."

I started calculating everything in my head. "She was six months pregnant when she moved out? How could I have not known something like that?"

"Mr. Mitchell we have had cases where mothers delivered healthy babies full term and never knew they were with child."

"Still, I should have been told. I missed out on so much of his life."

The woman opened her brief case and pulled out a bunch of forms. "I need you to sign these and we can do an oral swab on both of you today, if that is still okay?"

"Of course. How long until we know the results?" I asked.

"A couple days. In the meantime, we can petition the court for temporary custody. In an emergency situation like this, the judge will usually speed things up. We could know something as early as tonight if we turn this in before noon today."

"You can use my office. The computer and fax machine are in there."

"That is a big help. Thank you, Sir."

Savanna and Noah started walking down the steps. He never let go of her hand. Her face had no expression, but I couldn't blame her. I had no idea what I was going to say to her.

Noah and Savanna stood in front of me. "Do you like the house?"

He shook his head. "It's so big."

"It is big, but only because we wanted to fill it with cute kids."

He looked down at his feet. I grabbed his chin and lifted it up. "Would you like to live here and fill one of those rooms with lots of cool stuff?"

He said nothing, but as if it were slow motion, he let go of Savanna's hand and plopped his body against mine, hugging me tight. I wrapped my arms around his little body and took in his scent.

I had a son.

This was my child.

I was a father.

The two agents looked from each other and then back to Noah and I. "We are going to go outside and make some calls. Is it okay if the child stays here?" The woman asked.

"Of course."

When the agents went outside, I grabbed Noah and took him into the kitchen. Savanna always had some sort of ice-cream in the freezer. We sat him down on a high stool and leaned across from him watching him eat his ice cream sandwich. "Is it good?"

"Yes. I love ice cream. Mommy didn't let me have it. She said it would make my teeth icky." He looked sad again.

I reached over and touched his shoulder. "You miss your mommy don't you? It's okay if you do. My daddy died in an accident and I miss him every day."

The child's wet eyes looked right at me. "Did you cry a lot?"

I let out a cackle of air. "Yeah, I did. Savanna will tell you how bad it was for me. I didn't want to ever talk about it because it made me so sad."

"Yeah. Is she in heaven now?"

"Of course she is. She is probably looking down at you right now, being your guardian angel." I noticed that Savanna was saying nothing, but I couldn't step away from the boy to speak to her alone. She couldn't expect me to turn my back on a child I never knew I had. I was his father, for Christ sakes.

"So, what is your favorite thing to do? What do you like?"

"I like trains and dinosaurs and airplanes and army men. Sometimes I play legos, but Mommy stepped on one and she said it hurt like Hell, so I don't play them anymore."

We both laughed when he said Hell, but he had no inclination it wasn't a proper word to use. I reached my arm over and pulled Savanna tight against my body. As Noah concentrated on his ice cream, I turned to face Savanna and leaned my forehead on hers. "Are you okay with this?"

She looked at the little boy and then back to me. "I knew he was yours from the moment I saw those eyes. How could I not want something that is a part of you? You really didn't know about him did you?"

I pressed my lips against hers and held them there, until we heard Noah. "Ewww, you get cooties from that, ya know."

We both started laughing. "No way, cooties? Well, I am never kissing again then," I joked.

Noah started laughing.

I leaned over the counter again. "Noah, you are goin' to be livin' here with Savanna and I from now on. We can decorate your room in anything you want. In fact, Savanna loves to redecorate." I threw her a wink. "Does that sound okay with you?"

"You mean, I get one of those giant rooms?"

"Sure do!"

He looked sad. "I don't like the dark very much."

"We'll get you a big fat night light." Savanna interrupted.

"Do I have to call you Daddy?"

It caught me off guard. I had no idea what to say. After taking a deep breath and thinking about what would be the best thing to say, I sat down beside him. "Buddy, you can call me Colt for now, if that makes you feel better. I know we just met and this is all kind of new for both of us."

"But, you are my dad, aren't you? That lady said I was going to live with my dad."

I laughed. "Yeah kid, I'm your dad. I didn't know it until today, but there is no denying it. You look just like me kiddo. Wait until you meet my mother, she will go crazy over you."

"Is she an old lady?" He asked.

I started laughing. "She isn't that old. Would you like to meet her right now? She lives on the ranch too. In fact this whole ranch belongs to our family."

"Even the big fat cows?"

Savanna was rolling. "Every single one."

"What else is here?"

"Chickens. Lots of chickens. We grow our own vegetables. We have a few horses. There is a big pool at the main house where my mother lives." The little boy seemed so interested.

"Can we go see it all?"

I looked over to Savanna and she nodded. She leaned over to talk to Noah. "I think that you and Colt should take a ride on the golf cart and explore everything right now. Would you like that Noah?"

"YEAH!" He hopped down off his stool and grabbed my hand. It was the coolest feeling. "Come on, let's go."

I turned around to face Savanna and couldn't tell what she was thinking. As excited as I was that I had this beautiful little boy, I knew it wasn't going to be all peaches and cream with Savanna. We had lost our child tragically and I would never want to replace that void with another child, but Noah was mine. Savanna still wanted her own children with me. We needed to be able to talk about this before I got in way over my head and lost her. She had been so fragile and was still in therapy. I was very afraid that this was going to break her. "Do you want to come with us?"

She shook her head and I could see the tears forming in her eyes. "No, you go ahead. You have so much time to make up for. Besides, the agents are still working on his case. I will just sit here in case they need anything."

"I love you Savanna Mitchell. I hope you know that." I couldn't tell her I was sorry for all of this happening the way it was in front of the boy. He had lost the only family he ever knew. He needed to feel welcomed and loved. "And no, I had no idea I had a son. Darlin' I swear to you that I had no idea."

Noah grabbed on to me as we exited the house. He held my hand even after we climbed onto the golf cart. "So where do you want to go first?"

He looked up at me. "I've never had a grandmother before. My friends at pre-school have grandmothers and they buy them cool things. Will my grandmother buy me things too?"

He was so innocent when he asked that I knew he wasn't being selfish. He was too little to even understand that. "Trust me when I say, that you will probably get more gifts than you will ever even ask for. My mother is goin' to spoil you."

"Will she love me? My friend's grandmothers love them."

I stopped the golf cart and looked at him. "Noah, of course she will."

"Will you love me?"

My heart broke for him. I squeezed his hand and kissed the top of his head. Tears started forming in my eyes as I stared at my mirror image. "Buddy, I think that I loved you as soon as I saw you. I knew you were mine from that moment."

I have no idea what she was doing all the way out here, but Sam came running out of the woods. "Cool, a dog."

"That's Sam, she's our dog." Sam came up and jumped right on our laps, crushing poor little Noah. "Calm down girl. This is Noah."

Noah started petting her while she licked all over his face. Small giggles were coming from his little body and I couldn't help but love how perfect his laughter sounded to me. "I get to have a real dog?"

"Yes." I laughed.

Sam finally jumped down and raced us to the ranch house. Noah thought it was funny how she was trying to keep up with us.

I parked in front of the house and we both started walking toward it. Lucy must have seen us pulling up because she opened the door as we approached. She put her hand over her mouth and gasped, saying something in Spanish. I grabbed her on the shoulder. "Where is my Mom?"

She pointed toward the kitchen, but just stood there staring. My mother was taking a sip of her coffee as we walked into the room. She took one look at Noah and started choking. While she grabbed a napkin and cleaned herself off, she never took her eyes off of Noah. I was still holding his hand as we walked closer.

"Tell me I'm dreaming, Son?"

I crouched down to Noah's level. "Mom, I would like you to meet my son Noah. We just met today, but he will be staying with us from now on." There was no sugar coating things.

She kneeled down in front of Noah and started to cry as she ran her hands through his dark hair. "How is this possible? Did you know? Where is the mother? Where is Savanna? Is she okay?"

"Calm down." That was a bunch of questions. "I had no idea until about an hour ago. You know better than to even ask that. Krista *was* his mother and there was a terrible accident. She and her boyfriend were killed in a car accident. She listed me on the birth certificate, but never told me about her being pregnant. This is all a shock to me too, Mom." I patted Noah on the head. "Savanna is home with the agents assigned to his case. They are doing the necessary paperwork so that Noah can live with us from now on."

She cupped his cheeks and looked into his eyes. "There is no denying this child Colton. My Lord, he looks exactly like you." She reached over and kissed the top of his head, while still trying to contain her tears. "Would you like some cookies?"

"I'm not supposed to have cookies before lunch."

Lucy was standing behind me, still in shock. My mother looked toward her. "Well then, I guess we need to feed you lunch first."

I patted him on the back and whispered in his ear. "You ate an ice cream before lunch."

He giggled and put his head down. "I won't tell."

"Me either Buddy."

Lucy made Noah a peanut butter and jelly with no crusts. He ate every bite while I explained everything that happened to my mother and Lucy. They were still in shock, but to be honest, so was I. This morning I left the house thinking it was going to be a normal day. I had no idea that somewhere out there I had a child.

Just as I had suspected, my mother accepted Noah immediately. She ran up to her room and got old pictures from when I was his age.

Lucy started feeding him cookies while my mother pulled me to the side. "Son, how is Savanna with all of this?"

I shook my head. "I don't know. I haven't had a second alone with her. She says she is okay with him living with us but, not to be ignorant toward her, I just could never turn my back on my own child."

"Of course not. I didn't raise you to be that kind of man. I just think you need to really sit down and find out how she is handling this. The longer you wait, the harder it will be to get through. A child is a huge responsibility and with everything my daughter in law had been through this past year, I would say this could be a big breaking point. Don't get me wrong Colt, I couldn't be happier for you, but Savanna might not be as okay as she is saying."

My mother was right and it wasn't Savanna's fault. I couldn't expect her to come out of this without some hard feelings. "I will talk to her tonight."

Of course my mother dropped whatever she was doing and rode back to my house with us. She held Noah on her lap and talked all about the farm. He seemed interested and she was more than happy to keep him occupied. When we got to the house, we found Savanna on the porch swing. Shockingly, Noah jumped off my mother's lap and went running for Savanna. She lifted him up onto the swing with her. That little kid wrapped his arms around her and stayed like that. Savanna hesitated then finally let her arm fall down over his body. She shrugged as we climbed up on the porch. I didn't know what to say. Noah obviously really trusted her. He would need that to be able to adjust to the changes in his life.

I leaned down to kiss my wife and thankfully she kissed me back. "Hey Darlin', Mom can't get enough of the kid."

"I knew that would happen. He is super cute." Savanna looked down at Noah who was smiling at her.

"You're pretty." He giggled.

"Well, you are a cutie."

"Are you going to be my Mommy now?"

Everything stopped.

My mother and I said nothing as we stared into Savanna's shocked eyes.

Chapter 16

Savanna

I had no idea what to say to the child with his arms wrapped around me. He was the cutest little boy I had ever seen and I wanted to be completely in love with him. For the past two hours I had cried, laughed, called my mother, cried some more and then finally just sat in silence.

Was I even right to be feeling hurt?

Did I have the right to cry?

If Colt knew I was the reason our baby had died, would he have really wanted me to be a mother to Noah? I felt the vomit rising in my mouth as I tried to tuck that secret in the back of my mind. I was so tired of reliving it every single day. I needed to move on, but doing that would require me to live with the lie, with the knowledge of what I lost.

Noah continued to wait for me to answer and as the tears fell down my chilled cheeks, I brought my lips down and kissed the top of his head. This was Colt's child and I could never abandon him. "Is that what you want? I mean, you don't have to call me Mommy. Savanna or Van is fine with me."

"Van is a funny name."

"It's my nickname."

"Can we watch T.V. now?" Obviously, he was finished with our conversation.

"How about I take you inside and watch with you. I think your dad and Savanna have some things they need to talk about." My mother in law took Noah's hand and they disappeared into the house.

Colt sat down next to me, grabbing my hand and kissing it, before setting it down in his lap. "Are you okay Darlin'?"

I shrugged. "I want to be. It's all just so fast. It's just so overwhelming."

He reached his arm around me and pulled me close to him. "Savanna, I love you with all of my heart, but you know I can't turn my back on that kid. I wish we would have found out differently, but I can't regret finding out about him."

I reached up and touched my husband's stubbly face. "I love you too baby. I know what this means to you and I will do everything I can to help you raise him."

He looked down at my hand and creased his face up. Without looking back at me he started to talk. "If we are goin' to do this and add more children to this family, he is goin' to need you to be his mother. Now, I know this is all so fast, but you are ready to be a mother. We talked about adoptin' if you couldn't get pregnant again. There is no difference. He already has my last name Savanna. I'm not askin' you to replace his mother, but she is gone and you are here. Losin' a parent as an adult is hard enough, but I can't imagine what that kid is feelin'. He needs solidity. He needs us both."

A knot was forming in my throat and I wanted to agree with Colt, I swear I did. Instead, I buried my head into his chest and began crying my eyes out. Of course, Colt pulled me into his chest tighter and held me there, placing kisses on top of my head. "I'm so sorry you have to make this decision Darlin'."

"I just don't know if I can do this Colt."

He pulled me away from him and looked into my wet eyes. "Don't you dare think about givin' up on me Savanna. I couldn't bear to lose you."

I shook my head. "I will never leave you Colt. I swear it."

"Can we do this together? Please can we welcome this little boy into our family and keep with our plan of fillin' this house with more children?"

He wiped my tears away with his thumbs. "Of course Colt. I will do whatever I have to do for our family."

He held me tight again and I could feel his body trembling. Colt was crying, which was something I had only seen a couple of times. He sniffled into my shoulder. "I can't believe this is happenin'. Thank you Darlin', thank you so much."

Once Colt and I finally calmed down from our dual emotional breakdown, we remained on the porch swing in each other's arms. We could hear Noah inside talking to his new grandmother about everything under the sun. Colt and I were also taking it all in, considering we knew nothing about the child.

When we finally went inside, my mother in law insisted that we were going to have a huge welcome dinner for Noah. The kid was ecstatic.

Soon Aunt Karen, Lucy and Conner showed up and we had a house full of people. Sheriff John showed up later and the older women went into the kitchen to start dinner. Noah was having a great time with all of the attention he was getting.

The most interesting part of the whole day was the way that Noah wanted to be around me. Colt hadn't left his side, but he continued to favor my attention over everyone else's.

At one point he tugged on my leg and I crouched down in front of him. "Can I have trains in my room?"

"You sure can. Would you like to go shopping with me tomorrow?" I asked.

"I want to go too." Colt's mother interrupted.

We were interrupted by a sudden knock at the door. Colt walked over and opened the door, revealing the two agents assigned to Noah's case. "Sorry to barge in again. We have the temporary papers all signed and approved. When the documents are filed and the tests come back, we can get everything finalized and then you won't hear from us anymore."

"So, Noah can stay? Like..he can stay with us from now on?" Colt was beside himself.

"Our job is to find a home that is in the child's best interest. You and Mrs. Mitchell can provide this child with a home and a stable environment. The courts will always side with the biological family first before they even consider putting the child into foster care. It will still be a few days before the papers are filed with the court system, but Noah is all yours." He handed Colt a file. "This is all of Noah's medical history, as well as a copy of his birth certificate and social security card. As you can see, he was given your name at birth."

"How come I never found out about him? Why didn't the state require child support?"

"The mother has to file for that. From what we gathered from the deceased woman's father, she was involved and living a few towns over with her fiancée. There is no way you could have known unless the mother or someone told you."

Colt reached out and shook the agents hand as they exited the house. He followed behind them and came back with a few suitcases full of Noah's things. I watched the agents pull away from the house and turned back to Colt and Noah. They were opening up the bags to look through them. Colt got this look on his face and started fanning the bags. "These bags stink. I guess your Mommy started smokin' again huh?"

Noah looked up at Colt. "Do you smoke?"

"Nope."

I walked over and grabbed the bag, noticing the smell myself. "How about we wash everything so that when we get your furniture tomorrow we can fill your drawers with clean clothes?"

"That sounds good." Colt agreed.

"I get all new things...and a new room too?" The little guy seemed shocked.

Colt patted him on the head. "Buddy, you can have whatever you want."

Probably not the best thing to tell a little boy, but he was very overwhelmed.

The family stayed and had a huge spaghetti dinner for Noah. The child seemed to really fit right in. Colt made it a point to hug and kiss me even more than normal. I appreciated it so much that he was making an effort to be by my side during the transition. He had come so far from the man who used to shut everyone out. I never wanted to lose that.

As our family began to clear out, the three of us were left in the house all alone. I still couldn't believe that we had just acquired a child in just one day. I had a feeling that maybe Sheriff John had made some calls on our behalf. I could hardly believe it was protocol to leave the child with strangers after one day. John knew the judge in town, and since he had been sheriff for so long, it made sense that people probably owed him a bunch of favors by now. It didn't hurt that Colt's family was the richest in the county and donated a bunch of money every year to different events and organizations.

It didn't even matter how it all came to be. Noah was here with us and he didn't have to leave. Colt was so happy and it made me happy too.

We tucked Noah into the guest room for the night, but after about an hour, I heard the door creaking open to our bedroom. A little boy in dinosaur pajamas came walking over to my side of the bed. "I'm scared."

It was the cutest thing I had ever seen. I suddenly realized how Ty could fall in love with Bella so helplessly. I reached my arms out and pulled the little boy into bed with Colt and I. Once I got him between us, I tucked us both in and accepted him into my arms when he cuddled his little body against me.

I laid there for a while, just stroking little pieces of his hair. I had wanted a child of my own for so long. Being a mother was so important to me and here was this child, who obviously needed and trusted me. Maybe it was God's plan all along for him to come into our lives. I kissed the little boy's head and let myself fall asleep, feeling like that empty hole in my heart could actually have a chance to heal.

I woke to Colt talking to Noah. The sun was up and they were both leaning on their elbows in bed. Noah was telling Colt about a mean kid in his preschool. Colt was making faces and reacting exactly the way that Noah wanted him too.

I giggled and caught their attention. "Good morning sleepy head," Colt said as he tossed an extra pillow my way.

"Not everyone likes to wake up at the crack of dawn," I mumbled.

"We have a big day today. Conner and I are going to paint Noah's room while you and Mom are out buying his furniture."

"Sounds like you have it all planned out."

"My dad says that we can paint it blue and green. Do you like blue and green? Green is my favorite. What is your favorite color?" The little boys sudden burst of conversation was unexpected. Colt began to laugh at me, as I tried to take in everything that had just come out of his mouth.

"Green is a nice color Noah. My favorite is blue."

"Blue is cool too. Do you think I could put spaceships on my ceiling?" He asked.

I sat up and walked toward the bathroom. Noah followed behind me, not realizing I needed a private moment. It was a good thing the toilet had its own private door. "Be right back," I said as I closed the door to relieve myself.

When I came back out he was standing there with his hands behind his back waiting in the same spot I had left him. I gave him a quick smile and grabbed my toothbrush. "Can I brush my teeth too?"

Colt came in behind me and kissed me on the shoulder before reaching in the cabinet to grab one of the extra toothbrushes I had bought during one of my extreme couponing splurges. "Here Buddy. It might be too big for your tiny teeth though."

He reached as far as he could, but couldn't wet his toothbrush under the water. Colt lifted him up and let him sit on the sink. We all three brushed our teeth in unison. It was a simple mundane action, but it was so sweet. This was the family interaction that I wanted all along.

When Colt would spit, Noah would spit. He copied his father's every move in fact. I came out of the bathroom to see them straightening the bed. He tossed the little boy on it and started tickling him. Noah laughed so hard as the two of them bonded. I leaned on the door frame, just watching how happy they were.

Our day of shopping burned little Noah out. At first he was so excited, but as we needed to fill out paperwork and drive to different places, he got tired. By the time we were on our way home he had fallen asleep.

Colt met us outside and offered to carry the sleeping little guy up to our bed. His mother, Conner and I started getting everything out of the car. By the time we made it up to his room, Colt was already back in Noah's room. "What do you think? Think we did good?" He asked.

I looked around the room. I don't know when they had the time, but they had painted the room green and blue. Hung from the ceiling were different planes and spaceships. "It looks amazing. He is going to love this."

"Conner found him some glow in the dark stars too," he added.

They both seemed so proud of their hard work. Colt's mother had paid the furniture company to deliver it to our house. We could hear the trucks coming down the gravel driveway, so I ran downstairs to meet them.

Within thirty minutes we had his whole bedroom suite set up. The big surprise was that we had found a real bed in the shape of a train. Since it was a special order, Colt's mother bought the floor model. This was her first grandchild, so you can imagine how much spoiling was going to occur. It worked out better because I had no idea how the thing was originally put together. It came apart in five pieces, but it was giant. His mother smiled from cheek to cheek as the guys got it all set up.

She had managed to buy him the furniture and also a whole slew of new clothes. I bought him all of his bedding, curtains and some cool toys for his room. It was no wonder he was conked out in the other room. I was about to fall asleep myself.

Noah slept for two hours, allowing us ample time to get his room set up. Conner and my mother in law finally went home, leaving Colt and I alone. I considered going into the room and sleeping right next to him, but my excitement for him seeing that room was too much to handle.

I sat on his train bed, setting up his toys on the built in book shelves. Colt hung his curtains and was arranging them as

Noah walked into room. He put his hands over his mouth and looked around.

Colt put his hands on his hips. "Hey Buddy. What do you think? Did we do good?"

He ran toward Colt and wrapped his arms around his legs. "WOW!" He shouted.

We ended up ordering pizza after spending the next hour playing with all of the cool new things in his room. For someone that had just came into our lives, it felt like he had always been there with us.

The next few months went by fast. We got Noah enrolled in a preschool program close to home. He was excited to wear a cute little uniform everyday like the bigger kids did. Of course, he wore a uniform because it was an elite private school, not that Noah cared anything about that. He made new friends and no longer got picked on by other children.

He and Colt spent a bunch of time together, in fact, he often went to work with his father. Colt had taught him all about the chickens and even some things about the cattle. He thoroughly enjoyed the tractors and riding them with Colt. Sam no longer slept on our bedroom floor. She found a new spot in bed with Noah. Noah couldn't have been more happy about it, considering he didn't like being alone very much.

I wasn't going to therapy as much and I actually felt good every day I woke up. We planned a huge trip to Disney World with Miranda and Ty in the fall and Noah was so excited to be able to see Mickey Mouse.

He and Bella finally got to meet and they were the cutest little pair of cousins. While they visited we had a professional photographer come and take pictures of them together as well as family photos of both of our families. I bought every single pose and hung them all over the house.

Colt had finally got in touch with Krista's father and visited him at the nursing home. He gave Colt lot's of old photos of Noah that Krista had given him. We wanted Noah to always be able to remember his birth mother. She had brought him into the world and spent her last breath loving him. We hung her pictures in his room along with new ones.

Social services came out for one visit and never contacted us again. We had sole custody and nobody could ever take Noah away from Colt.

Noah saw a therapist for the first two months he lived with us. We did it as a precautionary measure, but were relieved when the doctor said he was coping with the loss of his mother and change in his life very well. Colt and I spent every single free moment making him feel like he belonged with us.

For the longest time Noah called me Van. He liked that I had such a funny name. One day we were at the park. Colt and I were sitting together on a bench watching him play with the other kids. This cute little girl came walking over to us to tell us she had a new baby brother. As we gave her our attention, a very jealous Noah came over and climbed onto my lap. He interrupted her and put his face in front of mine, taking away my view of the little girl. "I love you, Mommy."

His words took my breath away. I forgot all about that little girl as I hugged that jealous little boy. "I love you too, Noah. So much."

"Why are you crying?" He asked.

"You called me Mommy."

"Are you sad now?"

"No Buddy. I am so happy. You make me so happy." I squeezed that little kid so tight as Colt rubbed my shoulder.

I was wrong about not being able to be his mother. My life revolved around that child and it was wonderful. I would never forget the baby that I lost, but Noah made me treasure every single day of being his parent.

Chapter 17

Colt

With the addition of Noah to our family, Savanna and I didn't exactly have a lot of alone time. She became so focused on being a mother that our time together just seemed to be put on the back burner. I wasn't complaining, she was an awesome mother. Noah was crazy about her.

Aside from his three days a week in preschool, they spent all of their time together. Savanna was an only child and I could relate somewhat, but I also got to grow up with my younger cousins, where Savanna didn't have that.

I think sometimes she enjoyed playing with toys and being his pal. I had come home several times to them playing army men, or building giant Lego towers. I think part of the reason he adored her so much was her ability to play like a four year old.

Savanna and I had decided to get him a pony and start teaching him how to ride horses. She wanted to be the one to show him everything about it. I remember the day that horse trailer pulled into the ranch. Noah went flying out of the house, just waiting to see what his horse looked like. He had spent an entire week trying to guess it's color and height.

His pony was white with brown spots and he named him Atticus. It wasn't a common horse name, but his first choice had been Toilet Paper Butt. We spent a half hour explaining that toilet paper combined with butt was not an appropriate name, and whichever one of his friends that told him that should be ashamed of themselves.

Savanna taught him the basics, first showing him what every part of a horse was called. Next she taught him how to saddle up his pony. After the first day he was busting to ride. While I took him out on one of the combines, Savanna saddled the pony up and gave him a test ride. We had bought him off of someone we knew and a little girl had been the previous owner. The pony was used to being ridden.

That following morning we saddled up one pony and two horses and went for a family ride. Savanna held on to a separate set of reigns to prevent Atticus from running off with our four year old son. We kept the horses at a slow pace, never letting them gallop or canter. Noah wanted to let loose, but Savanna did one hell of a job keeping him calm.

After a couple weeks she finally let him start riding without guidance. I bought him some boots and a cowboy hat so he could be the real deal. It was fascinating watching him grow right before my eyes.

Since we never got time alone, I had surprised Savanna with a trip to a cabin in the woods. I'll admit that my intentions were only on one thing, but she never complained when I gave her the news. My mother took Noah gladly for the whole weekend, promising to not buy him a small island while we were gone.

It was so nice to get away with my beautiful wife. I had missed her so much physically. We spent every single day together, but I still missed her. Before Noah came into our lives, things weren't exactly perfect. We had suffered so much and even though his coming into our lives made us stronger, we were still lacking the physical aspect of our marriage.

Our son had some kind of built in radar for intimate moments and many times he had come in the room right before the big moment was about to happen. Colt called him CB behind his back, as opposed to actually saying the word cock block. He was a little kid. He couldn't have known that he was interfering in our special time together.

The cabin was very secluded and unbeknownst to Savanna, had a very large Jacuzzi tub in it. I made sure to pack all of our groceries so we never had to leave once we arrived. I didn't want to share my wife for the entire weekend.

I carried her into the cabin and sat her down so she could take in the glass wall facing the back of the house. A view of a lake was behind the small house.

"It's beautiful here." Savanna turned around and wrapped her arms around me.

I pressed my lips against hers, keeping them there for longer than we were used to. Her tongue stroked my lip, causing me to open my mouth for her. As our tongues started to meet, I felt her hands reaching up my shirt. I kicked the front door shut as she pushed me back up against the wall. Our kissed intensified and as our tongues continued to mingle. I could feel my cock hardening in my jeans.

I swung Savanna around lifting her up, pressing her against the wall. I freed my hands and let them wander up to her soft breasts. Her skin was like silk and I went slow, watching her expression as I did it. I ran my hand in between them and then back down to her stomach. She wrapped her legs around me, forcing her hips to thrust into me. I pressed her harder against the wall as I covered her mouth with mine.

"I need you naked." I said through our kisses.

With both of my hands grabbing her ass, I carried her over to the couch and tossed her down. She backed up enough to start stripping out of her clothes right in front of me. I removed my shirt and started unzipping my pants, letting them fall to the floor. Savanna removed her bra and bit down on her lips as she squeezed both of her nipples, making them hard for me. I grabbed her stretchy pants and ripped them off of her, tossing them behind us somewhere.

With one swift movement, I picked her up carried her to the bedroom. She slipped down my body and climbed into the bed, making sure that her ass was right in my face. I grabbed the back elastic of her little thong and pulled her back toward the edge of the bed. My fingers began running where the tiny fabric fell over her ass. I moved the fabric over to be able to slip my fingers inside of her folds. She groaned feeling my fingers down there in her tender spot.

With her ass in the air and her face down against the blankets, I reached my other hand over her back and then slowly grazed one of her breasts. My two fingers slipped into her wet channel, while she continued to rock back and forth against them. Seeing her so turned on was almost too much for my deprived ass to take. I pulled my fingers out of her needy body and flipped her around. With one jerk, I pulled off her panties and spread her legs wide open. Savanna moaned when I stood there looking at her perfect body. My hands were on her knees as I slid down in between her legs, taking my first taste. Her sweet musk filled my mouth and I couldn't get enough of her. My hands spread her open more and I held onto her thighs while

I began licking on her swollen nub. Savanna's body began to buck against my face, causing me to lick even harder. She screamed out, louder than I had ever heard her do it before. Even after she fell calm against the bed, I still couldn't stop tasting her. Little trembles came every time I moved my tongue around.

My cock was throbbing to be inside of her. It had been way too long. I crawled up over her body, making sure to give each of her hard nipples some much needed attention. I loved how hard they felt against my tongue. I teased them with my teeth, licking every inch of her pink nipples.

Savanna grabbed me by my ears and pulled me up to her mouth. The pain was nothing compared to her eagerness to kiss me. I felt her licking my lips, tasting herself while she kissed me. One of my hands found her ass cheek and squeezed it hard in between my fingers. Her lips came off of mine while she cried out in pleasure.

Her fingers drug down my back causing me pain, but also ecstasy at the same time.

I thrusted my girth all the way inside of my wife. She cried out as I filled her with my size. Her tight little walls were slick with her juices, but still tightened as I thrusted in and out of her.

Savanna took her legs and flipped herself on top of me. Her beautiful hair flowed down over her breasts. I watched her play with her nipples, shaking them with her fingertips. She didn't know what she did to me. I needed her so much.

I grabbed her waist with both hands and grinded her into me. She ran her hand through her hair as she picked up her own pace. Her body was wet with sweat and it glistened in the natural light coming in the window. Savanna grabbed my hand and sucked hard on my wedding ring finger. She closed her eyes and thrusted her body back further, causing my girth to go in even deeper. Her ass was lifted and then coming back down against my sweaty skin. The faster she moved the closer I got. I closed my eyes and called out as I felt myself filling her.

Savanna's hot body collapsed on top of me, showering me with kisses. As her lips pressed over mine, she pulled away to get the words out. "I. Missed. This."

We fell asleep there on the bed, never parting from each other. It didn't matter that it was hot, or we were sweating profusely, I wasn't willing to let her go, not even for a second. I needed to feel her body and her love for me.

We had reconnected and I planned on doing it over and over again until we had to go home.

We both woke later and finally unloaded the car. Savanna chose to only wear my shirt I had on, while I threw on some jeans to walk outside in. Once we got our groceries and coolers put away, we had a snack and decided to sit out on the back deck to watch the sun set.

Savanna walked in the house and came out in only a pair of cowboy boots. I literally spit and my beer went flying out of my mouth and nose. She leaned against the railing showing off every inch of her body to me. "That is the hottest thing I have ever seen in my life, Darlin'."

"Do you want me Colt?"

"Um, is that a trick question?"

"Say you want me. Tell me how you want it," She ordered.

I licked my lips and sat up further. "I want you Darlin'."

She turned around and ran her hands over her perfect ass. "Do you want to bend me over right here? Would that turn you on, Baby?"

Oh fuck....

I stood up and walked over to where she was still bent over, rubbing her ass cheeks. I ran my hand up the small of her back. With one hand I pulled her up to stand with her back against my body. She stuck my fingers in her mouth, biting down on them. "Oh God! Don't stop talkin'."

I pushed her back down to a bent over position, keeping one of my hands pressed firmly against her back. I let my jeans drop to the deck. My hard cock pressed against her ass and I almost sensed she wanted it back there. I slapped my hardness against her soaked entrance and she moaned, knowing what was coming.

"Fuck me Colt. Fuck me so hard."

"Oh Darlin'." I grabbed her hips and slipped right inside of her. She grabbed the railing and held onto it while I pounded my shaft inside of her. I reached my arms up and put them over hers, using the railing for my benefit as well. My body smacked against her ass with each thrust and soon Savanna was crying out, her screams being heard all across the lake. I followed her lead and filled her for the second time. Unlike our first time, Savanna separated us immediately, kissed me full on the mouth and walked back into the cabin, without saying a word.

I stood there naked with a big ole smile across my face. This was the best idea I may have ever had.

Later that night, Savanna and I curled up next to the fireplace. She lay inside of my strong hold, stroking my arms with her fingertips. "This is nice. Thank you for bring us here Colt."

I kissed the top of her head. "We needed it."

"It's so different having a kid. I thought we would have more time for each other."

I laughed. "Yeah, we don't have any alone time."

"Maybe if we didn't hog Noah up for ourselves all the time, we would have more. Your mother always offers."

I kissed her cheek and then pulled her head closer to kiss her lips. "Maybe she could keep him every weekend."

We both laughed.

"Are you happy Colt? Are you upset things changed between us? I mean, not just with Noah. With the baby we lost too."

She turned her body to face me and I cupped my hands around her face, letting my forehead press against hers. "Darlin' I couldn't be more happier than I am right now, aside from havin' another child, there is nothin' else I could ever need. You have no idea how much I appreciate you bein' that boy's mother. Steppin' up like that made me love you even more Savanna."

It was the truth too. She didn't even realize how amazing she was.

"When he came into our lives so suddenly, I was so unsure of myself. I think I was afraid to love another child, but I fell so in love with him. I couldn't help it. Now, I can't imagine not being his mother. He makes me so happy."

Her words were beautiful and she meant every single word. She had been there when he got his first cold after he had moved in with us. I was all panicking and she instinctively knew exactly what to do. She stayed in his room with him, went out and got him a vaporizer, took him to the doctors, made sure he took his medicine right on schedule. She went into this Mom machine mode and in some ways never came out of it. Noah was always her first priority and I loved that about her.

"You make him happy. That kid lost everything and you welcomed him into our family, makin' it so easy for him to transition. You keep the memory of his mother alive and have never been negative towards the whole situation. Do you have any idea how amazin' you are?"

She shrugged. "It never hurts to hear it over and over again," she teased.

"Well if I need to remind you every single day, I will."

She wrapped both of her legs over top of mine, almost straddling me. Her head went into my chest. "What happens if we can't get pregnant again? What if I can't give you another child?"

"I have to believe that God won't do that to us. Darlin' you have been through so much hardship. You have proven to be an amazin' mother. We will have another baby. It may take a while, but I'm never goin' to go anywhere. If it doesn't happen than we will spoil the hell out of our son and be the best parents to him that we can be. Don't even get yourself worried about that."

"I would never want to replace Noah, but I just want to be able to give you a child too. I want Noah to have a brother or sister one day. I dream about him talking to my belly. It's beautiful Colt."

Her words were so sincere. I wished I could have told her without a doubt that we were going to have more children, but the truth was we just didn't know.

"Let's take our life day by day Savanna. Maybe if we don't think about it so much good things will happen."

We laid there together in front of the fire until I carried Savanna's sleeping body to bed.

Since Savanna always was the one to take care of our family, I woke up early and made her breakfast. After we ate, we spent the morning in the Jacuzzi tub. We had connected on a deeper level than ever before and I felt so close to her.

We finally left the cabin to explore the lake. I rowed a tiny boat out to the middle of the lake and we had lunch out there all alone. Savanna seemed so relaxed and I could tell she was really enjoying our time away. I couldn't help but miss Noah. For months we had spent every single minute with him. It was hard to not look over my shoulder for him every once in a while.

"What are you thinking about?" She asked.

"I kinda miss Noah, I mean don't get me wrong, I'm havin' a great weekend bein' here alone with my wife, but I can't stop thinkin' about him."

She started laughing and shook her head.

"What?" I asked.

"It's just funny, because I feel the same way. I feel lost without him."

"Well, we can see him tomorrow. It isn't like we are away for a whole week." I explained.

"Or, we can go home tonight and surprise him."

I wondered if she was joking until I saw the excitement in her eyes. "You seriously would rather go home than spend one more night alone with me?"

She climbed toward me, causing the boat to rock. "I would love to spend one more night with you, but I also wouldn't mind going home to be with Noah."

She climbed on my lap, giving me kisses slowly all over my face. "If you keep kissin' me, I won't be able to make a rational decision."

As much as we missed Noah, Savanna and I decided to stay one more night at the cabin. We owed it to ourselves to enjoy our weekend away together. Although, when Sunday came we packed up the car and headed home. I guess we expected Noah to be all bent out of shape over us leaving. Instead, he was too preoccupied by a remote control plane my mother had purchased him. He and Conner were too busy flying it to even notice us pull up to see him.

Once he got the plane landed safely, he basically told us that Conner would bring him home when they were done, at a later time.

Savanna and I sadly got back into the car and drove to the house without Noah. It was great that he was spending time with his family, and that they all loved him so much, but I wasn't sure I liked sharing him.

Conner finally brought Noah home after a couple of hours. He was only excited to see us for the first ten minutes and then he was off to watch television like we had never gone anywhere.

"Guess he didn't miss us." I reached around and hugged Savanna from behind.

"Guess not."

We both laughed.

Chapter 18

Savanna

Our weekend away was wonderful and Colt and I seemed to both enjoy ourselves equally. We needed to get away, even though I missed Noah like crazy. That little guy had been exactly what I needed to turn my life around and get out of the depressed stupor I had been living under. Every single day with him made me so happy.

I loved being a mother. I always knew I would, but actually being one was just unexplainable. It didn't hurt that Noah was the cutest kid ever. He looked so much like his daddy and I got such a kick out of watching them interact.

Colt didn't dredge up the past very often. I know it hurt him to not know about Noah and experience everything in the first years that he missed out on, but he pushed past it. With Krista losing her life, we were Noah's only parents and with that meant that we would experience his life in its entirety, where she only got the first three years. Some days it really made me sad that she couldn't be in his life to see what a perfect son she had.

I didn't know much about Krista, except for the fact that she came from nothing and she had a brother that was in some band now. Her father was a deadbeat and now lived in a nursing home. Apparently, her fiancée got them out of the trailer they were living in and offered them a much better future. Even though she never told Colt about Noah, the little boy knew about his father. Noah told Colt, more than once, that his mother always said one day he would meet him.

When Colt went to talk to her father at that nursing home, he explained that the longer Krista waited, the harder it got for her to do it. He explained that Krista's fiancée had always wanted to adopt Noah, but since Colt was on the birth certificate, she wouldn't be able to do it without his signature. I guess she knew that when Colt found out he had a child, there would be no way in Hell he would sign him over.

I was always taught in church that everything happens for a reason. The past few years had proven that theory time and time again. Noah was my angel and I fell instantly in love with him. Being his mother was the easiest decision that I ever made. We couldn't wait to make our family even bigger.

Colt and I had left me getting pregnant up to God. I never went back on the pill and just had hopes that one day we could add more babies to our perfect little family. Noah had started to ask if he could have a brother or sister as well.

It all started because we had put him into T-ball and he was very interested in the siblings of his teammates. One night after a game, we went out for dinner and he flat out asked us what we were waiting for. I started laughing, but Colt was the one to have to explain that babies didn't exactly get dropped off by a flying bird.

Noah would still ask at least twice a week when his brother would be getting here. Yes, he only wanted a brother.

The day we found out was unexpected. Our hot weekend of lovemaking must have sealed the deal.

Six months after Noah walked into our life, we found ourselves standing over the little white stick again. Noah included.

While Colt and I looked away, our Son, stared at it. "It's changing! Mom, I think you have a baby in your belly button."

My belly button?

We peeked over to see two blue lines appear on the strip. "Oh my God! I'm pregnant."

"So how long till it pops out?" Noah asked.

Colt and I couldn't even celebrate before bursting into laughter. "Nine months Buddy. The baby has to grow first."

"What? That is like five years from now. I will be all grown up," he said in a serious tone.

"Sweetie, you are only four and nine months is less than a year. Your brother or sister will be here in less than a year."

"Just a brother Mommy. It has to be a brother." Noah put his hand on his hips and spoke.

"We will love it no matter what. We have to help take care of Mommy though. Can you help do that Noah?" Colt asked.

"Heck yeah. I will make her peanut butter bread." Noah announced.

Sounds delicious.

Noah stepped down from the step stool we bought him. He followed us into the bedroom. "Will Mommy get fat now?"

Ugh....Kids...

We are having a baby and he wants to know how fat I will get.

After laughing, I sat on the bed and tried to calm down my excitement. "I will get a big belly so the baby has room to grow."

"Even if you get fat, I will love you."

"Well, thank you Noah."

"Can we name the baby Scooter?"

"Probably not." I laughed.

"How about Sasquatch? That would be so cool to tell my friends I had a brother named Sasquatch."

"Noah, I think Mommy and I will name the baby a better name that suits our family." Colt explained.

"Will it be bald? Bald people are scary."

I fell back on the bed laughing. I couldn't hold it in.

Colt tried to stay serious. I watched him clenching his jaw, trying to contain himself. "Bald people are not scary. Every person is different."

The questions continued for the next few weeks.

We were probably wrong in some ways to include Noah in the early part of our pregnancy, but we never wanted him to feel left out. I got past my first trimester and was feeling good about carrying the baby to full term. Noah was a good little helper and when he gave me a hard time, Colt was always close enough to give me some space.

It was always important for Noah to know about his birth mother, Krista. I never knew her and therefore had nothing against her. What happened to her was so tragic and I hoped that she didn't suffer. Noah never talked about the accident. The therapist he used to see said that he spoke about it once and didn't remember much. He thought his mother was just sleeping. How much can a three year old understand?

At any rate, it was also very important to me and Colt that he be included in everything baby related. We decided, well Colt decided, he wanted the sex of the baby to be a surprise. Noah was not too thrilled. We took him to our sonograms and he kept trying to sweet talk the nurse into whispering it in his ear.

Of course, Colt's mother insisted on buying him every kind of 'big brother' item she could find. He had about five shirts, including one in camouflage, two hats and even a sign for his room. We let him be involved in the decorating of the baby's room too. He insisted that we move his playroom to the far end of the hall and give his new brother or sister the room closest to him, because he wanted to help with nighttime feedings. We knew it wasn't going to happen, but he didn't have to know all that. So with Noah's help, we picked out an Americana theme. With the help of Aunt Karen and my mother in law, we were able to decorate every inch of wall space with some kind of red white and blue item. We found a great crib bedding set and ordered all of the furniture.

Maybe we were jumping the gun, decorating things so early, but we were just so excited. The doctors were saying that my pregnancy was normal and healthy, and that we had nothing to worry about.

The next couple of months flew by and I was almost to my third trimester. With the exception of Noah's riding lessons, in which I was not participating in the riding part, I didn't do much at all. Lucy had little to do at the main house, so my mother in law had arranged that she take care of me and our house more.

We would end up chatting the day away, especially when Noah went out to work with the guys. Ever since our trip to Ty's farm, he had been obsessed with chickens. We had both kinds of chickens at our ranch. We grew baby chickens for large poultry companies and also raised chickens for eggs. Colt gave Noah the sole responsibility of taking care of the chicken coop. His daily duties were to collect the eggs, hose out the crap and make sure they were all accounted for. You never knew when a fox was going to a have late night feast.

Colt got his little 'mini me' son a matching John Deere ball cap for when they worked together. It was the cutest thing. Even his uncle Conner got in on the hat party. Of course, I took a million pictures and added to our family wall in the house.

Ty and Miranda had decided to bring their other horse Thunder to live at our ranch, so Noah was thrilled to be able to play with his cousin Bella and to have another horse to ride. We invited them to stay at our place, but we knew they would be more comfortable at the main house. Miranda and Bella still had their rooms there and it gave them a little more privacy. Even after being married for over a year, the two of them hadn't exactly settled down. They fawned over each other every chance they got.

We tried to visit with them every couple of months. It was important for us to keep the kids close.

Bella and Noah were instant friends from the first moment they met. I will never forget the first time they saw each other. Since Noah is eight months older than Bella, he made the first gesture. We had greeted them on the porch. Of course Noah stood behind his father, nervous about meeting someone for the first time. Ty was carrying Bella in his arms and slowly sat her down in front of us. When she reached up to hug Colt, it took Noah about two seconds to walk around his father and see who was getting all of his attention. Colt knew what was going on, so he sat Bella down and the two of them just stared at each other. Noah still had a hold of a huge bit of Colt's jeans.

He put his hand on his son's head. "Noah, this is your cousin Bella."

"What's a cousin?" He asked.

Ty bent down and touched Noah's chin. "It means that she is your family."

"How long is she goin' to stay here?"

"Only for the weekend, Kiddo," Ty explained. He stood up laughing and shaking his head. "Like father like son. He looks so much like you, it's unreal, dude."

Before Colt could respond, we heard chatter from the kids. "Want to see my room?"

"Okay." Bella took Noah's hand and they disappeared in the house.

Of course, Ty had some obnoxious comments when they were out of sight. "Dude, have you taught him about the birds and the bees yet? I don't know if I'm okay with my daughter going into a little boy's room yet."

Miranda nudged him in the side. "Ty, shut up! It's cute."

For the whole weekend the two of them played like they had known each other their whole lives. In fact, we had to keep checking on them because they never came down for food or drinks. They were inseparable.

After that first initial visit, us adults promised that we would also try to get together as much as we could. Ty and Miranda were the second most excited people to find out that Colt and I were expecting. Since they were hoping to get pregnant themselves, it made us having babies at the same time more exciting.

Family was the most important thing in my life and I had the best one out there. I was so happy and had everything that I had ever wanted. I couldn't wait to meet our newest addition.

Chapter 19

Colt

If someone would have told me that through tragedy something good would come, I wouldn't have believed them last year, but seeing my son and my wife proved that theory to be true. Savanna and Noah were my whole world and the fact that he loved her so much, made my life feel complete.

When we found out we were going to have another baby all I could feel was relief. Savanna loved Noah like he was her own, but I knew that having a baby meant the world to her. To add to the excitement, Noah was just as excited. In fact, he couldn't wait to meet his brother or sister, although he was really hoping for that brother.

I knew I was torturing both he and Savanna, but I wanted to be surprised. This was our first birth and it needed to be as exciting as possible.

With Ty and Miranda arriving any moment, Noah was running around the yard like a maniac. He had already planned out he and Bella's whole weekend, starting with showing her how he could drive his own golf cart. Bella had just turned four and Noah was getting closer to five. He always took control of their plans. Bella never seemed to care. The two of them could spend hours playing with rocks as long as they had each other.

Being that Bella needed to spend time with her grandmother while they visited, Aunt Karen had planned to take both kids to her house for the first night. Noah didn't spend the night at places, other than my mother's house, unless Bella was in town. He went wherever she went. So, while Aunt Karen had a fun night planned for the kids, Savanna and I had planned a night of cards.

Savanna couldn't drink, due to her pregnancy, but she didn't seem to care in the least. She had been the one to drive to the liquor store and stock up the fridge with what everyone liked. She had also spent the past two days cleaning everything in the house. I have no idea what made her do it. Lucy kept the house perfect and it wasn't like she had to impress Ty or Miranda.

At any rate, my wife was pregnant and I tried to not argue with any of her decisions, even when they were ridiculous. Speaking of ridiculous, she was now on this kick about having our baby in a bathtub. She forced me to sit up with her one night and watch two women having babies in their tubs. After I saw the water turning a shade of red, I had to get up and walk in the other room. Not my wife though, she sat there eating popcorn like it was an Emmy winning flick.

Like all of her ideas lately, I ignored her. I knew it would be pushed aside by some new idea she got in her head.

Ty and Miranda arrived at our house a little after dinner. Bella had unhooked herself from her seatbelt and was already flying out of the door when we walked outside. Clear across the field, I could see my son running toward us, waving his hands.

Savanna came out holding her growing baby bump and gave everyone a smile. Miranda climbed out of the car and gave me a big hug. "Hey Cuz."

"Hey yourself," she replied.

Just like every time, Ty went running up toward Savanna. He normally picked her up and spun her around, but as he got closer to her he stopped dead in his tracks. Savanna stood there looking at him. "What?"

"It's just....well it's your tits. I barely recognized you with those giant melons." He immediately started laughing and held his arms out to her.

"I missed you too." Savanna shook her head as she pulled away.

Ty grabbed her hands and stood back looking at her. "Seriously Van, you look great. Pregnancy looks good on you. The boobs do too."

I walked up and put my arm around Ty. "It never gets old with you does it?"

"Nope, never." He leaned in close to me. "Dude, they are huge. Don't tell me you aren't loving that shit."

I cackled and cleared my voice. I said nothing, but the smile on my face says it all. He was right, Savanna's breasts were huge and I was loving every second if it.

Once Miranda and Savanna had given each other big hugs, Ty and I took the truck to drop Thunder off to the pasture.

There was no doubt in my mind that he was going to be happy to see Daisy again.

We got halfway down the lane and Ty was drumming on his knees. He had a huge smile on his face.

"What is up with you? I know for a fact your daughter was in the car on the way here, so what gives?" I asked.

"My wife says I can't talk about it."

I knew he was busting, so I decided to use reverse psychology on his ass. "Fine, I didn't really want to know anyway."

He immediately turned to face me. "Dude, Miranda is preggers. A miniature me is growing inside of her."

I shook my head at how he announced it. "I kinda figured. That is awesome Cuz. Savanna is goin' to be so freakin' excited."

"We just took the test this morning, so it's really early still. I just can't wait dude. Izzy is going to go nuts when she finds out. I don't think I can be like you guys and not find out what it is. I want to know right now and it had only been one day."

I started laughing. "Yeah, Savanna isn't too happy about waiting either. I didn't do it to make them suffer. I want to experience the whole natural surprise."

"Dude, fuck that! There is no way I can go nine months and not know."

"To each his own Cuz. Have you talked to Conner today?"

"Miranda sent him a text message earlier. He said he might stop by later."

"Might? What the hell does that idiot have to do that is more important than seein' his family? Sometimes I wonder what that boy is thinkin'."

Ty started coughing he was laughing so hard. "You should have seen when he came out to our place for that one week. He wanted to go out drinking every damn night. By the third night, I couldn't even function. He parties way too much. I know I used to be bad about it too, but he just drinks until he becomes completely belligerent. It really pissed Miranda off. We didn't want him acting like that in front of Izzy."

"He works his ass off in the day, but we don't see him much at night. He never complains and always shows up the next mornin' to work. I don't know what to do about him."

"Have you thought about what we discussed last time we visited?"

"Yeah, I reckon' we can look into it. You do know what has to happen if we proceed, right?" Ty and Miranda were inquiring about branching out the cattle business to his family farm. Things were going really good for them and they wanted a new venture that would be profitable. With my contacts, and Conner helping them get it all started, it was a great opportunity for both of us.

I tell ya, Ty really had his shoulders on right. Everyone was so upset about he and Miranda at first, but everything we thought we knew about that boy was dead wrong. He was one hell of a father, a devoted husband, and a pretty smart businessman. He managed their money and knew exactly what he needed to do to make sure they never had to worry about anything. It didn't hurt that he and Miranda would eventually get the farm. He would never have to pay a stiff mortgage, not that I did either. We were both very fortunate.

"I guess we can talk about more when he is around. I don't want to do it if he is all drunk though. He thinks he knows everything." Ty wasn't lying. Conner was unmanageable when he was drunk. The man was sailing down a dangerous path and he really didn't seem to give a shit what anyone thought about it. Having Savanna and Noah had taken my focus off of Conner and his endeavors. He was a grown damn man, for Christ sakes. He needed to grow the hell up and be responsible.

The moment Thunder went trotting in that corral, Daisy came right up to him. Atticus stayed in the corner of the pasture while the two lovebirds got reacquainted. Ty and I stood there laughing at the two of them for a couple minutes, before heading back to be with the girls.

As we approached the house, we saw Noah and Bella on one of the golf carts. He knew the rules and how fast he was allowed to go, so when I saw them flying past us, I got a little ticked. I slammed on the brakes to our cart and whistled through my two fingers. Noah's golf cart came to an abrupt halt. "Noah Shelton Mitchell! Get your little butt in the house right now!" I ordered.

My son's face turned bright red as he passed us. He refused to look our way. Ty covered his mouth to hide his laughter. Bella looked scared to death. When they got ahead of us, I followed the two of them to the house. Noah jumped off the golf cart and started to run in the house. "Get down here boy!"

I rarely had to raise my voice, so he knew he was in trouble. He looked down at the ground. "Do you know why you are in trouble?"

"Yes, sir."

"Noah, if you aren't allowed to ride that fast alone, why would you do it with Bella?" I asked.

"Because she told me to," he answered sadly.

I glanced over at Bella, who was ducking behind her daddy. Ty knelt down on the ground. I could tell he was trying so hard not to laugh. "Iz, did you tell him to go faster?"

She nodded her head up and down. Ty was a sucker. He bent over and kissed her on the forehead. "Don't do that again, Sweetie. You both could have gotten hurt and if something happened to you Daddy and Mommy would be so sad."

"Okay, Daddy."

"Go in the house with Noah. Me and Uncle Colt will be right in." Bella listened to her father and walked right into the house. We could hear them talking as soon as they got out of our sights.

"Sorry about that."

"Yeah, she is her mother's child I see." I joked.

"Ha ha, douche bag. I get it. You are saying my daughter moves fast like her mother aren't you?"

As funny as that was, it was not what I meant. "No, asshole. I mean she is ornery like her mother. Jesus, why would I say that about a four year old?"

Ty shook his head. "Shit! Sorry. You know that when it comes to Izzy, I get all overprotective."

"And Miranda," I added.

"Duh! It's my job."

We headed into the house and already I could smell that Savanna had something good cooking. The smell of cinnamon and something else filled my nostrils. I ignored whatever Ty was saying behind me as I made my way into the kitchen. Savanna was bent over the oven. I reached down and grabbed her hips pulling her into me just enough to catch her attention. "What are you doing?" She asked startled.

"What are you makin' that smells so darn good?"

"Miranda and I are making pumpkin rolls. I mix and bake and she spreads and rolls."

The room filled with mine and Ty's laughter, while both girls stood there looking like they had no idea what was going on.

Savanna put her hands on her hips, her little belly protruding. "What the heck is so funny?"

I looked over and Ty, who literally had tears rolling down his face he was laughing so hard. "Darlin' you just said that Miranda spreads and rolls. Do you get it?"

Miranda put her hand over her mouth and began laughing with us. Ty walked over to her and kissed her on the cheek. "She is so good at it too."

Savanna rolled her eyes. "You guys are so stupid. You know what I meant. If you want any of these treats you better get your asses out of my kitchen."

She took the oven mitt and swatted it at Ty. "Get out smartass!"

I followed behind Ty trying to avoid the pregnant woman swatting the oven mitt. Ty walked upstairs toward the sound of the kids laughing. When we got into the hallway, we peeked inside the playroom door. Noah and Bella had put one of Savanna's sexy nighties on the dog. Ty walked in the room and sat down with them calmly. "What are you two doing to Sam?"

"Playing dress-up, Daddy," Bella answered her father.

Ty tugged on the lace outfit. "Where did you guys find this cool outfit?"

"It was in my mom's drawer. We wanted to find something pretty because Sam is a girl," he explained.

I hadn't heard her walking up behind me, but I heard Savanna gasp and turned around. Her face was already as red as a beet. "Oh my God! Noah, where did you get this?" She walked toward the dog and tried to hide the outfit with her body.

Even though Savanna thought she was morbidly obese, she actually didn't even look pregnant from the back. Her body had stayed small, all except for her belly. So, the fact that she was standing in front of us trying to block a dog, actually did nothing.

Ty took complete advantage of her embarrassment. "We can still see it."

She looked at me like I was somehow responsible for all of it. "Are you just going to stand there and let this happen?"

I shook my head and laughed at her. When she started to get mad, I pulled her into my arms. "Darlin' they are just playin'. They have no idea what the outfit is for. Just let them play."

She leaned into my chest and gritted her teeth when she talked. "I don't want Ty seeing my underwear."

Unfortunately, Ty heard her. "Don't get your panties in a bunch. I have no interest in your underwear, Sweet Cheeks."

She walked out of the room throwing her hands in the air. "Whatever!"

I leaned down to Noah. "Next time just ask Mommy first. There are some things that are too expensive to be puttin' on the dog."

"Yes, sir."

We left the kids in the playroom and went back downstairs. The women were sitting at the kitchen table. Miranda was slicing the pumpkin rolls and I could feel my mouth watering. "I get the first slice," I blurted out.

"Says who?" Savanna tested.

"Since you are carrying my child, I guess you can have the first slice." I leaned over and wrapped my arms around my seated wife. "And also because I love you."

She reached her hands up and touched mine. "Good answer, and I love you too."

Conner never showed up to play cards with us. In fact he never even stopped by to say hello to Miranda, Ty, or even Bella. Obviously, I hadn't noticed the extremity of the situation.

We all had a great night, even though Miranda never came clean about their growing surprise. I understood them wanting to wait, since they had just found out earlier in the day. There was no rush, but I knew Savanna would be thrilled. It meant so much to have our kids be close. The way that Noah and

Bella played together was crazy. I knew they would always be close.

We called it a night around midnight. The kids had conked out in Noah's room and we insisted that Bella just stay the night. After they had taken an hour long bubble bath, the kids had put on their pajamas and settled down to a Disney movie. Within fifteen minutes they were both sound asleep. Of course, it took Ty and I a good twenty minutes to clean up the bathroom floor. Even with three feet of bubbles, we knew they couldn't get baths together much longer.

We called Aunt Karen and told her not to worry about taking the kids for the night.

I started thinking about when I was a kid. I clearly remember a time when Ty and Miranda got a bath together. They were probably two or three years old and his parents and my parents went out while Aunt Karen babysat. Ty and Miranda probably had no idea about it.

Once they headed to the main house, I climbed up the steps and slid into bed with my wife. She was reading one of those what to expect books. She looked so cute with her little belly under the covers. Her little book was resting on her stomach. I laid my head across it, pushing the book out of the way. My fingers slowly removed her blankets and shirt, revealing her bare skin. I pressed my lips on her stomach. "Daddy loves you, little one."

Every night I would talk to my baby, even if Savanna had already fallen asleep. I loved to feel the little one moving around and kicking at me. Noah still got excited when the baby would kick while he was around. He would start laughing and carrying on. I knew he was going to be a good big brother because he was already a great son. Even though I missed out on a lot of his life, I knew we had so much to look forward to. Savanna had given me the family I wanted us to have. She made life worth living and could never know the extent of my love for her.

Chapter 20

Savanna

We woke up to two little kids crying. Apparently they woke up and started jumping on Noah's train bed. From the force of both of them jumping at the same time, one of the bedrails came loose and it sent them tumbling on top of each other. Noah had a big knot on his forehead and Bella was holding her elbow. In only a pair of boxer shorts, Colt carried the kids to the kitchen and gave them both bags of ice for their injuries.

He came back up to bed stating that they were settled down and watching cartoons. I heard him turning on the shower and looked over at the clock. It was only seven in the morning and breakfast at Colt's mother's house wasn't until nine.

Through the crack in the bathroom door, I could see my husband taking off his boxers and walking in to the shower. He closed the door behind him, but I could still see him through the glass. The water ran down his face and he leaned forward against the shower wall. His perfectly sculpted body looked so hot soaking wet. I just stood there staring at him for the longest time.

I don't know whether he sensed me, or it was just a natural reaction to look out, but he turned and caught my eyes with his. A half smile came across his face as he bit down on his lip. He never moved. "You goin' to just stand there or come in here and join me Darlin'?"

Feeling a bit sexy for being caught watching him, I pulled my shirt over my head as I approached the bathroom. While still walking toward him, I shimmied out of my panties. He turned around and opened the shower door, with his arms open to greet me. Just to be safe, I reached back and locked the bathroom door. I'd rather them knock for a second than walk in and see us naked.

Colt's wet arms pulled me into his chest. His scruffy face tickled as his lips brushed against mine. Wet fingers traced over my big belly. I turned my body around and rested my back against his chest. Colt took both hands and held onto my baby bump while his tongue played with my neck and my ear.

He nibbled on my shoulder and I moved my head to the side, so he could have nothing in his way. "I love you."

The vibration of his voice sent chills between my legs. I turned my body around and nestled my head under his chin. My hands played with the water on his chest. I grabbed his body wash and starting washing his chest, taking my time with each nipple. I pushed him against the shower wall as far as he could go. He traced his fingers over my ass cheeks before squeezing them in his big hands. A small cry escaped from my mouth.

"I want you," I whispered.

Colt walked forward, causing me to walk backwards until I hit the shower wall behind me, with his hands still on my ass. He kissed my lips before sinking down to kiss the skin between my breasts. He kissed my belly before reaching his final destination. His hot tongue wasted no time stroking against my wet sex. I closed my eyes, since I couldn't see past the baby bump, and tried to focus on what his tongue was doing. My hands naturally brushed through his dark hair, grabbing a bunch and not letting go. I used my hold on his hair to direct his face. As I did it, I heard a deep groan coming from between my legs. The vibration of Colt's voice added to the electric sensations moving through my body. My legs began to feel weak, but Colt steadied me, by spreading my legs open further and holding me on my inner thighs. He pushed all of the shampoo forcefully off of the small bench seat and brought one of my legs up to sit on it, before burying himself between my legs again. I reached up and grabbed the top of the frame to the shower door, holding on while my body began to convulse with pleasure. Colt's mouth lingered as his tongue played with my exhausted nub. Small shrills hit me every time he did it.

When he finally stood back up, my hands instantly found his hard cock. He stood in front of me, positioning it between my legs, while he stood there kissing me. My slippery hand began stroking it. I lathered my other hand up and used it to stroke faster. This time it was Colt falling back against the shower wall. I pressed one hand against his chest holding him still while the other worked to stimulate his rock hard cock. He could barely manage words to speak. "Not like....not like this Savanna. I want you Darlin', please." More low moans escaped from Colt's mouth as he closed his eyes and enjoyed how my hand was making him feel. He pulled my face up to his. "I want you so bad."

I took one look at Colt's eyes and my stroking slowed. His utter sexiness was something I found impossible to resist. The water fell down his head, while he cupped my face with his hands. Perfect lips pressed against mine, followed by a very skilled tongue. As if it were in slow motion, I felt my body lifting up and being pressed against the shower wall. I reached my arms around Colt's neck and felt it slide inside of me with ease. Our lips were still touching as low moans came out of both of us.

Our skin slapped together as he thrusted himself in and out of me. He continued to kiss me as he removed his entire penis, to only force it deep inside again, each time leaving me wanting it more. Just the size of his girth, rubbing against my inner skin forced a rush of bliss with each thrust. I played with his hair as he began to speed up the pace, no longer teasing me with pulling it out.

I could tell he was about to finish. He held on to me tighter, pushing me against the wall harder and harder, until he pinned me still, holding me tight, while his lips stilled against mine.

My feet were slowly set back down to the shower floor, while Colt leaned against the wall, trying to catch his breath. I had no idea how long we were in the shower, but the water was starting to get cold.

Colt leaned over and kissed me before grabbing me a towel and wrapping it around my body. I loved watching him walk around naked. His ass was sexy as hell.

As we entered our bedroom we could hear voices coming from downstairs. I instantly felt horrible for leaving the kids unsupervised for however long we had. Colt dressed quickly while I followed suit. By the time we made it downstairs, we were standing face to face with Ty and Miranda, who were laughing their butts off.

"Care to explain what you two were doing up there?" Miranda was still laughing when she said it.

My face was turning a bright red shade. I shrugged my shoulders.

"Well, while the two of you were," he stuck up his fingers to quote, "'cleaning the bedroom', our children decided they wanted to have glasses."

I had no idea what Ty was saying or why they were laughing. The kid's backs were facing us, and they seemed to be behaving. "What are you talking about?" I asked.

Noah heard my voice and turned around. In black magic marker he had two giant raccoon circles on each eye, with a line connecting in the center. If that wasn't funny enough, Bella turned around and had a matching pair of magic marker glasses. "Aren't they cool, Mom?"

Colt just stood there scratching his head. Miranda buried her laughter in Ty's chest, while he stood there waiting for me to respond. "Noah, where did you get the marker?" He was over four, obviously he knew where we kept them, but I had to ask.

"In Daddy's office. We were just playin'." Noah explained.

It took Miranda and I two kind of soaps to remove the permanent marker from our children's faces. Due to the fact that we got so occupied with the kids, Ty never brought up mine and

Colt's shower sexcapade. With the combination of Noah and my pregnancy, Colt and I didn't have a lot of sex time. When it became available we took advantage.

My husband had patience, I had to give it to him, but everyone had their breaking point. Pleasing him and keeping him happy was something that I considered important. Was it really wrong to shut the door for some alone time? Noah knew where to find us and how to get our attention. He was famous for beating on the door, then asking why we locked it in the first place. There were a couple times I swore Colt was just going to sit him down and explain how we were making babies, so he would stop asking.

At any rate, we got the kids cleaned up and all headed to the main house for breakfast. The three older women were there at the table, drinking coffee. A buffet style set up was on the island, just like every breakfast at Colt's mother's house. Everyone greeted each other and started catering to the kids. Colt's mom had bought them a little kid table and they felt all cool about having it for themselves. Us adults made our plates and settled down at the table.

When the kids finished they went into the family room to watch television, while the adults stayed around and talked. Conner came walking in the door about a half hour later. He had some brunette around his arm and a pair of sunglasses on his face, even though it wasn't even sunny. In fact, it had been raining on and off for a couple of days. We all stopped talking and watched as he and his flavor of the week made a plate. They took their food out to the pool yard without saying a single word to any of us. I don't know why, but I looked over toward Ty and Miranda. He was clenching his jaw and looking outside. Even though I was looking right at him, when his fists pounded on the table, I still jumped. Out of reflex I grabbed my belly while I watched Ty get up and start walking toward the pool yard door. Colt slid his chair out and followed behind him.

Miranda stood up and took off after the guys. I looked at the three older ladies, my mother in law, Aunt Karen, and Lucy, and wondered what in the world was happening.

Colt's mother grabbed my hand. "Everything will be okay. Just let the guys handle it."

"What do you mean? What don't I know?"

Conner's poor mother put her hands into her face and started shaking her head. "I can't believe I let things get this bad. What am I going to do? He is going to end up hurting himself or someone else."

"Let's just hope that Colt and Tyler can help him." Lucy added.

I tried to listen in, but could hear nothing. They weren't really giving me any hints on what the heck was happening, so I walked outside to where Miranda was standing.

Conner and the mystery girl were sitting at a table eating their breakfast, while Ty and Colt stood over them.

I whispered to Miranda. "Are you going to explain?"

"Conner is out of control. He is partyin' too much, drinkin' himself belligerent. We don't know how to get him to stop. He won't even associate with us anymore. Colt is workin' so hard to make this cattle deal work, and Ty and I can't be responsible for him if he moves in with us. His parents aren't goin' to be okay with him comin' in drunk every night. He probably doesn't even know this girl's name. It's pathetic!"

"I guess I haven't had very much time to notice. I'm really sorry. Between Noah and this pregnancy, I've been so preoccupied." I explained.

"Exactly, I don't want to be dealing with his drama with morning sickness. It's bad enough." Miranda stopped talking immediately. She looked at me and smiled. "We just found out yesterday before we came. I just wanted to wait until I was further along to tell everyone. Please don't be mad. I wanted to tell you last night, especially after Ty told me he slipped and told Colt. I honestly thought he would have told you this morning."

I looked over at my husband and shook my head. "He is going to get it for keeping such exciting news from me." I pulled her into a hug. "Our kids are going to be so close again. This is awesome, Miranda. I bet Ty is just out of his mind excited. I know he was counting down the days to start trying."

"Oh my gosh, Van, you have no idea. He ran around the house jumping up and down for at least an hour. The car ride here was unbearable. Keeping it from Bella was even harder. His knee was shaking so bad in the car, it felt like we had a damn flat tire. Every second we have been alone, he is touching my stomach. My God he cannot keep a secret, it is ridiculous."

We both started laughing. Our celebration conversation was cut short when we saw a paper plate being thrown toward Ty's face. The mystery girl backed up away from the table. As Ty wiped the food off of the front of his body, Colt and Conner stood face to face, screaming at one another.

They kept pushing each other, finally Ty getting in on it, making it even worse, obviously.

"I am tellin' you to back the fuck off, Colt. It ain't none of your damn business," Conner yelled.

Colt pushed him back and got him sitting in the chair. "It is my business when you are supposed to be workin'. What the hell is wrong with you? What are you on, man?"

He stood up and pushed Colt to the side. "Get out of my face, Colt. Mind your business and stay out of mine. Don't you have a wife and a kid to tend to? It don't matter what I am doin', cause it ain't none of your concern." He took his hands and motioned for Colt to move out of the way.

Ty walked in front of Colt and shoved Conner to the ground. "This shit will not happen when you come to stay with us. I will not have my daughter and my pregnant wife seeing you this way. Get your fucking ass up, take that little bitch home and clean yourself up Conner, or this whole deal between us is done!"

Obviously, Conner hadn't heard the pregnant part. He shoved Ty hard, making him lose his balance. He went ass first into the pool. Conner started walking away and I watched as Miranda went flying toward him. He stopped when he reached her. "Move, Randa."

She didn't say a single word, but instead, slapped him right across the face. He quickly grabbed her by the wrist and began to shove her out of the way, forcefully. Colt was coming from one direction as Ty leaped out of the pool and clothes-lined Conner to the ground. Wet fists pounded Conner in the face. "If you ever lay a fucking hand on my wife again, I will kill you. She is pregnant you piece of shit."

Colt pulled Ty off of Conner and he just laid there looking at his sister. "Randa, I wouldn't have hurt you, I swear it."

She held her hand out for Ty and they walked into the house without saying another thing to him. I turned to Colt, who was running his hand through his hair trying to figure out what the heck had just happened.

Conner started getting up, but ended up just sitting up looking at both of us.

"Get your shit together Conner. If you ever come into my mother's house and disrespect her again, you will have to answer to me. Dammit boy, grow up. I don't know what you're doin', but you better stop. You ain't got shit without this family, Cuz."

Colt grabbed me by the waist and walked me back into the house. I still had no idea what was going on with Conner, but obviously I was the only one who didn't know. I guess there were more things Colt hadn't told me.

The three women had gotten up from the table and were helping Lucy clean up. I started to walk over to offer a hand, but Colt grabbed me by the hand and pulled me into the small powder room. The space was confined and I had no idea what was going on. "Are you okay?"

"I want you and Miranda to take the kids to our house." Colt stared at me like I was supposed to read his mind.

"Care to fill me in on what the hell is going on? We were just having breakfast and then you're outside fighting. What is wrong with Conner? What aren't you telling me Colt?"

"Sugar, I'm not really sure. It's definitely alcohol, but I reckon' it has to be somethin' else too. I don't want you involved in this."

"Conner has been fine, Colt. I don't understand?"

He ran his hands over his face. "He has been actin' funny for months, but the alcohol abuse has become an issue. He doesn't have a father and neither do I. You know I feel obligated to look out for him. Can you just please take the kids and Miranda and just go to the house. Ty and I will stay here and try to talk some sense into him. There is obviously something else goin' on that we don't know about."

I put the toilet seat down and sat, giving us a bit more breathing room. "If he is abusing drugs or alcohol, how could we not have noticed? I mean, I know he likes to drink and go out, but I never thought Conner would get himself involved in something so dangerous."

I was feeling like my breakfast was coming back up. Colt was very protective of Conner, so I knew if something was really going on, it was not going to be easy for him to deal with. With Miranda in good hands and living out of state, Colt had been able to relax more and worry about his younger cousins less. Now I wondered if he was somehow blaming himself for not noticing this before it got this bad. "Colt, this isn't your fault. No matter what is going on with Conner, it isn't because of something you did, or didn't do. You have to know that." I grabbed his hands and looked right at him.

He leaned down and kissed me on the head. "Darlin', Krista's dad was a big time drug abuser. I don't know how many times I had to hear her talkin' about him spendin' all of their money and not takin' care of himself. There were times where he wouldn't even wake up for days. I don't want this from Conner. I won't let him ruin his life."

There was no use arguing with Colt about his family. He wasn't going to give up until he knew Conner was going to be alright. I stood up and kissed my worried husband. "I love you baby. I will see you when you get home. Don't forget that you promised the kids they could ride today."

A half smile was displayed on one of his cheeks. "I won't forget, Darlin." He lifted my chin up. "I love you."

"I love you too."

Miranda and I grabbed the kids and headed to the house. Neither one of us talked about her brother. I could tell she was anxious about her brother, but she focused on the kids and nothing else.

Chapter 21

Colt

The last thing I wanted to do was some kind of intervention on my cousin.

Ty and Miranda hadn't come here to visit to deal with something like that, but we couldn't let it go any longer. Ty and I had been working hard to try and expand the family cattle business. Conner was the biggest part of the operation. Without him, our plans would have to be put off until we could afford to find someone with all of the knowledge that I had trained Conner with.

I knew Ty was frustrated, but I wasn't sure of the extent until I started paying attention to Conner's actions. His stunt at breakfast was the last straw for me. He blatantly had brought a complete stranger into our home and didn't even have the decency to introduce her, or thank my mother.

By the time that Ty and I walked the girls out, Conner had already taken the girl and gone back to his house. We hopped on the golf cart and rode toward my Aunt Karen's place.

Conner's truck was in the driveway, as well as a car I didn't recognize. Ty and I looked at each other before walking right into the house. I led the way through the kitchen, until I reached the living room.

Conner was being straddled by the girl. Thankfully, they were both wearing clothes. I would have liked to say that was the worst part of us barging in on them, but I was wrong. A tiny bag of white powder was laying on the table, along with a rolled up dollar bill and a half snorted line of coke.

They obviously hadn't noticed us walking in, or the door shutting behind us, because they were steady making out. My cousin's hand was slipped down into the front of the girls jeans. She sat up and began rocking back and forth. I looked to Ty to roll my eyes, but he was just staring at the drugs on the table. I nudged him with my arm, grabbing his attention.

At the same time, we each headed over and grabbed the couple by the arms, separating them. Ty was closest to the girl. He pulled her by the arm, shoving her into the kitchen, while I held on to Conner.

"Get your hands off of her!" He yelled.

I could hear Ty yelling from the kitchen. "Get your shit and get out of this house. Did you know that Conner's mother is dating the sheriff? How about we call him and have him come over right now. I'm sure he wouldn't see too kindly about the drugs all over the living room."

Conner looked down at the table and turned his gaze away from me. A loud crash sounded in the kitchen and Ty came walking in. "She's gone." A car motor started outside, followed by someone skidding away from the house.

Ty came into the room as I shoved Conner onto the couch. I stood up preventing him from moving while Ty dusted the paraphernalia off the table. I watched him walk toward the bathroom and then heard the toilet flushing. He washed his hands and came back out to stand next to me, shaking his head at Conner the entire time. "Do you have any idea how much of my money you wasted?" Conner said rudely.

"You have got to be kidding me right now. We just caught you doing drugs and you are worried about how much money we wasted? Dude, you need help." Ty was so frustrated.

Conner wouldn't look at either of us. He just sat there laughing for no reason. I leaned over and smacked him straight in the jaw, his face turning as my hand made impact. "How long has this been goin' on?" I asked.

"There ain't nothin' goin' on. Me and that girl were just havin' a good time. Not everyone is as uptight as you two pussy's."

He crossed his arms over his chest and looked from Ty to myself. "You were using illegal drugs. How long has this been goin' on?"

"What? Me havin' a good time? Livin' my life to the fullest? Givin' the ladies a good time?"

Ty looked at Conner and shook his head. "You need fucking help!"

"Fuck off, Tyler. I'm so sick of hearin' your mouth. Why don't you take your perfect little family and go the hell home. This ain't any of your business." Conner's eyes were halfway open when he was speaking to us. The drugs were obviously kicking in.

"It is my business when your sister is crying herself to sleep over you. Do you have any idea how much she wants you to come stay with us? It's killing her seeing you like this." He shook his head again. "Shit, man, you didn't even come to say hello yesterday. Izzy talked about seeing her Uncle Conner and you didn't give her the time of day. You're pathetic, man. How could you pick some strung out chick over your flesh and blood? How could you hurt Miranda?"

Conner put his hand over his face and leaned his elbows on his knees. "Whatever man. Please just leave. I don't feel like hearing any of this right now." He never moved his hands.

I sat down on one side of my cousin, while Tyler sat in the chair across from us. "We ain't leavin'. It's ten thirty in the morning and you are drinkin' a beer and snortin' coke."

He started to laugh. "That shit ain't even mine. My girl likes doin' that. It makes her all freaky and shit. Not that either of you two fuckers would know what a good party with a girl looked like. You walk around with your fingers up your asses all the time. You wouldn't know a good time if it hit you in the face."

I was losing my cool, clenching my fists to try and hold in the anger. Conner was shit faced. It wasn't even noon. How could I not have seen how bad off he was? This was a disaster. A fucking nightmare.

"You can either get your act together, or get the hell off the ranch. Those are your options Conner."

"Screw you Colt. You ain't gonna do shit to me. Just get out of here."

In one leap, Ty was on top of Conner with his hands around his throat. Conner was punching the hell out of Ty, but he kept holding him by the throat. Somehow, Ty had managed to flip him around in a head lock, while Conner pounded on Ty's face. I pried the two of them apart and sat between them. Ty said nothing as he got up and walked out of the house. I don't really think it was about him, it was the fact that he was hurting Miranda.

I stood up, ignoring the look on Conner's face. "You have twenty four hours to get your ass clean, or you need to find somewhere else to live and work. I will not have drugs on my property and be an enabler to you and your habits."

Conner said nothing as I walked out into the kitchen, but I did hear the loud sound of a beer bottle smashing against a wall.

Ty was outside sitting on the golf cart. I hopped on and he immediately started driving away from the house. "It's much worse than I thought. I'm real glad you brought it to my attention."

"He ain't coming to my farm like that Colt. This could ruin everything you know." Ty had wanted to branch out the cattle business for over a year, so this problem with Conner was a major issue for him and his family.

"It won't ruin everything, but it will definitely set us back. I can't believe his mother knew nothing about this."

"She is so serious about John now and besides, Conner is a grown man. He should be able to be responsible for his own actions. I think she has a right to finally enjoy her life. It had to be hard to not date for all of those years. She had to do it for the kids."

We pulled up at the cabin and saw the girls sitting on the porch swing. Noah and Bella came whipping around the corner on two Hot Wheels vehicles. One was a Tractor and one was a Mustang. They were giggling, trying to race each other. "Sorry ya'll had to deal with this on your visit."

Ty put his hand on my shoulder as the kids flew by us. "Hi Daddy!" Bella waved.

"Hey Sweetie!" He turned to look at me. "This isn't your fault Colt. Conner just needs an eye opener. He needs something that will change the person he wants to be. You and I both know what that is like."

I nodded. He was right. Ty and I both knew what it was like to find something that made us want more out of life. I don't know how much I had changed for Savanna, but Ty was a different person. I'd hate to tell him that he turned soft, but it was true. All he cared about was being with his girls.

"How'd it go?" Miranda asked from the porch.

Ty skipped all the steps but the last and hurried over to where she sat. He leaned against the railing as I came up to meet him. "Not exactly how we pictured it."

"What's that supposed to mean? Oh my God, Ty, your face." Miranda stood up and approached Ty, holding her hand up to her husband's face. "Did he do this to you Babe?"

Ty grabbed her hand and pulled it away from her face. "I'm fine. I pounced on him first. He was just trying to get me to let him go," he explained.

"I think he was still drunk from last night." Miranda thought she knew the worst of it.

"He was drinking when we got there, Baby."

Ty pulled Miranda into his chest and kissed her on the head. "He can't come stay at the farm like this. I can't be pregnant and responsible for him too."

"I know, Baby. Don't worry about it right now. He obviously didn't hear us mention it, so we can focus on you having a good first trimester and then figure out what to do about Conner. As of right now he isn't our problem to fix. Colt gave him an ultimatum and hopefully he does something about it." Ty stroked Miranda's hair as he spoke to her.

"If he knows what's good for him he will cut his shit out. I wasn't lyin' when I said those things Ty."

He looked over at me. "I know, Cuz, I know."

Miranda was really bent out of shape about her brother. After Ty and I finally dropped the conversation, she went inside and called her mother. We could hear her raising her voice in the office. I don't think that my aunt was saying she wasn't concerned, but I think she just didn't know how to handle her grown son. Aside from drinking and driving, we really weren't sure what else he was doing. Sure, he was caught with drugs, but Ty and I couldn't prove they were really his.

Savanna stayed outside with the kids, while Ty and I started watching a ball game and drinking some beers. The kids came in yelling that it was time to ride the horses, but we still had about a half hour left in the game we were watching. They went back outside huffing and puffing that we were meanies. A few minutes later we heard them outside laughing and playing again.

Miranda finally came out of the room and winked at Ty before she went outside with Savanna.

"It's pretty cool we are both going to be Daddy's' again." Ty announced.

"Yeah, it is. I just can't wait to be there for the birth. I missed out on so much with Noah."

"The birth is crazy. It is scary and disgusting and beautiful all at the same time. Do you have any idea what their shit looks like?" I had to remember that I was talking to Ty. Of course he was going to bring this up.

"Yeah, I hadn't put too much thought into that part of it."

He started laughing. "As much as I wanted to be with Miranda that first night we were finally together, there was this flash right before of what it looked like down there the last time I had seen it. Dude, I was scared shitless."

"Not that I want to even talk about Miranda like this, but I have to believe that you of all people would have still gone through with it."

He shook his head and busted out in a loud uncontrolled laugh. "Yeah, there is no way I could have said no to her. She had me from the first kiss. Everything else was just a bonus. Besides, it ended up looking nothing like I remembered. Trust me when I say I have it memorized in my head. Every little inch of it."

The grin on his face showed me he was just playing into my disgust of hearing about it. I tossed a pillow at him. "You're sick."

"Yeah, I know."

I decided that talking to Ty about Savanna's birth was a mistake. He was lucky to have been there for Bella to come into the world. If it weren't for that day, he and Miranda probably would have never gotten together. Looking at Noah now, made me regret not seeing him as a baby. All of those first experiences that I had missed out on. I knew we would have a lifetime of new ones, but it still hurt to know I could never have those back. I would never try to replace that with our new baby, but I was very excited to experience them. I wanted to see those first steps, or hear the first words.

Krista's dad had made sure I had pictures and Noah's baby book, so I could at least read about them. The first thing he said was 'ba ba', a word he used for his bottle. He got his first tooth at five months and took his first steps at nine. The pictures of my little boy were cute, but they didn't fill that absence of not being there. Noah would never judge me for that. I think the kid loved me before he had even met me. I still didn't understand why Krista did what she did, but she never kept it a secret that I was his father. I had to believe that she always did want to tell me.

I started thinking about Conner and how upset his father would have been if he saw how his son was behaving. The company he was keeping was what was bringing him down. The girls kept getting more rough looking and obviously had introduced him into a new kind of party life.

None of us kids were raised to take up with people that lived like that. We knew better. I had to assume that this was Conner's way of dealing with his loneliness. He was drowning himself in booze and women to get through not having happiness for himself. It wasn't like the rest of us were gloating in happiness, but it was hard to not see it when you lived on the same property and were related.

My cousin was engulfed in some sort of infomercial about rags you hook on your feet and polish your floor with. I shook my head before calling for his attention. "Hey Ty, what if movin' away will help Conner out? I know you are worried, but if he is at your place he doesn't have access to the things he has here. Everyone knows Conner here and they put him on some kind of pedestal. If he moved out of the state, he wouldn't know anyone. You would be his only means of communication. I just don't see him changin' if he still lives here."

Ty shook his head and leaned his elbows on his knees. He clapped his hands together and kept shaking his head as he talked. "I don't know man. I'm willing to do whatever we need to do to help him, but this shit is not something I know anything about. If he is using drugs, I can't allow that shit in my house, or my parent's house. And frankly, I don't want that kind of shit happening around my daughter."

"I get that, but I don't think it will happen. We need to get him as far away from here as we can for a while. Other than to force him into the military, this is the best scenario."

Ty didn't say anything for a good two minutes. I noticed him glaring out the window at the ladies swinging on the porch. "Let me talk to Miranda. I don't want to say yes or no without really talking to her about it first."

A weather alert came on the bottom of the screen, catching our attention from the conversation we were having. It was a severe weather alert for our county. They were calling for strong thunderstorms with high winds that could potentially create funnel systems, turning to tornados. "Damn, we picked the wrong weekend to visit." Ty joked.

"It says we are under the warnin' until nine tonight. I guess we better get the girls and the kids inside and call to the main house in case they don't know what's goin' on."

Ty got up and walked outside, while I dialed my mother and let them know about the storm. Sam came running into the house and went right upstairs. She only did that when she was afraid. I had no sooner got off the phone, when I heard the women calling the kids names. I went out to the porch with the rest of the adults and waited to see the kids coming around from the side of the house.

After a good five minutes of calling, Ty and I looked at each other and started walking down the porch steps.

"Where could they have gone? The golf carts are here. His battery operated cars are here. Do you think they are hiding?" Ty suggested.

Thunder rumbled in the distance and I had noticed that the wind was picking up. "Noah doesn't like thunder storms. If they are hiding then we will see him any second running for the house."

I felt confident that any second my son, and my niece would come walking up to us. The girls were standing on the edge of the porch looking all around. "Colt, please go check the barn. They are probably with the horses." Savanna started to walk down the steps. The sound of the wind chimes on our back porch echoed against the woods. I could tell the wind had really picked up by the loud clatter of them.

Ty and I headed toward the barn where we kept the horses. "I'm surprised that we can't hear Thunder. He starts getting loud when storms come in."

We both looked at each other and started hauling ass toward that barn. My greatest fears were confirmed when we opened the door and only saw Daisy in her stall. Ty threw his arms up above his head. "Fuck! Goddamn it!"

"Go get the Gator. We can cover more terrain with it. I have to go tell the girls what's goin' on."

Ty went flying out of the barn, while I jogged over to the girls, who were standing on the porch. "I was sure they would be in there." Savanna looked so disappointed.

"I got somethin' I need to tell you both."

The girls looked at each other and I watched their faces change from frustration to fear.

Chapter 22

Savanna

"What do you mean? Do you know where they are? What is going on?" I was frantic to find out where our kids were. The weather was picking up and they needed to get inside before it started raining.

Colt creased his brow and couldn't look me directly in the eye. When he finally did, I could tell there was something wrong. Instinctively, I put my hand on my belly and took a few steps toward him. "Tell us Colt. What is going on? Where are they?"

"Darlin', we can't find them and the horses are missin'."

No! No! No! This can't be happening....

My stomach turned into knots and my heart started pounding. I heard Miranda gasping behind me, then felt her reaching her arm into mine. At the same time, Ty came whipping around the corner on the Gator, a cross between a golf cart and a four wheeler. I turned my direction back to Colt.

"Ty and I are headin' into the woods to look for the kids. You two stay here and call us if they come home. Call my mother and tell her to be on the lookout at the main house and try to hunt down Conner. If the kids are on the horses, we are going to need his help."

Colt leaned over and kissed me on the forehead before he hopped on the vehicle with his cousin. Ty started pulling away from us. "We will find them." His voice carried as the guys disappeared from out of our view.

I started to cry immediately and Miranda pulled me against her chest. "They'll find them Van."

"I hope you're right."

The rain started coming down harder as Miranda and I headed into the house. We frantically both went after our cell phones and started calling everyone with a phone on the ranch. I didn't expect Colt's mother or Aunt to go searching through the woods, but they did go out and check all around their vicinity. John happened to be over Aunt Karen's, so when we called, he and Conner set out to start looking themselves.

Once our phone calls were done, it was hard for both Miranda and myself to remain calm. The sun was starting to set and the rain was really coming down. In the horizon, large bolts of lightning lit up the sky.

Our children were out there somewhere. If they were anywhere near Thunder during this storm they were in danger. I didn't know if I could bear to lose another child. Noah meant everything to Colt and I.

Poor Miranda stood by the front door, hugging her arms around herself. Tears strolled down her face. Noah had been riding for over a year, but I knew that Bella was not as experienced. Noah wasn't even great at it himself. His little body was too small to maneuver a pony, and especially a horse.

God, please help us find our kids.

"Miranda, I'm so sorry this is happening. Noah knows better than to get on a horse by himself. Maybe Thunder just got out by himself and the kids were never with them. Maybe they are just hiding somewhere."

She covered her face with one of her hands. "Bella doesn't like thunder and lightning. Ty knows that too. She hides in his arms every time there is a storm. There is no way she wouldn't have come inside by now. Something bad has happened. I can just feel that something is wrong, Van."

"Don't talk like that! We don't know that. We just saw them a little while ago riding around having fun. We were outside the whole time and never heard anything. If they got hurt they would have cried."

I was trying to comfort Miranda, but also myself. She said nothing, but went flying outside. I followed behind her, wondering if she saw one of the kids. Instead, we saw Atticus coming down the driveway, running around neighing. As if seeing the pony running free wasn't enough, I noticed the horse had a saddle hanging loosely to the side. The reigns were hanging down to the ground as the pony paced around the yard.

It was dark outside and the only thing that gave us light was the flashing of the lightening. Miranda headed toward the pony, but I grabbed her and pulled her back onto the porch. "No, wait! I will never forgive myself if you get hurt. Just let the guys catch the pony."

Miranda turned around and sat down on the porch. She was sobbing. I sat down behind her and hugged her as close to my body as I could get her. My big belly wasn't helping too much. "They were on the horses, Van. They were on the horses," she kept repeating.

Teaching Noah to ride was something that had made me so proud, but now I worried if my teaching him had been the wrong thing to do. Our children were out there somewhere, they were alone, in the dark, and afraid. It was hard to not think that they weren't hurt or worse.

I didn't know how to comfort Miranda when I was petrified for the safety of the kids myself. If something happened to them I would never forgive myself.

Miranda pulled out her phone and started dialing what I assumed was Ty. I must have been right because I heard his voice pick up. "Have you found them?" She asked through sobs.

"What do you mean? Well, you have to keep looking. I know...yes, but I can't sit around here and do nothing. Ty, please, I need to do something."

She hung up the phone and buried her hands into her face.

I grabbed her hands. "Miranda, what is it?"

She shook her head and avoided looking directly at me. "They found Noah's hat."

"What do you mean? Where?"

"In the woods, somewhere in a thicket. They said they saw Atticus runnin' and found the hat a few minutes later. They ran into Conner and John and they are all lookin' for them. So far they haven't heard a single peep from either of them. Where could they be Van? Where could they be where they can't hear us callin' for them? I can't just sit here waitin' for word. I have to go look for my daughter." She got up and started walking toward the front door.

As I watched her bending down to put on her shoes, she turned back toward me. "Miranda, wait! I'm going with you."

There was no hesitation in my voice. My son was out there somewhere and I felt responsible. There was no way in Hell that I was going to let her go out into the dark, while it was storming, alone. I ran back into the house and grabbed us a couple of flashlights and two jackets. They weren't waterproof but they would at least keep us warm for the time being.

As we headed out into the woods, reality really hit both of us. It was pitch black outside. We were heading into the dark woods, while heavy gusts of wind were blowing and the rain was pouring. Loud cracks of thunder caused us both to jump as we joined hands and continued trudging through the forest.

Miranda and I both took turns calling the children's names. We would walk a few feet and shine out the lights all around the area, before continuing forward. I'd taken many walks in these woods and Miranda had grown up on this property, but it didn't really help at night time. Getting lost in the woods was easy to do, especially without the light of the moon to guide us.

In the distance we could hear one of the gator's motors and voices calling the kids names. They were too far away from us to get their attention.

As the vehicle got further away from us, I got excited when I heard the sound of crackling leaves heading toward us. As it got closer, it sounded like more than one person coming our way. Miranda and I stopped, while shining the light in the direction of the sound.

A group of deer came leaping over a thicket, almost trampling on top of us. We both screamed and fell back onto the wet ground.

I turned back toward Miranda and noticed she was holding her leg. She had fallen on a patch of briars and had tiny thorns stuck all in the back of one of her legs. She was trying not to cry out in pain, but I knew that part of the skin was sensitive and she must have been in agony with the amount of them stuck in her.

I got her to flip around and with only a flashlight, I started removing the thorns one by one. She was crying out as I pulled each one of them out of her. When I got everyone that I could see out of her leg, I helped her stand up. She steadied herself and we began moving forward again.

Miranda was still in pain from her fall, but we held onto one another as we kept going further into the woods. Every few seconds we continued to take turns calling out the kids names, with no response.

"My God, where could they be Van? The guys have been searching for over an hour now. Do you have any idea how many acres of land we have to search?" Miranda hunched over and started crying worse. "I can't believe this is happening. I can't lose my daughter. I just can't lose her Van. She has to be okay."

I rubbed her back and tried to think of what to say. "We will find them. Noah is a smart kid. He has been going out hunting and fishing with Colt. He knows about the outdoors more than other kids his age. You know he wouldn't let anything happen to Bella. You have to know that Miranda."

She nodded her head and wrapped her arms around me. "I just want to find them, Van. We. Have. To. Find. Them."

I looked her dead in the eye. "We will. I won't give up until they are home safe. I promise you that."

We started moving again, only pausing to search with the flashlights, or when the loud crash of thunder startled us. The rain wasn't as bad as we walked under the trees, but the wind was wreaking havoc on anything dead in the forest. All around us we could hear limbs breaking and falling to the ground. Without being able to see our surroundings, it was impossible to know whether a limb was going to come tumbling down on top of us, or even a whole tree.

I didn't want to admit how scared I was, because that meant that my child had to be even more petrified. I thought about the day he came into our life and that first initial moment when I considered not being able to be his mother. Guilt washed over me as I began to wonder if choosing to raise him had caused this chain of events. Was I the reason that those two children were out there somewhere, alone, in the dark?

All I ever wanted was to be a parent and Noah had given me that, how could I have let him out of my sight tonight? How could I have let this happen?

This time I was the one crying. Miranda stopped and started to hug me. "I'm sorry for freaking out. We have to keep moving."

"What if we don't find them? What if Colt never forgives me for showing Noah how to ride? My God, I would never be able to even forgive myself. Miranda, what have I done?"

Miranda stood there in the pitch black with me. She didn't respond to me at first, causing me to cry harder. "This isn't your fault. One of us should have seen or heard them. We should have known they were up to no good. You can't blame yourself for this Van. Colt would never want you to do that."

I squatted down, holding my belly, and feeling the baby inside of me moving around. "I don't know what to do. After everything I have been through, this has to be the worst. My baby that I lost was hard to deal with but, but Noah is real, he is here with me every single day, loving me and calling me Mommy. It is my job to protect him. My little boy is out there somewhere and I don't know what to do to bring him home, to bring them both home."

Miranda grabbed my shoulders and started shaking me. "You have got to calm down, Van. We aren't goin' to find them if we stay here. Noah is a smart kid and if he is anything like his father, he is somewhere safe. Colt has taken him huntin'. He has to know of places to go." Miranda suddenly froze. Her eyes got real big and she grabbed my hand and started pulling me along, without giving me an explanation.

"What is it? Why are you pulling me?"

"I think I know where they might be." She kept going without turning around.

"What do you mean? Where?"

"Keep moving and I will explain" Miranda's slippery hands were doing a good job holding onto mine. We each had a flashlight and shined them in front of where we were walking. The ground was slippery and quite a few times both of us slipped on wet tree limbs on the ground.

"When we were kids, we used to go out to this old rope swing and swim in the lake. On the way there sits a bunch of little clusters of rocks and a large stream. Some of those clusters are actually like mini caves. They are only about four feet deep and not closed off from the elements, but they will keep you dry."

"Why do you think they could be there? How far is it away?" We kept walking even though my body was exhausted. I refused to tell Miranda to stop going. We needed to find the kids. I wasn't going to rest until we did.

"I don't know for sure, but they would be scared and want to hide somewhere dry. It is the only place I know of. Even if they aren't there, we can call the guys and have them pick us up."

"How do you even know we are headed in the right direction? It is pitch black out here?"

Miranda stopped walking and bent over to catch her breath. I held on to my tummy and waited for her to answer me. "We passed this tree we used to carve our names on a ways back. We crossed over the trail we used to ride our four wheelers on. The lake is up ahead. I'm not sure what part we will come out at, but I will be able to find the little hole they may be hiding in."

I stood up and got a few more deep breaths in before we started treading through the slippery woods again.

Miranda had been right. Within five minutes we came out to an opening. When the lightning struck across the dark sky, I could see the reflection of it in the water in front of us. Miranda pulled me along the water's edge and began calling out for the kids again. She pulled out her phone and started dialing on it before holding it up to her ear. "Babe, it's me. You and Colt need to meet us at the water.....I don't care Ty, we couldn't just sit there waiting it out. Yes, she is fine. No, we haven't found them yet. Yes. Okay. See you in a sec."

She turned in my direction. "They are about five minutes away. He is goin' to call Conner and have them come here too. He said they found Thunder running around in the woods. He is pissed we left the house."

"Let's just keep looking." Colt was going to be irate, but Miranda was right, we couldn't just sit there doing nothing while our children were in danger.

We walked past three little covered spaces with no sign of the kids. I continued to call out into the night for Noah and Bella. Knowing that the guys were on their way, I let go of Miranda's hand and sat on a large rock next to the lake. My stomach was knotted up and my legs were exhausted. I rubbed on my calf muscles while Miranda stood behind me flashing her light around. She continued to call out to the kids. The water was running from the woods edge and draining down into the water. I sat on the rocks watching it pour in. The muddy water was flowing fast all around us and with the winds picking up, nothing was secure. If the children were anywhere near this place, they were in grave danger. One false move and they would be carried away by the strong current.

When we heard the Gator heading toward us, I knew that we had run out of time to find the kids on our own. Miranda and I had exhausted all of our ideas of where our two children could be hiding. The headlights lit the area around us, and soon Ty and Colt were running in our direction. Colt held out his hand for me and I grabbed it and stood up, but my foot lost its gripping and my hands were too wet for Colt to grip on to. The water was draining so fast into the lake from the rain. The large rock I was standing on gave way, sending me sliding right down with it and straight into the water. One second I was holding on to my husband and the next I was being pulled away from him.

All I could think of was Noah and my unborn child. We didn't have time to waste on saving me. They had to focus on the kids. I needed to save myself.

My first concern was the temperature of the water, but it wasn't too freezing. The second thing I was worried about was something hitting me in the stomach. I brought my knees as high as they would go. It wouldn't protect me from pointed branches, but large items such as rocks would not get to my belly. The current was pulling me toward the center and grabbing hold of something was becoming more difficult.

Colt yelled my name as I went under the water for the first time, fighting the current. I grabbed at everything that I could to try and steady myself. Colt continued to run along the water's edge. He was screaming my name, never losing sight of me. He dove right into the water after me, swimming with the current to reach me faster. When I felt his strong arms grabbing me, I knew I would be safe. He grabbed a log that was half in the water and half out and we sat there waiting for Ty to get to us. As Ty slowly made his way out onto the log, something caught my eye. Actually, I don't know why I looked over, but when I did I saw something I never thought we were going to see again.

Two little kids were cuddle together under the shelter of a bunch of rocks and logs. "NOAH!" I screamed at the top of my lungs. As Colt climbed out of the water and he and Ty pulled me to safety, I just kept yelling for my son. "NOAH! NOAH!"

The guys shined a light in the direction I was pointing and saw the two kids. They went flying toward them, leaving me standing there shivering with anticipation of holding Noah in my arms. Ty and Colt came walking out into the opening and as the storm continued to flash lightening across the sky, I saw two beautiful children being carried in the arms of their fathers. They were soaking wet and both crying, but we found them. We were all going to be okay.

Chapter 23

Colt

That there had to be the scariest moment of my entire life. I thought Savanna being taken was hard, but not knowing if I was going to find my child was terrifying. I would never want to watch my wife slipping out of my grasp and falling into that water again, but if she hadn't, we never would have found them. Ty and I had to climb and maneuver over a bunch of wet limbs and a slippery embankment to get to them. There was no way we could have spotted them unless we were in the water.

Savanna helped save them both.

Conner and John pulled in as we got the other Gator. They jumped off and grabbed the girls, not wasting any time getting them back to the house. Ty and I held our kids on our laps as we followed behind the other Gator. We were a good ten minutes drive away from the house. I still couldn't believe the kids had gotten this far away from us.

The ride back to the house seemed to take forever. The kids were weeping, but neither of them would say a single word.

The wind was dropping trees all around us and three times we saw John and Conner ahead of us having to take different routes, due to fallen timbers.

John rushed Savanna into the house, while Miranda and Conner stood waiting for us to pull up behind them. We never let go of the kids as we rushed them into the house. I could hear Savanna fighting John from upstairs. He must have been insisting that she change into dry clothes before she came down to worry with the children. She was very pregnant and her safety was a major concern.

John came down shaking his head as he walked toward both of the kids sitting on the couch. Miranda and Ty went running up the steps gathering blankets and dry clothes. Both of their lips were purple and shivering. Ty and Miranda started removing Bella's wet clothes while I did the same to poor Noah. He wouldn't look directly at me, and I went to lift up his arm, he screamed out in agony.

"What is it? What hurts?" I asked.

He just kept screaming and screaming. I had to get his shirt off to see what was going on. I jumped up and ran into the kitchen for a pair of scissors. I was as gentle as I could as I tried to remove the shirt. Noah continued to cry out, even when he saw Savanna hurrying down the steps toward him.

Through his cries, I heard him say 'Mommy'. She crouched down at his side and rubbed his little head.

"Mommy's here, baby. Mommy's here." She helped me remove the rest of his clothes and watched his body tightened up as we moved the shirt away from his injured arm. From Noah's shoulder down to his elbow was black and blue, and I could tell from one single glance that it was completely dislocated.

Savanna and I looked at each other, while behind us we heard Conner. "I will drive."

If things weren't such an emergency. I may have worried about Conner's sobriety, but he seemed like he had his head on straight and was determined to get us there safely.

He knew, as well as everyone in the house, that Noah needed immediate medical attention. I looked over at Ty and Miranda and got a good look at Bella. She had some dried blood on the side of her head and some scratches on her arms. Miranda had a washcloth and was trying to clean the mud off of the child to see the extent of her injuries. Ty turned around to face me. "We need to take them both to get checked out. They could have concussions and shit."

I was trying to remain calm around the children, and I knew Ty didn't like to curse around Bella, so he was obviously in a nervous wreck. "Let's go then. I think Savanna needs to get checked out as well."

She nodded and walked over to grab some shoes. I got Noah some dry pants on, but wrapped a blanket around his body instead of trying to dress him with a shirt. The boy was in excruciating pain.

We ended up having to take two of the ranch trucks to the hospital to accommodate the whole family, and even my mother and Aunt Karen showed up moments later.

We were thankful that the hospital wasn't too crowded and took the kids and Savanna back within fifteen minutes of us arriving there.

Although we were put into separate rooms, we were able to keep checking on each other since the emergency room was not crowded with patients. Bella had minor scrapes and some bruising from where she fell off of the horse. They did some x-rays and other tests to check for concussions and any internal bleeding, but she seemed to be just banged up.

Savanna was immediately hooked up to monitors and seen by an OBGYN. The baby was fine and they even left the monitor on so everyone could hear the heartbeat. Just as an extra precaution they did a sonogram and offered to keep her overnight for observation.

Noah was the worst off. He had a gash on the back of his head, that required two stitches. His shoulder was dislocated. He had one broken rib and a broken arm, in two places. They had to re-set his arm and I can't even explain the agonizing sound that came out of my son when they did. They gave him something for the pain that also seemed to relax him and allow him to rest.

Even though he did not have a concussion, they were having him stay overnight as well.

With Bella being discharged a few hours later, The family started to head out, leaving me with just my immediate family. Once Savanna knew that the baby was okay, she became adamant that she be able to share a room with Noah. I think under normal circumstances it wouldn't have been possible, but the nurses were very kind and got Noah moved into Savanna's room. He didn't really need to be hooked up to any monitors, so it wasn't necessary to transfer all of the equipment over.

Once Savanna had Noah by her side, she started to relax. Her blood pressure had been high due to the anxiety of the night, but it went back to normal almost at the exact moment our son came into the room. She held his hand and kept watching him.

I was still pretty angry that she had gone out and risked her safety, but I knew we wouldn't have found Noah otherwise.

I tried to sleep while my family slept, but I think my adrenaline was still in full force playing out every moment in my head. When all this was done and we were home safe, I was determined to get to the bottom of why my son thought it was okay to sneak on a horse he wasn't familiar with. I never wanted to bust his little butt until this stunt he pulled. That boy had put not only his life, but his cousin Bella's life, in danger.

The thoughts of punishing my son were interrupted when I heard Savanna's voice.

"Hey Baby."

"How you feelin' Darlin'?"

"My legs are killing me, but I feel better now that I know everyone is okay. Colt, I'm so sorry that I went out into the storm. I couldn't sit at home just waiting. I had to go out and look for them."

I shook my head. "I'm not goin' to say I'm not angry with you. What you did was reckless and you put not only yourself but our baby in danger. If something would have happened to you I couldn't live with myself."

"Nothing happened. Well, nothing terrible. We are all okay Colt." Savanna knew things had happened and she could have lost that baby. I was pissed and she needed to know it, but at the same time, I was so damn happy that they were safe now.

"Savanna, what you did was careless, but you are the reason the kids are safe now. I don't know how to feel about it when you're the only reason for that. I love you Darlin', but please be more careful."

She started to cry. I watched her look over at Noah and caress his little hand with hers. "I just love him so much, Colt. I couldn't spend one more second not knowing he was safe. I'm not sorry for what I did and if I had to make the choice again, it would be the same. I'm his mother and it is my job to protect, even if it means risking my own safety."

I figured that it was best if I just dropped the conversation all together. Savanna was pretty clear about her feelings. None of us could get much sleep at the hospital, so when it came time for them both to be released, we rushed out of there to get home to our comfortable bed. Of course Savanna wasn't ready to let Noah anywhere out of our sight. She put the boy right between us in bed and had her arm around him immediately.

She loved that boy so much, it brought tears to my eyes.

The family started showing up some time after lunch. My mother and Lucy brought a whole spread over to feed everyone. Bella was attached to Ty and she and Noah hadn't really said much to each other.

Savanna put a show on for Noah and Bella to watch and they sat there together not saying much to one another. We all just kept watching them, wondering why they couldn't talk to each other. Finally Miranda went over and squatted in front of them. "Hey, you two. What's goin' on? How come you aren't sayin' much to each other?"

They both shrugged but refused to look toward the other.

"I think we would all like to know what exactly happened yesterday. Who had the idea to get on those horses?"

They finally looked at each other before looking back at Miranda. Savanna had sat down across from them, while the rest of us stood behind the couch. I leaned down and patted Noah on the shoulder. "Buddy, you need to tell us all what happened. I know last night was scary, but we need to know what happened."

"I don't want to get in trouble," he said sadly.

Miranda grabbed his knee. "Noah, Sweetie, we aren't askin' because we want to yell at you. We just want to know so it never happens again."

The little guy put his head down and stared at his knees. "Bella wanted to. She said she knew how."

Bella started crying and we all turned in her direction. "Bella, did you tell Noah you knew how to ride?"

"I'm sorry, Mommy." Bella cried harder and Miranda put her hand over her mouth in shock. Ty came up beside her and lifted his daughter's face.

"Izzy, Honey, why would you do something like that? You know better than to do something like that."

"I know, Daddy. Please don't be mad." The little four year old leaned forward against her father's chest. He wrapped his arms tightly around her and kissed her head.

"Iz, you can't do anything like that ever again." He pushed her away to be able to look her in the eyes. He took his thumbs and wiped them away. "Do you understand me?"

"Yes, sir." She put her head down again and continued to cry.

"You need to apologize to your cousin."

It seemed like Bella found it to be hard to look over at Noah. I suppose it was the first time she had ever lied to him and it made her feel awful. "Sorry, Noah."

"Okay," he said quietly.

I cut off the apology. "How did the two of you even get up high enough to saddle the horses?"

"We stood on the feed buckets," Noah replied.

I shook my damn head and let out a chuckle. Of course he knew to do something like that, he was my child after all.

"Well, you know you shouldn't have done it, even if Bella said she knew how. Neither one of those saddles was tight enough to ride."

"I won't do it again, I swear." Noah looked so sad, even after Savanna came over and kissed him on the head.

"So who fell off first?" Conner asked from across the room. Of course, when I looked over at him I couldn't help but notice the beer bottle in his hand. My focus was on the kids today, not my cousin.

"I did. Thunder got spooked from the storm and threw me off. He took off right away. Bella hopped down to help me, but Atticus ran away too. We were scared of the storm and kept hearin' noises, so we hid," Noah explained.

"Honey, how did you maneuver over those rocks while you were in that much pain? The embankment was slippery." Savanna waited for Noah to reply.

"Bella and I held hands. Once we got inside, it was too slippery to get back out."

"Noah, we should all be so angry with you, but since you both are home safe and went through so much, we aren't goin' to punish you. This will never happen again, Son. Do you understand me? You could have been killed. Both of you." The more I looked at my injured son, the more grateful I was to have him home. Last night had been rough on everyone, I couldn't imagine being a little child and going through that dark storm with those injuries.

Two pregnant women had battled weather and horrible conditions to save their children. We were physically and mentally drained. Even though Savanna and I had taken a nap, I could tell she was still tired.

The kids settled down and finally started talking to each other after they realized they weren't in trouble. It was kind of cute how they were protecting each other. I wondered if they sat in that protected spot and talked about it.

The family all seemed to calm down after lunch and we spent the rest of the day together. It was still raining outside and with Noah's arm in not only a cast, but also a brace, he couldn't play with much. After they ate, he and Bella cuddled up on the couch and watched some movies. Us adults played some cards in the dining room and sat around catching up.

Ty and Miranda were leaving first thing in the morning to go home, so after everyone except for them left, we sat down and talked about our idea for Conner. At first, Miranda didn't like our idea, but after we really explained the situation, she seemed to ease up and agree with us about it. She knew that it would benefit not only Conner, but the whole family if he moved out to their farm.

Conner may have been going through some hard times, but he was damn good at his job and he knew exactly what to do to get Ty started up and running. It would be easy for us to talk him into going there if he didn't think it was just to get him clean. We had talked about this business opportunity for a long time. He would never suspect it to be anything else.

Everything was going to work out with Conner and our new business venture. At the end of the day our decisions were about protecting our family.

Chapter 24

Savanna

It was hard to say that Ty and Miranda's visit wasn't disastrous. I felt horrible and wished I could somehow make it up to them. I kept trying to replay the kids disappearing in my head. There was no way of knowing they would pull a stunt like they had, but maybe I could have prevented it if I were paying more attention to them.

Even though I talked to Miranda almost every single day, it was still different when they came to visit. So, when they came for weekends, I got so excited and spent all of my time trying to entertain and make sure we all had a good time. I knew the children weren't just my responsibility, Miranda was there as well and she would never have blamed me for it. I just felt horrible that it had happened.

We watched with sad eyes as their family pulled away from our house and set out on their long ride home. An instant emptiness filled my heart every time they went home. Even with all of the people my age that I had met in college and in town here, they never gave me the friendships that Ty and Miranda gave me. I guess them being my family was also another reason.

We were all pretty nervous with the Conner situation, but right before they pulled away, Ty made sure Colt knew he would have the room ready for Conner by the end of the week. I was kind of thinking that Conner would have an issue about moving away from everything he knew, but he took the news calmly, even thanking Ty for giving him a chance to make things right.

I don't know if it was the boy's intervention that scared Conner or him being out there during our family emergency, but something had been an eye opener. He had even woke up early with Ty and helped him load up the car. Then he and Bella went for a ride on the golf cart, before everyone headed over to our place.

Noah was a sight for sore eyes. The poor little guy still felt bad for what they had done. He was in so much pain still, but tried his best to hang out with Bella. He let her draw all over his cast, leaving little room for the rest of the family and his friends at school.

After watching everyone leave, I turned around to see my sad little boy sitting on the porch. I approached him and lifted his chin with my hand. "They will be back to visit soon, baby."

"Mom," He was beginning to transition from Mommy to Mom. It was both cute and sad all at the same time. I guess that is what happens when you are entering kindergarten. "will I ever be allowed to ride a horse again?"

I let out a sigh before sitting down on the step beside him. Colt was standing behind him and sat on the step above us. I guess he wanted to be in on the conversation. "Noah, what happened yesterday was an accident. I know right now you think everyone is mad at you. We aren't really mad. It's just that we love you so much and couldn't imagine if anything ever happened to you."

Before I could continue, Noah interrupted. "You mean something like what happened to my mom Krista?"

Colt patted Noah on the head. "Yeah, Buddy, like that. You already know that doing something like that can get you hurt. We spent half the night in the emergency room because of it."

"I know Dad. I didn't mean to cause trouble. I just wanted Bella to have a good time. I told her my Dad was a cowboy and she said I wasn't old enough to be a real cowboy. I figured if I rode around on the horses, she would believe me."

Colt leaned down and kissed Noah's head. "The next time you get a bright idea like that, you need to clear it with Mom or I first, you hear me boy?"

"Yes, sir."

I leaned in toward him and kissed his cheek. "We just don't want anything happening to you, Noah. We love you so much."

"I love you too, Mommy and I love Daddy. I'm real sorry for what I did. It won't happen again. I need to be a good boy so that I can be a good brother." He reverted back to Mommy when he was sad.

Good to know....I get to be called Mommy when he is emotional.

"That's right! You do need to be responsible so that you can set a good example for your brother or sister," I agreed.

"My brother, Mom. We all know I am having a brother."

Colt and I both laughed. Colt rubbed him on the head. "We will love the baby either way, right Noah?"

He sighed and shook his head. "Yeah, I guess so. I just really want a brother."

"Sisters are really cool too. You would get to be her protector." I tried for all these months to get him to not care if it was a boy or girl and he just wouldn't budge.

"They can't play with tractors or legos and they wear those stupid bows in their hair." Noah spoke like girls were the devil. It was quite funny, even though Colt and I were both worried the baby was going to be a girl and totally devastate our son.

"Sweetie, little girls can play with tractors and legos. They don't have to always wear the bows in their hair, and they most certainly don't have cooties."

"Not all of them," Colt added sarcastically.

I looked up at him. "Not helping, Babe"

He just kept grinning and threw me a wink. I had to laugh at him, making a joke out of something that really scared me.

We were interrupted as tiny drops of rain started hitting us. We followed Colt into the house and plopped down on the couch. Noah was playing with his cast, dragging his fingernail over it. "It itches."

"I had a cast a few times. You know what I did?" Colt asked.

"What?" Noah was so curious.

"I got a stick and stuck it inside to get the itch out."

Noah's eyes got huge. "Does that really work?"

We started laughing at our son. "It sure does. You want me to go find you a nice stick?"

"Colt, seriously?"

"Darlin', he needs to itch. I will hook him up." Colt disappeared out of the front door, only to reappear with a stick in his hand. "Here, Buddy, try this."

I watched my son shoving a dirty stick down his arm. Immediately he screamed out.

"What happened?"

"I guess it is still sore inside, that's all. It's cool. It doesn't itch anymore."

I rolled my eyes at Colt, who still had a smile on his face.

We hung out at the house for the rest of the afternoon until we had to go to Colt's mothers for dinner. It was always the same family atmosphere on Sunday's. Thankfully, Conner decided to only grant us with his presence. We ended up staying over there until it was close to midnight.

By the time that Colt and I got Noah to bed I was exhausted. My gorgeous husband had other intentions. For some reason the house had been hot when we got home. I stripped down to my bra and panties and sprawled across the bed on my back, letting the ceiling fan cool off me and my giant belly.

Colt never took his eyes off of me as he unbuckled his belt and jeans and walked out of them. His strong arms pulled his shirt away from his muscular body. I watched his arm flex where the mustang tattoo sat and I bit down on my lip.

In only his boxers my sexy ass husband came crawling across the bed toward me. Now, I have to say that my choice of bra and panties were not what I would have called sexy. Aside from not being able to see past my stomach, I didn't really wear a lot of sexy underwear to bed. I needed to be as comfortable as possible. Colt was already having to compete with my pregnancy pillow Miranda had got me. I loved that thing, but Colt said it was a CB pillow, because it always blocked him from getting any.

I heard a low grumble as he positioned himself between my legs and pressed his lips on my belly. In retrospect, I knew I wasn't that large. I had gained fifteen pounds and it was all in my stomach. People told me every day they couldn't tell I was pregnant from the back.

I still had about three months to go and knew my belly would soon double in size. I tried to eat right, but I always had thoughts of not being able to turn my husband on when my weight got too high. So, as Colt's hands slowly removed my granny panties, and I heard the low groan coming from his chest, I knew that he wasn't going to let me rest until he got some much needed attention.

"Are you hot Darlin'?"

His hands traced over my sex and I gasped at how good it felt. "Yes, plus I didn't shave my legs today." I was getting lazy, I knew it.

In one swift pull, I was in Colt's arms being carried to the bathroom. He sat me on the edge of the sink and walked over to the shower, grabbing shaving cream and a razor.

"Holy Shit! Babe, what are you doing?"

Colt ignored me, getting down on his knees and wetting my legs with a rag, before putting shaving cream on the leg he propped on his shoulder. "Trust me Darlin'. I'll never hurt you." He kissed my foot and started spreading the cream evenly.

I gasped when I felt the razor gliding across my skin. Colt took his time licking his lips and even took quick glances at my naked crotch. It used to make me feel uncomfortable, but everything that man did now made me horny. Maybe it was my hormones, but I couldn't get enough of him. In fact, there were times when I was home alone and had to call him, because just thinking about him naked made me wet for him.

Colt finished with one of my legs before repeating the process on the other one. I had to admit, it felt good, after I got over the initial shock of what he was doing. It tickled, especially when he got to my inner thighs and let his hands linger there. When he finished with the second leg, he used a washrag to wipe off the excess shaving cream. He glided the warm rag up and down my thighs, making sure I felt it through my whole body.

As the rag went flying back into the sink, I felt my legs being lifted as my body was shifted to be lying on the cold marble vanity top. He put his finger up to his lips when I started to say something. I felt the back of his hand rubbing me between my legs, before he began to spread the shaving cream all over my sex.

This was hot!

It was so hot that the fear of being cut was long gone. What replaced it was a sudden heat covering all of my body. As Colt continued to spread the shaving cream, for obviously way longer than it should have taken, I watched my stomach rising and falling as my breathing increased. If I thought I was hot in the bedroom, well now I was burning up.

Colt's naked body was now standing over me, staring at his task at hand, or in hand.

"You okay Darlin'?"

I saw the razor in his hand and all I could think about was him touching me again. The absence was killing me, making me pant for more. "Yes, I love you. Please don't stop."

Colt spread my legs as he slowly began shaving where I could no longer see. I did a good job keeping myself hairless and had made an appointment for a waxing, unfortunately for the salon, Colt had other hair removing plans.

I could feel him moving my skin around, as well as feel every single glide of the razor against my skin. Colt used his hands to test and make sure he hadn't missed any spots. He turned on the faucet and filled the rag with fresh water before placing it between my legs to removed the shaving cream. Every swipe of that rag made my body buck.

Colt liked what he saw. He found my eyes and then moved his gaze to my chest. Without letting me off of the cold porcelain sink, he leaned down and removed my bra. Colt let the air hit my nipples and they hardened right up for him. He licked his lips before dragging his tongue over one of my nipples. My hands reached up and grabbed his hair. I pulled him up to my mouth and kissed him roughly, teasing him with my tongue as he pulled away.

"I want you, babe."

I moaned as his fingers penetrated my sex. "Oh Darlin', there is no denyin' that. I can feel it for myself."

He cupped one of my breasts and licked it again, never taking his eyes off of me. His fingers moved slowly backing in and out of me. "It...feels.....so...goooooood!" The words were stretching, because I couldn't think and react at the same time.

He brought one of my legs up and spread them wider as he spun me around and wrapped my legs around his waist. "Time to get into our big bed." My arms wrapped around Colt's neck and he held me as his strong arms carried me to our bed.

He laid us down gently and found my mouth right away. Gentle, soft kisses soon turned into carnal desire. Colt had to use his arms to prevent from laying on my belly, so it was easier to just flip him over and straddle his fine ass myself. I wrapped my legs around him, suggesting we trade places without having to stop kissing him. He knew what I wanted and happily obliged.

His large erection brushed against my leg and I let out a moan just knowing that it would soon be inside of me. Making love to Colt was always so intense. Between the size of him and how nurturing he always was, he could make me orgasm multiple times. The intensity of knowing his hard shaft was down there ready to slide right in, turned me on so much. I reached my hand down and grabbed his erection. After feeling it, I couldn't help but want to see it.

I slid down further, still holding on to his girth. My tongue slid over the tip, making him shiver underneath of me. I blew on the wetness, before licking it again. This time I filled my mouth with saliva and let it fall out over the tip of his shaft. My fingers spread it over him, using it as lubrication.

He stuck his arm behind his head and watched me playing with my tongue. I kept my eyes on him watching me, trying so hard not to close his eyes. When it filled my mouth, he let out a groan and his eyes closed tightly before he reopened them, biting down on his lip.

The more I sucked, the more sounds came from deep inside of his chest. I had to reposition myself a few times, to keep comfortable, but my mouth never left its task. Soon, Colt was grabbing my hair and closing his eyes more and more.

He never told me to stop, but as I could tell he was getting close, he pulled me up by my hair and shook his head, before kissing me on my lips. His strong arms lifted me until I was lined right up over his hard shaft. I scooted just enough to slowly drop down over his hardness, letting him slide inside of my hot sex. It was always tight and painful at first, but I had come to like it. My first orgasms always happened in the first couple seconds of initial friction. Just like usual, I cried out for Colt as my body began to tremble over top of him. He groaned as I whispered his name and collapsed over his mouth for a full blown make-out session.

Colt sat us both up, allowing me to hold on to his strong shoulders. He began lifting my still trembling body up and down by holding on to my ass. I used my legs and began rocking against him harder. My hands dug into his back as I felt another explosion coming my way. This one lasted longer than the first. I knew my nails were digging into his skin, but I kept my hold on him as the unbelievable sensations traveled all over my body. Colt bit down on my shoulder as he matched my climax. Instead of letting me rock back and forth, he kept me still, until he was able to move again.

I let go of his back and accepted his mouth on mine again. I loved his tongue and the way his full lips felt when they were wet. He pressed his forehead against mine. "I love you so fuckin' much, Savanna. I know we have had a rough couple of years, but we got through it. We have a son and beautiful baby comin' in a few months. Being married to you was the best decision I ever made. Thank you for this life Darlin'. It's everything I ever wanted."

Tears fell down my face. "Colt, there is no place else I would rather be then here with you, with our children. You have given me the most perfect life. Begging you to kiss me that first night was the best decision I ever made."

"Darlin', forcin' you to go to that damn bonfire was the best decision I ever made. That little number you wore was insane. It made me think things I shouldn't have been thinkin' that's for sure."

"I wore that to piss you off because you could never have me," I admitted.

He laughed and looked right at me. "Savanna, I wouldn't have taken advantage of you that night, but I'm pretty damn sure if I wanted you, I could have had you."

I lightly smacked his chest. "Are you being cocky?"

"No, I just see the way you look at me. You think I didn't notice it? Dressing like that to get my attention. You weren't just doin' that for that night. You were proving a point that you didn't look like a boy anymore, and my God Darlin', you didn't. You were the prettiest thing I think I ever laid eyes on."

"You weren't so bad yourself."

"Yeah, that's why it only took you a couple days before you couldn't resist my southern charm."

"Are you being serious right now? You're really that sure of yourself?" I wanted to know. He was being very ornery.

He started laughing, while stroking my arm. "Well, I reckon in the big picture of things that maybe I wanted it to happen. I mean, don't get me wrong, I didn't want to betray my cousin, but once I knew that you weren't really together, well that was a game changer for me. I wanted you so bad and walkin' away just wasn't in my mind. The more time we spent together, the more I knew you were the one for me. I just needed you to know it too."

I ran my hand over his face and leaned up to kiss his lips. Of course, I had to lay sideways to cuddle with Colt nowadays. "Falling in love with you was so easy. I tried to deny my feelings, but there was no way I could have ever been happy without you."

"Look at how happy we all are now. I know we have been through some hard times, but we have the best family and we are so close. I never could have pictured our life would be this way, especially with Ty."

"Ty is the reason I have you Colt. For a while I wanted to hate his guts, but I see my life with you and thank him every single day. Besides, I have never seen two people more made for each other than he and Miranda."

Colt kissed my forehead. "Except us Darlin'. We were also made for each other. At least, I know you were made for me."

"Except for us, babe."

Colt held me until I finally fell asleep, with only thoughts of our beautiful life in my mind.

Chapter 25

Colt

There was nothing better than waking up and feeling my baby kicking. Savanna was still asleep, but I couldn't help sliding over and putting my head over her belly. It didn't matter to me whether we were having a boy or a girl, I just couldn't wait to meet him or her.

Savanna stirred in bed and let out a little cackle when she saw what woke her. She ran her hand over my shoulder and through my hair.

I kissed her belly and smiled. "Mornin', Darlin'."

"Hey Baby," she whispered.

"I was just spendin' some quality time with the newest member of our family."

"I can see that. I was wonder......." Savanna was cut off by a fat yellow lab and a boy running in and jumping on our bed.

"Wake up! It's raining. Can Dad stay home today?" Noah climbed up between us, hugging his mother. He also bent down and kissed her belly. "Good morning Ninja."

"Ninja?" Savanna and I both laughed at the same time.

"Yeah, wouldn't it be cool if we named him Ninja? We could dress him in karate clothes and he would be super cool." My son's imagination made us both laugh.

"Noah, we can't name the baby Ninja. You really need to prepare yourself in case it is a girl."

"I have girl names too. You wanna hear em?"

Something told me that I should have said no. "Sure Buddy."

"I like Bella."

Savanna interrupted him. "Sweetie, we can't name the baby Bella, because it is already your cousin's name."

"But that is the only girl I like."

I looked to Savanna who was really cracking up. "Mommy has a book with all kinds of names. Maybe we could look at it together today, because guess what?"

"What?" He seemed excited.

"I'm staying home!"

We'd never taken care of an infant, albeit I never had any doubts about Savanna's mothering skills. If you asked our son, he would tell anyone that he had the best mother on the planet.

It just so happened that the day consisted of the worst rainfall we had seen so far this season. I had enough employees that on days like these I could stay home with my family. Of course, after having company over the weekend, we had run out of all of our favorite food and snacks, so we were forced to go out in the mess to fill our cupboards back up.

I made us all pancakes for breakfast, at both of their requests. Noah helped me as much as he could with one arm. He liked to make monster shapes and snakes. Savanna got out the cool whip and made him a six inch high stack of sweetness. Noah ate every single bite and sat back rubbing his belly. "Mmmmmm, thank you, Daddy."

"Did ya like em?" I asked, even though I already knew he did.

"Yup. What's for lunch?" Our son, the bottomless pit.

After helping my little buddy get dressed, we all climbed in the truck and headed to the grocery store. Savanna hated it when Noah and I went along, because we ended up buying all sorts of junk to eat. Noah and I together were her worst nightmare. We knew how to work as a team to get her to cave and buy what we wanted. He found it to be very fun, in a sneaky kind of way.

We'd been in the store for a good twenty minutes. Noah was riding on the back of the cart while I steered from the front. Savanna was behind us with her coupon contraption. She was totally involved in those damn things to notice where she was going. As we passed a couple in the center of the aisle, I turned around to make sure she was paying attention to where she was walking.

Before I could open my mouth to warn her, she collided with the female and her hand basket of groceries. Coupons went flying into the air, as did the woman's groceries. They both crouched down and began picking up their things. At first Savanna was only worried about picking up the mess and apologizing, but as I bent down to help my wife, I watched her get a good look at the lady.

They were both apologizing one minute and then in a frozen stare the next. We all stood up at the same time, in which Savanna grabbed our cart and headed out of the aisle one way, while the other couple went the opposite direction.

When I reached her, she was breathing heavy and basically hiding out in the corner of the store. I finally made it to her side and pulled her into my arms. "Darlin', what is goin' on? Did you know them?"

She looked up at me and had tears in her eyes. "Call the police Colt. Call them right now."

I had no idea what was going on, but as I pulled out my phone, I watched my wife hauling ass up one of the aisles. The nine-one-one operator came on the line asking what my emergency was, but I had no idea what to say.

After deciding to just have them send a cop to the grocery store, Noah and I went running after Savanna. She was standing by the window, in between two giant sales ads. With her coupon book in one hand and a pen in the other, she started jotting down something. I got closer and saw it was a tag number and the make and model of a car. "Savanna? Tell me what this is about."

Both Noah and I were standing there waiting for her to explain. She was trying to talk, but hyperventilating instead. A cashier came running over, handing her a brown bag to breathe into. She grabbed Savanna by the arm and sat her down on a nearby bench. I stood over her waiting to find out what the hell was going on. Savanna was holding onto her belly, but not acting like she was in any pain.

After a few minutes and the sound of police sirens in the distance, she looked up at me. "They were the ones with Tucker, the ones the police never caught. They were the ones that helped him take me. They took our baby from us Colt."

I crouched down to my knees and pulled her into my arms. "Jesus, Darlin' I had no idea."

She shook her head against my shoulder. "It's not your fault. You didn't know." She began crying heavily and I couldn't make out her words. Noah sat down beside his mother and held her hand. He surely had no idea about what was going on, but he sure as shit did a good job supporting her. Through her tears she leaned down and kissed his head.

"It will be okay, Mommy."

"Thank you, Baby." She looked up at me and finally started to calm down.

The police came in shortly and were directed toward us. Of course, they wanted her whole statement, which required us to go to the station. After paying for our groceries, we stopped by the station and Savanna talked to the original officer on the case. He was very kind to her and she finally calmed down after time.

The police put out a bulletin about the vehicle and the two passengers. Savanna never had a name for them and with

Tucker dead, she never seemed to care about what happened to the other two people. It was later that afternoon that she explained she had received a letter stating they were closing the case about a month before. At the time, she was so focused on Tucker being dead and what she had to go through, that she didn't seem too concerned about the other people involved. Tucker's mother was never charged on account of lack of evidence. Her attorneys played some bullshit scenario that Savanna couldn't have been in her right mind after being kidnapped. They claimed that her overhearing a telephone call did not prove his mother was on the other end of that call.

With Savanna home safely, and suffering from major post traumatic stress, we didn't talk much about it. She saw a doctor and through therapy and medication, she finally got better. What really healed my wife was Noah. He made her forget the pain and look forward to our future.

My son held true to being Savanna's biggest supporter. In the police station, he stayed by her side, clinging to her. On the way home, she sat in the back seat next to him, while he was still holding her hand.

Noah was a good boy. He never asked questions, but just stayed close to her for support. It was the same case once we got home and she started to relax. Instead of going upstairs to his playroom, he cuddled with his mother on the couch. After a couple of hours, he finally fell asleep still attached to her. I carried him upstairs to his bed, before coming down to sit with Savanna.

"You okay, Darlin'?"

She leaned her body into mine. "I'm sorry for losing it today. I saw them and everything that happened came flashing back into my mind. Our baby, the miscarriage, I just couldn't handle it Colt. I know that neither of us will forget our baby, but that just brought back all of the bad shit too."

"Darlin', you don't have to apologize to me. If I could trade places with you and take away that pain, I would in a heartbeat, you know that. I hate that you went through that."

"I just panicked. One minute I was apologizing for bumping into her and the next second I am running for my life again. I can't explain it any better than that."

I kissed the top of her head and ran my fingers through her hair. "Try not to let it bother you. You positively identified the other two people involved. You gave them the vehicle. They have their names and will catch them Savanna. They both have records and they will be put away for a long time. They will be held responsible for what they did."

She sobbed in my arms and finally, after some time, her sobbing subsided. "There is something I have to tell you about that night, Colt. I can't keep it from you any longer."

My stomach immediately knotted up. I couldn't imagine what she needed to tell me. My first thought was that he raped her. The saliva was building up in my mouth just thinking about someone doing that to my wife. A part of me didn't want to know, but I knew I had to. "You can tell me anything, Darlin'."

She shook her head. "Not this Colt. If I tell you this, then you probably won't want me anymore."

Is she nuts? I could never not want her.

"That's not possible, Sugar."

I brushed the tears away from her face and waited for her to start talking. She looked down at her wedding ring and began twisting it around. "When Tucker took me I was so afraid. All I could think about was getting home to you and keeping our baby safe. He had me tied up in that basement by plastic wire ties. At first he wasn't physically violent. He was verbally threatening me, but he never inflicted physical violence on me, aside from subduing me."

She leaned over and took a drink of her water. "He kept leaving me alone in that basement. I could hear him upstairs talking to the two other people. A couple times he came downstairs to check on me. Every single time he left me alone, I did everything I could to free my hands from those ties."

"I saw your wrists Savanna. I know what you had to do to get free." I ran my hand over her face, moving the hair out of her eyes.

She shook her head again and looked right at me. "He came down this one time saying he was going to make a phone call and that I had to tell you I was okay, so I guess he could get your money. Tucker didn't know that I had freed my hands. I wasn't going to sit around waiting to be found. Nobody would have known where I was. So, I waited until the right moment. He went upstairs and I tried to climb out of a window. He came flying down those steps and ripped me from the window, causing me to fall all the way down to the concrete floor."

I was picturing it all playing out in my head and all I could see was how petrified she must have been. "You don't have to tell me anymore, Darlin'."

"No Colt, I do. You need to know this." She wiped her tears and looked back at my face. "I tried to fight him, to protect myself and the baby, but he kept kicking me and hitting me. I felt that boot go into my stomach and my side. I felt what was happening inside of my body, Colt. Tucker killed our baby, but I couldn't put all of the blame on him."

I cut her off. "What are you talkin' about? Of course you can blame that son of a bitch for it."

She shook her head again. "No Colt. As he was beating me, he was telling me that hurting me was never the plan. He was beating me *because* I ruined his plan. It was my fault he laid a hand on me. It was my fault our baby died. I killed our baby. It was me. I did it, not Tucker. If I would have just sat there and waited, our baby would have lived. It was all my fault."

I pulled her into my chest. "Jesus Savanna, you can't believe that. You were trying to escape from being kidnapped. You didn't kill our baby. Don't you ever think that way. Darlin' I would never blame you for what happened. You need to get that out of your pretty little head. Tucker Chase did all of this, not you."

She cried so hard in my chest and I couldn't blame her. She had been carrying around that guilt for over a year. It was time for her to understand she wasn't to blame.

"How can you not be mad at me Colt? If I would have just listened to him, our baby would be alive today. It's my fault for trying to get away."

I cupped my hands over her face. "You listen to me right now and you listen good. You are not to blame for what happened to the baby. You acted on instinct to try and survive. You were trying to save our baby and yourself. What happened was a horrible accident, but you are not to blame for it. Don't you ever say that again Savanna. Please don't ever even think that." I pulled her back into my chest. "I thought I was never going to see you again, Darlin'. I was so scared over it. Losing our child was awful, but losing you would have ended me. I don't want to ever be without you. I will miss our first baby forever, but I will never ever blame you for what happened. You never should have been in that basement in the first place. If it's anyone's fault, it's Miranda's for bringin' that piece of shit into our lives."

Savanna pulled away from me and shook her head. "No, I will never blame her. People make their own choices in life. Miranda was never anything like Tucker. She had no idea he was capable of being the person he became when they first met. I will never blame her. I love her too much to put the blame on her."

"Then stop blamin' yourself. It ain't nobody but Tucker's fault."

She agreed by smiling. "Okay, I will try."

For the rest of the evening we all three lounged around the house. Noah woke up from his nap and claimed he was dying of starvation, so Savanna made us all grilled cheese sandwiches. She cut Noah's in the shape of a heart, which he got a big kick out of. He still ate the cutoff pieces, claiming the crusts were the best part.

We sat around the kitchen table laughing and carrying on and I felt like somehow something had changed. Savanna seemed at peace.

Chapter 26

The next three months went by so quickly. The bigger I
got, the more Noah and Colt did for me. I wasn't helpless, in fact
I spent most of my days trying to reorganize the entire house
and Colt's garage. He was fine about the house, but when he
came home to me standing in the garage in one of his winter
coats, putting screws into jars, he lost his temper with me.

It was funny, he never raised his voice. He got this mad
look on his face, that was more sexy than scary and he pointed
to the door to the house. I took a second to finish up what I was
doing before stomping back into the warm house.

The winter was rough and we were being pounded by
another snow storm. It didn't help that I was in full nesting mode
and bored out of my mind. Every drawer, cabinet, and closet in
our house had been completely organized. I even went on a
binge and made photo collages for the whole family. I was out of
my mind. Our little baby had begun moving around so much at

night that I wasn't getting any sleep. I had two weeks to go until my official due date and I was going totally insane.

Sunday morning came and I knew we were at least going to trudge through the snow to get to Colt's mother's for Sunday funday. Noah had been going in and out of the house constantly. Colt was trying to clear me a good path to walk to the truck, I felt bad he had to go through such hard work just for me to have dinner at his mother's house. Noah had already built three snowmen and I was running out of household items to use for the faces. We were out of grapes, carrots and buttons, as well as toothbrushes. He used the toothbrushes instead of pipes because he learned smoking was bad for your health.

By noon, I had dried his snowsuit three separate times, washed the foyer floor around ten times and done three loads of laundry. When Colt said it was time to head over, I was beat. I threw on a pair of his sweatpants from college, that were old as shit and came walking downstairs. I looked like the abominable snowman.

"Darlin' is that what you're wearin'?" He knew as soon as he said it that it was a mistake. You NEVER talk about a pregnant woman's attire.

"Yes, this is what I'm wearing. Why? We are going to your mother's not a fashion show."

He started to say something, but bit his tongue and changed his tone. "I was just wonderin' if you are goin' to be comfortable, that's all." He smacked my ass as I walked past him.

"Seriously? That hurt."

"You liked it. Stop your complainin' before I take you upstairs and give you some more." I knew he was teasing as I watched our son jump off the couch.

"I'm ready too!" Noah came to the front door in a pair of superman underwear, a hoodie and a cape, as well as giant red rain boots.

Oh, Good lord!

"Noah, Honey, what on earth are you wearing?" I asked.

"This is my superhero uniform. I need to be ready in case you go into labor, Mom."

Colt and I started laughing. Noah gave us a dirty look as Colt patted his head. "Buddy, you need to put on some pants for now, but when we get to Grandma's you can wear your uniform in the house."

He went running up the steps toward his room and I could hear his drawers opening to his dresser.

I looked to Colt who was still laughing. "I can't believe you told him he could take his pants off at your mother's. What has gotten into him anyway?"

"He is excited about the baby, that's all. I'm excited too."

Obviously...

"Well I do hope you don't start taking your pants off at the dinner table too."

"Darlin', I will be taking them off as soon as we get back, because there ain't nothin' sexier than seein' you in those old sweats."

Smooth talker!

I grabbed his cheek and pulled him down to me for a kiss. "Good come back."

"Are ya'll ready to go or what?" Noah came whipping down the stairs and started opening the front door.

Since it was an icy mess outside, Colt held my hand and slowly helped me walk down the porch stairs and then to the truck. He lifted my fat butt up into it with no strain on himself. It was really nice to have such a strong man. He patted my backside as I slid in.

He winked at me. "You liked that didn't you."

I leaned back out to whisper in his ear. "I will take care of this friskiness later on."

"You promise?"

I nodded as I watched him walk around the truck and help Noah to get in. I'd been so exhausted recently to worry about my appearance, but just moments before pulling up to the house I realized I hadn't even checked my hair. Colt was laughing at me as I tried to flip my hair up in some kind of neat ponytail with just my fingers as a brush.

Colt opened Noah's door and he went running into his grandma's house. Lucy would holler at him for getting the floor all messed up. Colt came around to my side and helped me get down. "You okay, Darlin'?"

"Yeah, it's just hard getting around. This little person inside of me has run out of room."

"I bet. Come on, let's get you inside the warm house."

Colt held my hand and led me into the house. He sat me down on a chair and started pulling off my boots. After he removed my jacket, we headed into the living room. The house was super quiet. I should have expected they were up to something.

I loud ensemble of 'SURPRISE' was being yelled from the hoard of people in the room. I jumped from being startled and got butterflies from the excitement. Noah came rushing to my side. "It's a party for my new brother, Mom."

"Maybe sister," I whispered in his ear.

I was greeted by everyone, including Miranda and my mother. I was so glad to see them that I almost didn't notice Bella sitting on Ty's lap in the corner. He nodded his head and gave me a wink, before turning back to talk to my dad and Colt.

Colt glanced over and mouthed the words 'I love you'.

I mouthed, 'you too', before directing my attention to all of the lovely people in the room.

My mother's arms wrapped around me. "Are you surprised? Did Colt tell you about it?"

I looked back over toward where Colt sat and saw him smiling. "No, he didn't tell me. Do you think I would have worn this," I pointed to my clothes. "if I knew this was happening."

"You look fine, Sweetie. My God, Noah has gotten so big. I can't get over it. Your father and I told him he could come spend a couple weeks this summer at our house. Of course, Tyler heard us and insisted he stay a week with them too."

I started laughing. "He and Bella just love each other so much. It would be nice for them to have all that time together. Although, with Miranda and Ty being pregnant, I don't know how they will handle a newborn and our two rug rats."

"Honey, if you are worried they will steal some horses, you have to know they wouldn't try that again." She sounded confident, but I knew my son, and the things he did to impress his cousin.

My mother and Colt's mother led me over to a corner chair and started handing me gifts. I was surprised that Miranda was around four months pregnant and she already had a little baby bump. It was her second pregnancy so I guess that was why.

She sat down next to me after giving me a big kiss, and started writing who my gifts were from.

"I can't believe you're here."

She reached for my hand. "Van, Ty and I would never miss this. We love you, Cuz."

"I love you too, so much. I hope you both know that."

She looked over at Ty and he gave her a big smile. "We do. So, did you pick out any names yet?"

"Aside from SpongeBob Square pants and Ninja Joe?" *Like that was ever going to happen.*

We both started laughing. "Have you and Colt picked out any names?"

"It's a surprise."

"Of course it is," she teased.

After opening the room full of presents, Colt and I had enough diapers to probably supply Ty and Miranda's baby as well as ours for the first two years. I have four sets of crib sheets, over twenty bottles, seven soft blankets, and a wardrobe of clothes sized from birth to two years. We got all kinds of seats and gadgets as well as a couple baskets of baby necessities. Ty and Miranda got me the breast pump that she swore by. Of course he had to add something smart in the card about watching me try it out. I just laughed. At this point in our lives I knew that Ty joked about everything. I'd learned to appreciate him for his sense of humor and his love for his family, because at the end of the day that was all that mattered.

After the hour of present opening, the party headed into the kitchen. It was the biggest spread I had ever seen. There were so many cool foods shaped like baby things, some being butts and rattles. Ty came over and showed me a plate with two cupcakes that he had purposely put two favors on top to look like nipples. "Van, look at what I'm eating for dinner."

"You would think with a daughter and a baby on the way, you could at least act right in public," I teased.

He smacked my ass and shoved one of the fake boobs into his mouth. "Never!" With a mouth full of cake he bent down and gave his daughter the other cupcake. I couldn't help but burst into laughter. Bella took her cupcake and licked it. When she didn't like the icing, she gave it to Ty, who ate the spot she had licked. She thought it was funny as I started to gag. "Aunt Van thinks Daddy is gross."

"My Daddy is the funniest person in the whole world." Bella leaned over and kissed Ty.

"I think you might be right kiddo."

Ty walked over toward the guys while Bella pulled me toward the large cake on the dining room table. "Look Aunt Van."

Wow!

The cake was a giant copy of our last 3-D sonogram photo. It was quite a difference seeing it so much larger than the smaller picture I was used to looking at. "It's so cool." Noah came up behind me and stood with Bella, looking at the cake.

"It's pretty amazing isn't it?"

"Is that how big the baby is now?" Bella asked.

I started giggling. "No. The baby will be small and we can hold it in our arms when it gets here."

"Well, I hope my mom's baby won't be that big. Then it would be an ogre like Shrek." Leave it to my kid to assume ogres were real. *Really? Ogres?*

Since the kids had found the dessert table, their attention went from the size of the baby, to how many desserts they could both eat before they threw up. I watched them for a couple moments before my mother caught my attention. She and Colt were sitting up at the breakfast bar, already involved in a conversation. I made my way through the crowd of family and friends and sat down next to them. "Were you really surprised, Sweetie?"

"I had no idea. Colt did good keeping this secret from me." I moved forward so I could get a good look at my sneaky husband's face.

"Colt was telling me that they want to induce you if you haven't gone into labor in the next two weeks. When you both find out a date you need to let me know. It's going to be hard for me to get a flight in little notice. If you make it to the induction date it will give me ample time to plan. You know your father and I don't want to miss it."

"I know. I was just kind of hoping I would deliver before that. This baby is just too stuffed in my body. I think it's time it blessed us with its presence."

"Oh Sweetie, it will be here when it's ready. You can't rush perfection. I'm sure you can make it a couple more weeks." My mother seemed confident. I didn't!

Aunt Karen got everyone's attention to play some yarn game. Apparently, you were supposed to take the string and guess how big my belly was. The closest person to guess how gigantic I was around, won the prize. I watched as the room full of men and women started taking spools of yarn and cutting out large strands, measuring them up to their own bellies.

It was quite comical until everyone was standing there with yarn that appeared to be over five feet long. I looked down at my big belly and rubbed it. *Was I really that gigantic? Good God!*

Colt came up behind me and shoved his yarn in his pocket. One by one the yarn was measured against my real body. I was so relieved when most of them were way bigger than I was. The people who were close lined up against the wall and waited to see who was the absolute closest. When everyone was finished, Colt pulled out his strand and reached it around my tummy. His strand was off by only one inch. Nobody else was that close, I was sure of it.

The room filled with laughter. "You cheater! Colt! You weren't allowed to play." Aunt Karen came up and grabbed the string out of his hand.

Everyone continued to laugh.

"So what do I win?"

She rolled her eyes and handed him a wrapped package. He opened it to reveal a small bottle of scented lotion. Colt got a huge grin on his face. He looked up at everyone in the room. "I bet this will make my ass smooth like a baby."

Even I began to laugh, but when I did something happened. I felt something warm and feared that I had just peed myself in front of our entire family. I closed my legs as tight as they could go, but continued to feel the gushing of warm liquid.

Colt stopped laughing and looked at my face. I slowly opened my legs to reveal the wet spot all over his sweat pants. "I think my water just broke," I whispered.

Colt stood up. "OH MY GOD HER WATER JUST BROKE!"

Chapter 27

Colt

The room filled with chaos as Savanna stood there in total shock. In the midst of all of our family, she was going into labor. Her mother and Miranda came rushing over to her side. I wouldn't say she was freaking out, but she definitely wasn't able to focus on anything.

She hadn't been complaining of having any labor pains, yet as soon as we got her standing and suggested she get cleaned up, she hunched over and grabbed the underside of her belly. We guided her back to the couch.

"Colt you need to head to the house to get her overnight bag. I will call the doctor and get her cleaned up. Grab her a clean pair of pants so that her legs don't get too cold going out in the cold air." My mother took charge of things, giving me orders on what I needed to do, but I just stood there.

Ty was standing over in the corner with Conner, but had walked over and grabbed me by the arm, pulling me out of the house. "Get in the game, Dude. You might have a baby by the end of the night."

I don't know whether it was his pep talk or the cold air hitting me in the face, but we both hopped into the truck and headed back to my place to get the bag that Savanna had gotten together for her hospital stay. Ty came into the house and waited for me at the door. I ran back down the stairs with her bag in my hand. "Did you get her clean pants?"

"Shit!" I ran back up the stairs to our bedroom.

As I came back down the stairs, I heard Ty laughing at me. "Dude, you have got to calm down. It is your responsibility to get her through this and remain calm. Right now you seem like you need to be bitch slapped."

I gave a little chuckle. "Sorry, I'm so nervous. I don't think I have ever been so scared."

"Dude, if I can get through it, you can. Just remember if it gets too scary stare at her thigh instead of her pussy. Don't take any mental pictures. It will haunt you forever."

We climbed back into the truck. "You give the worst damn advice."

"It's the truth. Seriously, you will be fine as long as you keep her calm. She can't see you freaking out. You have to be her rock."

Speaking of bitch slapping.....

"You sound like one of those fuckin' books Savanna keeps in our bedroom."

Ty responded immediately, "I watched my daughter being born and read the books when I'm on the shitter. Miranda knows it's the only time I will consider picking up a book. She got rid of all my Sports Illustrated and replaced them with baby mags."

Miranda is one smart girl.

We pulled back up at the main house to a crowd full of people. Ty ran the pants inside and when I finally got inside Savanna was already in the bathroom changing. When she came out she was walking slow, like she was in pain. I rushed to her side. "Darlin', what can I do?"

"The doctor said that since my water broke and I'm having contractions we need to get to the hospital. Lucy is going to keep the kids."

I was a little confused. "What do you mean Lucy is going to keep the kids? Where is everyone else goin'?" There was a whole house full of people to keep the kids.

"I want our families to be there and I already asked Miranda to be in the room with me. Her and Ty are the God parents and I think they should be there." She still wasn't making very much sense.

"Why the Hell would you want Ty in the room?"

She rolled her eyes at me. "Because he has been through this before and I can tell from the look on your face that you are already freaking out. He isn't there to watch and I guarantee he won't get anywhere near my nether regions, but you will need him, Colt. Besides, I hardly think I'm going to care when this baby starts coming out." She continued to walk toward the door. I held her hand and helped her get her coat on.

"We are going to follow you." My mother announced. Behind her stood Savanna's parents and my Aunt Karen.

Ty came running up in front of us. "Give me your keys. You sit in the back with your wife. I will drive." I got ready to warn him of his driving. "No worries. I will drive carefully and get us all there in one piece. Don't forget my pregnant wife is sitting in this truck too."

It actually did make me feel better knowing that Ty would do anything to protect Miranda. The weather was bad and the roads weren't much better. It was going to take us double the amount of time to get her where we needed to go.

Once we hit the main roads, they were worse than we suspected. Ty did a good job going slow, but even in four wheel drive we were sliding all over the road. The snow was really coming down again and visibility was almost non-existent. We were finally having to drive so slow that we ended up getting stuck. Luckily, I had just bought a brand new pair of chains for my tires. While Ty and I went out into the freezing weather to get them hooked to the tires, Miranda went ahead and called my mother to let her know that Conner would have to come get them and drive them in another truck capable of having chains. I knew they were somewhere behind us, but my main concern was making it to the hospital before Savanna delivered another Mitchell baby in the back of a vehicle.

It took us a good thirty minutes to get the chains out, untangle them, and get them on all four tires. When we climbed back into the truck, Savanna was really having a tough contraction. The winter storm made everything so quiet outside of the truck, but it was sure a different story as we climbed back in.

Miranda was hanging over the front seat, trying to soothe Savanna through her contraction. We hopped in the truck and started moving slowly again. The hospital was a good fifteen minutes during normal weather and being that it was so hard to see, I wasn't really sure how close we actually were.

Savanna laid down on my lap. I stroked her hair and watched her suffering through the pain.

"Okay, that last one was only three minutes apart. They are getting' closer Van." Miranda restarted the timer on her phone. She sat back facing forward in the seat.

"How far apart do they need to get before we start to worry?" I asked.

Savanna shook her head and tried not to cry. I could tell she was in a lot of pain still. She was holding onto her stomach. I reached down to feel it and it was as hard as a rock. "Darlin' tell me what to do?"

"Make it stop hurting," she cried.

"Sugar, I wish I could." I rubbed the sweat off of her face. She closed her eyes and tried to relax.

We passed a car that had slid off the side of the road. They were stuck in a culvert and trying to wave us down. It didn't help that I had a big old wench on the front of the truck. "Keep goin'"

Ty looked at me in the rear view mirror as he pulled over to the side. "Dude, at least let me tell them why we can't help. Miranda can tell Conner to stop and pull them out."

"Fine, make it quick. I don't know how to deliver a baby." I was really starting to get scared now. It wasn't something that I knew how to handle. My wife was in excruciating pain and there was nothing I could do to make it better. We didn't have the time to be stopping for people, no matter how rude it was. We had our own emergency situation.

Ty jumped out and came back in the truck a few seconds later. "They were cool about it. They said congratulations."

We arrived at the hospital a good twenty minutes later. Miranda had actually climbed over the seat and helped Savanna get through a couple hard contractions. When Savanna claimed she felt like pushing, Miranda ripped down her pants to make sure there wasn't a baby coming out. I think she was shocked at what it looked like down there, from the look on her face, but she finally regained composure and said she wasn't crowning and didn't need to push.

We pulled up at the hospital and a security officer came running outside to us. He flew back in and came out with a wheelchair. Within seconds, we were whisking Savanna upstairs to the maternity ward, while Miranda and Ty parked the truck.

By the time they made it up to the room, Savanna was already being changed into a hospital gown. They were prepping her for an I.V. and she was still trying to focus on her breathing.

The nurses were very responsive to what she was going through. They told her a few other relaxation techniques to help her through her contractions. Due to the weather, it took her doctor even longer to get to the hospital.

He walked into the room applying his gloves. In a brief moment he was already putting her legs up in the stirrups and giving her an examination. Part of me wanted to watch, but the other part of me didn't want to go anywhere near down there. I think most of it was Ty scaring the shit out of me. There were parts of my wife that I treasured and that was one of my favorites.

The doctor removed his gloves and scooted his stool away from my wife. "I'm going to go ahead and order the epidural. She's is at about nine centimeters. It won't be long now." He walked out of the room and left us.

I rushed to her side, kissing her on the mouth. "I love you, Darlin'. Our baby is comin'."

She opened her eyes as wide as they could get. "This fucking hurts, Colt. I changed my mind." Her face scrunched up as another contraction hit her again. I grabbed her hand and felt the power of the pain, through her nails ripping my skin open. I wanted to pull away, but knew doing so would only piss her off worse. I was at her mercy. She was in excruciating pain and I would do anything to take that away from her.

"You changed your mind about what, Darlin'?"

"Having eleven children. I don't want to do this ten more times. JESUS SHITBALLS, it hurts so bad." I shouldn't have laughed, but I couldn't help myself. Savanna's face was blood red as she focused on the pain.

Miranda came around and stood at the other side of Savanna's head while Ty sat in the chair behind me. He was being awfully quiet, probably reliving his first delivery experience.

Her contraction subsided and the death grip she had on my hand finally released. Miranda gave her an ice chip and rubbed her head. "Just breathe Van. Just keep breathing. It will all be over soon, I promise."

Through the doors came the anesthesiologist, who in turn made us wait outside, where we were met with the rest of our family. Miranda explained everything to them while I began pacing. After ten minutes we were allowed back into the room. Luckily, they let Savanna's mother and my mother come in with us. We all stayed out of the nurse's way as they got everything prepped. I noticed Savanna wasn't screaming out in pain anymore, she was just tightening up as her body contracted. "Is the pain better now?"

"Just a bunch of pressure. It still hurts, but it is much better. I'm sorry I screamed."

I kissed her dry mouth. "Savanna, I love you. You can scream as much as you want. Just deliver that little baby so you can see that it was all worth it."

The doctor and nurses came into the room, wearing surgical robes. They positioned themselves between Savanna's legs and got them into the stirrups. Ty went over to stand with Miranda, while I never moved from her side. The nurse brought over a mirror and positioned it so Savanna could see what was happening. "Oh my God! Why does it look like that?" She closed her eyes and refused to look. Out of pure curiosity I glanced down.

Don't pass out. Jesus Christ don't you dare pass out!

Ty was right. I don't know why but I looked up at him and watched him mouth the words 'told you'. I shook my head and gave Savanna a smile. "Focus on the baby, Darlin'. Don't worry about anything else."

Savanna, always being so modest, shocked everyone in the room. "My vagina is huge!"

We all just stood there, with nothing to say, until Ty leaned over and whispered in her ear. He kissed her forehead and she smiled as he pulled away.

Thank you God! I have no idea what just happened, but Ty was a freaking genius.

The doctor caught our attention. "She is ready to start pushing. Dad, you are going to need to hold this knee." Miranda stepped forward and grabbed her other knee and the doctor nodded.

"Okay, Savanna. I need you to give me some pushes. I'm going to count and I want you to hold it until I am done. We are going to repeat it until we get the baby out."

She nodded.

The pushing began. The first three times nothing happened. The fourth time I realized I couldn't stop myself from watching. A little head of black hair was starting to come out. The doctor looked over to me and smiled. "Looks like someone has their father's hair."

A few things happened.

I felt dizzy. My heart raced like it was running out of my chest. My eyes never left that little babies head.

I smiled back and listened for him to count again. Savanna didn't take long breaks in between pushes and the more she did it, the more exhausted she was becoming. During one push the head came almost all the way out and then went right back in. Finally, when she seemed like she couldn't push anymore, Savanna let out a scream as she gave it all of her might. The head and one shoulder came sliding out. The doctor grabbed the baby and it slid right out with ease. A little cry could be heard as the nurses took the baby and started cleaning it off.

"It's a girl!" He announced.

A girl? A girl? I have a daughter. I have a son and a daughter!

I hadn't realized I was crying until I felt the hot tears on my cheeks. I rushed to Savanna's side, stroking her tired face. "We have a daughter, Darlin'." I kissed her on the lips. "We have a daughter."

The nurses brought our little girl over to us, wrapped in a blanket. Her fuzzy head of black hair was covered in a little cap to keep her head warm. Little eyes were open and looking out at us. Savanna held out her arms and looked to me when she was placed there with us. I couldn't stop the tears and honestly I didn't want to.

Our family was all just standing there taking us in, most with teared eyes themselves.

"She's beautiful," I said as I leaned down to kiss my baby girl.

"She's perfect. Thank you, Colt Mitchell. Thank you so much for this life." I stood there with my two girls, accepting the slew of pictures being taken. The doctor finally finished with Savanna and left the room.

I looked up at my family and then back down to my little girl. "Meet Christian Michelle Mitchell!"

The family began filling the room with excitement. The middle name was after a cousin of Savanna's that had passed away. They were very close and it was important to her to have that. Christian was a name that Savanna and I had picked out that was both for a girl or boy. We both loved it and loved the nickname Chris for both a boy and a girl. To make our decision easier, Noah had finally requested the name Chris. Being that it was the only normal name he suggested, it all worked out.

After a few hours the room cleared out and just Savanna and I were there with our little girl. Savanna had already breast fed her once and she was sleeping so peacefully. While Savanna fell asleep herself, I held my little baby and just watched her sleep. A nurse came in and insisted I get some rest, so even though I didn't want to, I laid her down in her little hospital crib and slept in the recliner next to my wife.

"When can I see Noah?" I woke up to Savanna nursing Christian. She was playing with her full head of hair as she talked.

Of all the things, she already missed our boy. "My mom said she was goin' to wait until the roads were more clear before bringin' him out."

Just as I finished talking the door swung open. My mother came in first, followed by Conner with Noah on his shoulders. "Man, this kid was itchin' somethin' fierce to see ya'll."

Noah came running to me and I pointed to his sleeping sister. "She's sleeping, so you have to be extra quiet."

Noah crept up on my lap and looked at his sister for the first time. "She's so little," he whispered.

"She is only seven pounds and three ounces. That is pretty tiny for sure." Noah smiled when I explained her size. He didn't know much about weight, but he knew she was the smallest little baby he had ever seen.

"When can she play with me?"

"Not until she is older, Sweetie. She is still too little to play. We have to teach her to eat, and crawl and walk first." Savanna gave him a pat on the head after she explained.

He looked sad at first studying the little baby in his mother's arms. "Can I hold her?"

I looked to Savanna who just nodded. "Noah go sit in that chair with Grandma." I waited for him to get adjusted. "Hold out your arms, but don't squeeze her too tight." Gently I placed little Christian in my son's arms. He held her perfectly, studying her little face. The room got real quiet. "I think I might love her, Dad."

And that there was the most beautiful thing I had ever heard in my entire life.

Epilogue

Savanna

"I can't believe we have a daughter." We'd been home for a week and Colt still couldn't stop saying that. The ranch could have been falling apart and he wouldn't have noticed. He'd spent every waking second with me and the kids.

When Colt said that he didn't want to miss anything with Christian, he wasn't lying. That man gave her the first diaper change she ever had, the first bath, and her first tour of the house. He begged me to pump, so that at night he could get up with her and give her a bottle while I got some sleep. Several times I would wake up to an empty bed, only to find him rocking her in her nursery, singing softly to her.

As if Colt wasn't enough, Noah followed them around like a lost puppy. The three of them stuck together, watching television and just generally being entertained by a week old baby. Noah had adjusted to having a sister much better than we anticipated. He no longer even spoke about having a brother.

Instead he had changed his mind and was now the 'official sister protector'.

After my parents had finally gone home, everything started to get into a good routine for us. Colt did work for a couple hours in his office at our house, but he never left us alone. If I needed a nap he would take Christian into the office with him.

I couldn't have asked for a better father for my kids. Colt was perfect in every single way. How I ended up with him was something I will always wonder. His love for me was indescribable. His devotion to our family was unconditional.

Over the holidays' we got to see the family again. It was nice having Noah home from school for so long. He was always such a helper with his sister. Her face was starting to light up when she heard her big brother talking. In addition, when he gave her all of his attention she would smile from ear to ear.

I remember watching the two of them interacting and feeling so satisfied. Colt came up behind me and witnessed what I was seeing. Noah had Christian's little fingers in his. He was talking to her about how pretty she was. "Remember that time when he said all he wanted was a brother?" Colt's voice vibrated off of my back.

"I remember." We both let out a laugh.

"So, I was wonderin' if you meant what you said at the hospital."

I turned around and wrapped my arms behind Colt's neck. He gave me those beautiful green eyes to look right in to. "I said a lot of things at the hospital."

"Well, it was somethin' like you didn't want to go through havin' anymore children. I was kinda hopin' that you would change your mind. Darlin', I'm not askin' for eleven, but I would like three or four." Colt had a calm but determined look on his face. I turned back to look at our two kids. They were both perfect and I loved being their mother.

I brushed my lips over his and looked back into his eyes. "If they all look like that, we can have eleven."

He smiled and kissed me full on the lips. His mouth found my ear and he kissed it with his tongue. "Sugar, you just let me know when you want to start tryin'."

End of Book Three

Look For Risking Fate Jan 2013

If you enjoyed this book, please share a comment or review.

Let me know what you think of this book by contacting me at the following:

Somnianseries@gmail.com

http://twitter.com/jennyfoor

http://www.facebook.com/#!/JenniferFoorAuthor

http://www.jennyfoor.wordpress.com

http://www.goodreads.com/jennyfoor

Jennifer Foor lives on the Eastern Shore of Maryland with her husband and two children. She enjoys shooting pool, camping and catching up on cliché movies that were made in the eighties.

Made in the USA
Lexington, KY
22 November 2012